OFF KILTER

CATHRYN FOX

Discover other titles by Cathryn Fox at www.cathrynfox.com. Please sign up for Cathryn's Newsletter for freebies, ebooks, news and contests: https://app.mailerlite.com/webforms/landing/c1f8n1

ISBN: 978-1-998943-02-9
ISBN Print: 978-1-998943-01-2

RACHEL

"I don't know about this." I look up and read the big sign over Boston's hottest new pub—Kilting Around—as my friend Brodie opens the heavy door and gestures for me to enter. Nervousness takes up residence in my stomach as I step inside the busy establishment and look for a free table.

Honestly, it's not the pub I'm concerned about—it's quite lovely, actually—or the fact that there's a rough, tough, tattooed guy in a kilt serving beer. It's the business idea Brodie wants to run by me that has me filled with unease.

I point to the tatted-up server as he walks back to the bar. "Why are the guys wearing kilts?" I turn to Brodie, who also works here but has never mentioned having to wear a kilt before. "Do you wear a kilt too?"

Brodie puts his hand over mine and pushes it to my side to stop me from blatantly pointing. Oops. "Didn't I tell you that?" I shake my head no. "The owner is Scottish, and we all wear kilts." He winks at me when I crinkle my nose in confusion. "To give a real Scottish experience."

For the briefest of seconds, I consider what kind of Scottish experience Mr. Hot Scot in a Kilt over there might give me.

What the hell, Rachel?

Good Lord, the fact that I'm suddenly fantasizing about a man who looks like he might have committed murder ten minutes ago shows just how long it's been since I've been touched. Divorce will do that to you. An almost hysterical laugh bubbles up in my throat. Yeah, I think I'm losing it.

Brodie stares at me, no doubt assuming I've lost my marbles and he should probably bail, instead of running his business idea by me. "Are you okay?" he asks, and glances around to see what's holding my attention—and messing with my ovaries.

I pull myself together and smooth my hand over my skirt. "I guess seeing that guy in a kilt put me a little off kilter." I laugh, like a damn fool. "Oh wait, now I get why this place is called Kilting Around."

His brows knit together, and I'm pretty sure he's figured I've finally gone and lost my mind. Okay, it's true, I've been working too hard, trying to fight my way to the top in a male-dominated field, and take care of my son in a heritage house that's fighting back—literally. This morning, the sink nozzle thought it'd be fun to break and spray water up my nostrils. I'm also pretty sure there's an animal living in my walls. But that worry is for another day. When it finds its way free and tries to eat my face.

"Come on, let's grab a seat at the bar." I follow Brodie, and while I love his idea of creating a Dad for Hire business, I'm not sure it's for me. Sure, my son needs a man's influence in his life—his own father is barely around and I'm not saying that's a bad thing—but do I really want to hire a man to teach my son life skills?

While I'm not sure about any of this, I'm going to listen to what Brodie has to say. A year ago, I bought the house near his when I moved from the city to Gloucester, back to the small town I grew up in, wanting to be closer to my mother and give my son Lucas a fresh start after all the bullying at his elementary school. Brodie's been a great friend to me, and after a hard life that he only ever hints at, he wants to start a business and give back. I want to help any way I can.

Brodie waves to Mr. Hot Scot in a Kilt, and gestures to the beer taps. While I don't usually drink in the day, it's hot out, and Lucas is in day camp, and well...I could really use a cold one. I admire Mr. Hot Scot in a Kilt's tattooed forearms as he pours the beer, and a little moan of appreciation, one I have no control over, spills from my lips as he slides the drinks across the counter to us. I reach for mine, and my hand connects with his.

"Oh, sorry," I blurt out, my gaze lifting quickly. His gaze is dark, intense as it holds mine, and I try not to fidget under his scrutiny. Wait, did he hear me moan? Does he think it had something to do with him? Because it didn't. At all. Or much.

Okay, it totally did.

"I'm trying to get Tavish to sign up," Brodie says. "Unfortunately, all he does is growl no at me. The playground bullies would think twice about messing with Lucas with Tavish around."

"What?" I ask, tearing my gaze away from Mr. Hot Scot in a Kilt and work to focus on Brodie. "Who?"

"Tavish," Brodie says with a nod toward Mr. Hot Scot in a Kilt.

Mr. Hot Scot in a Kilt, or rather Tavish, grunts something under his breath and walks away. Wow, what a neanderthal. Hottest Neanderthal I've ever seen for sure, but Neanderthal none the less.

I lean into Brodie. "What's his problem?"

He snorts a laugh. "We don't have time for that." Producing a folder, he opens it and slides it toward me. "This is the contract and all the information." I open my mouth and he holds his hands up. "Just read it, see what we have to offer and think it over before you jump straight to no. The minimum contract is for six months, and there are ways to get out of it if it's not working."

I take a much-needed sip of my beer and it feels good on my dry throat. "I wasn't going to jump straight to no." Tavish walks back to the beer taps, and as I take in his big hard body, the needy part of me wants to jump straight to yes—to a fast hook-up, maybe in the back alleyway. Which is absolutely insane and completely out of character for me.

Clearly my ovaries and my brain aren't communicating.

"Look, you need help, Rachel." I take in the concern dancing in Brodie's blue eyes and feel a tinge of guilt. Maybe I've asked too much from him and he's tired of helping me out. He'd never complain or come right out and say anything, but I do lean very heavily on him. "You can't deny that."

"Nope, can't deny that at all." I stare at the papers before me, an uneasy feeling in my stomach as Brodie takes a sip of his beer. "I just...I mean, this is like bringing a stranger into our lives and how safe is that?"

"All the guys are vetted carefully by me."

"Was he?" I ask, my gaze raking over Tavish's tattoos, and rock-hard muscles. Nothing about him screams typical dad.

"Don't let the tattoos fool you. Underneath it all, he's a softie."

Tavish's head lifts, and he arches a brow, like he's giving Brodie a chance to take his words back before he takes him outside and gives him the pounding of a lifetime. Brodie just laughs. He's obviously not afraid of Tavish. I can't say the same for me. The hard, dangerous look about him, I weirdly enough find it kind of exciting...arousing. Good Lord, what is going on with me? Maybe I have heat stroke or something.

"Does he speak?" I ask quietly after Tavish walks away with a tray of beer.

"Only when it's necessary, and you'd be lucky to have him as a dad for hire."

Laughter erupts from the table beside us. Are they listening in, and think Brodie is out of his mind, too? "Really?"

"Former MMA champion in Scotland. No one will mess with you or Lucas when he's around, and even when you're not." Brodie holds his hands up and fists them. "He's good with his hands."

"Yeah, for fighting," I shoot back. Honestly, I don't need that in my life. I'm a peacekeeper by nature, and during my seven-year marriage, there was enough fighting to last a lifetime. I want to kick myself for staying that long. I thought it was better for Lucas, but I learned the hard way it wasn't.

He shrugs. "Not just fighting. He's good with his hands in other ways, too."

Unable to help myself, I turn on my stool and admire his big, battered tattooed hands as he distributes the beer. What would those hands be like on my body? My sex clenches and once again a small noise spills from my lips. I cover it with a cough, and take a big drink of my beer.

"Like what?" I ask, trying not to sound breathless.

"He makes rocking chairs. He's very handy."

"Oh wow." I'm actually surprised hands as big and powerful as his could create something delicate and intricate.

"He'd be able to help you fix things in that heritage house. He's not afraid to get his hands dirty, and what he doesn't know, he'll figure out." He sips his beer. "No more plumbing mishaps," he adds, like he's trying to sweeten the deal.

"Is he good with kids, though?" Am I seriously considering hiring Tavish? The man doesn't even talk.

All the better for what you want, Rachel.

Good God, what am I thinking? If I do sign with Brodie, the last thing I'm going to do is sleep with the dad I hire. Which means there is no way I could consider Tavish for the job. He hasn't spoken one word to me since I walked in the door, and I'm sitting here fantasizing about all the positions he could put me in with those strong hands of his.

Brodie turns to glance at Tavish and as if feeling our eyes on him, Tavish turns our way, a scowl on his handsome face. Brodie sighs. "Yes, he'd be great with kids. He just doesn't know it yet."

"Maybe he's not, and that's why he won't sign up."

"No, that's not it." There's something lost and sad in Brodie's eyes and it tugs at my heart. I thought he knew Tavish from the pub, but now I suspect they go way back.

"Were you guys friends in Scotland?"

"I wouldn't be alive if it wasn't for Tavish," is all he says as he turns his focus back to the papers, putting an end to the conversation. Something obviously went down years ago, and Brodie keeps it close to his heart. While I want to pry, I don't. Their past is not my business.

"I guess the point is moot, since he won't sign up."

"True." Brodie nods in agreement and drains his beer. He looks at mine. "Another?

"No, I have to stop at work before heading home."

"Are you still up for the VP of sales position?"

Now it's my turn to sigh. I'm the only female sales rep at MedFlex Pharmaceuticals, and I deserve the promotion over Jakob the snake, who has the perfect wife, kids and dog and plays golf with Matthew Callaghan, the CEO, but do I think I'll get it? Hell no. It's an all-boys club, with an impregnable glass ceiling for someone like me. "The decision will be made next week."

He smiles. "You'll get it. You deserve it."

I nod, appreciating his vote of confidence, but I'm a single mom who sometimes has to rush home to her son. They don't consider someone like that reliable enough. They want the married man who has a wife at home to take care of things. Maybe if they saw a guy like Tavish standing with me, it would shake them all up. Maybe they'd take me a little more seriously if they thought I had that kind of support.

That idea of Tavish intimidating them fills me with a morbid kind of glee.

Brodie gathers the papers and puts them in the folder. He holds it out to me. "You'll think about it?"

"I will." I slide off the stool. "Thanks for the drink. I'll see you tomorrow for dinner?"

"I think I might be taking a shift here, so I'll let you know."

I nod and head toward the door, and the strangest sensation crawls up my neck. I turn and spot Tavish standing at the bar talking to Brodie, but his eyes are burning through me. I step outside and a warm breeze cools my body down. Yes, something about Tavish makes me that hot. I tuck the papers into my bag, grab an Uber and head back to the office, where my car and a bit of work awaits me.

Inside our building, I take the elevator to our floor and the second I step off and see Jakob and our CEO Matthew Callaghan clinking glasses filled with amber liquid, my heart sinks. Jakob glances my way, a wry smirk on his face and it takes everything for me not to walk into his office and smack it off. God, I hate the way he thinks he can walk all over me.

No one would mess with you or Lucas if Tavish was around.

As I stand here, my disappointment turning to anger, Brodie's words bouncing around inside my brain, I can't help but think maybe I should sign the contract and find a guy like Tavish to be Lucas' dad...and my big daddy.

"**A**re you still covering for me tomorrow afternoon?" I ask my buddy Brodie as I pour a beer and slide it across the counter.

"That depends." I arch a brow and glare at him, bracing myself for what's about to come next. Dammit, I'm tired of repeating myself. "Are you going to sign up for Dad for Hire?"

"Right after you marry a fine lassie and have a dozen kids."

He laughs like he always does, since we both know that's never going to happen—for either of us. I support the organization he's building, but what do I know about being a dad? Fuck, I was taken from my own dad when I was a wee boy. Apparently in Scotland, you can't beat the piss out of your kid to toughen him up. You end up with your arse locked behind bars, and a kid who goes off to foster care, which in my opinion was never much better.

Nevertheless, that's how I met Brodie. We go way back and I'm here in Massachusetts, trying to rebuild a life outside of the MMA spotlight. He's responsible for helping me find work, not that I need the income. I made a fortune in the cage, but I need to get out of the house once in a while.

"Why do you need me to take your shift?" He wags his brow. "Hot date?"

I toss a cloth over my shoulder. Back home, women threw their panties at me. I was, after all, a well known UFC champion. Here I'm just a guy who serves beer in a kilt and I'm okay with that. It's true, I'm totally played out and want a simple life. My gaze goes to the empty stool beside Brodie, and something twitches between my legs. I'd have to be blind not to notice that way she looked at me—a mixture of fear and intrigue. She doesn't strike me as a panty-tossing kind of woman, and getting involved with a young mum is not on my agenda. I hated hearing her kid was bullied, though.

"I have a delivery," I remind him. "I sold two chairs to a woman in our neighborhood, and promised I'd have them to her by tomorrow afternoon at the latest. I'm just waiting for the stain to dry. Last month, shortly after I moved in, she was driving by when she saw me in the garage and stopped to inquire."

Intrigue dances in his eyes. "This woman..."

Why is he always trying to set me up? If I want company, I can find it. If I want a bed mate, I can find that too. I just don't want either.

Except maybe with the gorgeous lassie Brodie was just talking to.

Shite, what am I saying?

"Nice lady. Evelyn Hart." I grab the cloth on my shoulder and start polishing glasses. "Owns the bakery in town."

"Aye."

I angle my head and take in his smile. "You know her?"

He nods toward the empty stool. "Rachel's mother. You're right, nice lady. You should check out the bakery. She makes the best sticky buns. Rachel made them for me a few times. Delicious."

A very odd sense of jealousy grips me. "Are you and Rachel—"

"Friends," he interrupts.

I laugh as I take in his sheepish grin. "Turned you down, did she?"

"Something like that."

The door opens, and oddly enough, a part of me hopes it's Rachel coming back. It's not. It's Craig, here to replace me. "Thought so." I check the clock, and unknot the apron around my waist, hanging it on the hook behind the kitchen door. I wave to the owner, Gavan, letting him know I'm leaving and grab my helmet and coat.

It's still early enough for a relaxing ride along the coast. My home is about an hour from the city, but I don't mind the ride, especially on bike. The winter months might be a different story. I say goodbye to Brodie and he hollers after me to think about signing up for Dad for Hire as I step outside into the late day sunshine. I breathe in the city scents, and walk to where I parked my bike. Twenty minutes later, I'm cruising along the coast, suddenly hungry for sticky buns, and I'm not sure I mean the ones sold at Evelyn Hart's bakery.

I reach Gloucester and instead of going home, I head down the main street. I pass by the water tower. It looks newly painted and has *Welcome to the Scenic Town of Gloucester* written on it, and a picture of a clam to represent the fishing industry. Only problem is that the clam looks more like...well, let's just say it's questionable. I pull up in front of the bakery. I kill the engine, and I'm about to take my helmet off, when taunting noises from the community park behind the bakery grabs my attention. My thoughts instantly go back to Rachel, and her son. If there's one thing I hate, it's a bully.

Fire raging through my veins, I follow the path to the park, passing by a community piano that I've yet to see anyone play—properly, anyway. Not that I can play it. Music wasn't in my childhood, and it's too late for that now.

In the distance, I spot two boys around ten years old circling another boy, calling him names and teasing him about wearing girl clothes, even though he's dressed in jeans and a T-shirt.

Since I'm still in my kilt, I walk toward them as one kid pushes the boy to the ground. "Hey," I yell and take my helmet off.

All eyes turn to me, and the boy on the ground scrambles backward. I step up to him and hold my hand out. His eyes are full of wary suspicion as I try to help, and that's a good thing. He should be afraid of a grown-ass man—whether he's trying to help or not—on the playground. "What's going on here?" I ask.

"Nothing," one of the bullies says, and points to the boy on the ground. "He slipped."

"Is that what happened?" I ask the kid who's still in the dirt, narrowing my eyes to see if he's hurt. He has the same blue eyes as Rachel. I don't believe in coincidences, but all signs indicate this is her son.

"Uh, yeah," the blue-eyed boy says, and I bend, grab his elbow and haul him to his feet.

"You're in a skirt," the other bully says.

"You got a problem with that?" I ask and take a step toward him. Hey, I'm not a guy who likes to threaten or intimidate kids, but these little eegits deserve a bit of their own treatment.

The kids stumble backward. "I never saw a man in a skirt before."

"Now you have. If you have a problem with me, like you do with my friend here, now's your chance to show me. See, if you mess with him, you mess with me." Both boys shake their heads, and I wonder if their fathers will be on my doorstep later. I turn to the boy staring up at me with big blue eyes. "Where's your mother?"

"In the bakery."

"Let's go." I put my hand on his back and lead him away.

He looks up at me. "I like your skirt."

"Thanks, kid. Why were those kids bothering you?"

"I wore a skirt once." He looks down, defeated. "I probably shouldn't have done that."

"You can wear whatever you want. I do."

"I'm not big and strong like you." He looks at the tattoos spread along my arms. "I bet no one picks on you."

"You're right, kid, they don't. Have you thought about—"

A wailing cry cuts me off and I glance up to see Rachel coming our way. I hold my hand up to stop her. "Whoa." I'm not trying to abduct her son or anything.

"Back away," she screams, and holds her hands out like she's going to karate chop me or something. "Lucas, get over here."

"Mom, it's—"

"Lucas," she screams, her voice boarding on hysteria now.

I continue to hold my hands up and start moving away from Lucas. The boy glances at me with a hint of embarrassment. "She's been watching some show called Cobra Kai," he explains.

I nod in understanding. "It's okay. I was only trying to help."

"Get away from here." She pulls her phone out. "I'm calling the cops."

"You better go, kid."

Lucas walks toward his mom and she runs up to him, closing the gap between us. Suddenly her hand drops and her eyes go wide. "Tavish?"

I think she was so panicked, so focused on a man walking with her son, she didn't realize it was me. Her gaze drops to my kilt.

"I didn't realize." She takes deep gulping breaths. "I thought... I just saw the motorcycle out front, and your jacket and...Oh, God." She buries her face in her hands and as the sun shines down on me, I peel my coat off.

"It's okay. Everything's okay."

"No," she gulps out, her voice shaky as tears pool in her eyes. No doubt from the big adrenaline dump. "Everything is not okay."

Sensing there is a lot more going on here, and not really knowing what to do or how I can help, I walk up to her and do the only thing I can think of. I pull her into my arms and simply hold her. I'm not going to tell her not to cry, or that everything is going to be okay, because clearly she needs a good cry and I don't know if everything is going to be okay. The only thing I do know is the protector in me is ripping its way to the surface, wanting to take this woman and boy home and keep them both safe.

She sniffs and inches back. "I feel so stupid."

"No need."

A laugh that holds no humor bubbles in her throat. "You talk."

I shake my head. I can't even imagine what Brodie said about me. "Yeah, I talk."

She turns to Lucas and goes to her knees. Her small hands grip his shoulders as she searches his face. "Are you okay?"

"Yeah, I think Tavish scared Jared and Owen. I think they both shit their pants."

Rachel's lip quirks. "Lucas, no swearing." Her lids lift and she mouths the words, "Thank you."

I shrug. "Do you know their parents? I'm not sure this is over." I wipe the moisture on my brow.

"I'm not sure they'll admit to their parents that they were picking on Lucas."

Lucas pounds his fist into his palm. "If their parents find you, you can take care of them."

"Violence isn't always the answer," I tell him. Ironic, really. Considering I spent my childhood kicking ass. Sure, it was to protect those I cared about but still, and then I went on to make a name in the MMA.

Rachel's brows pull together and she glances around. "Wait, what are you doing here?" I'm about to tell her and she comes up with her own conclusions. "You decided to become a Dad for Hire?"

"No," I answer quickly. "I actually live here." I gesture toward the road, even though you can't see my place. "Moved from Scotland a month ago. Brodie didn't tell you?" She shakes her head and I continue. "He told me I needed to try your mother's sticky buns. That's why I'm here, in the park." She looks at me oddly, and I grin. "I don't think that came out right."

"Come on. I'm buying. It's the least I can do," Lucas says, and I laugh. What a funny little guy. He takes my hand, catching me by surprise. He tugs on my hand and my heart, and I glance at Rachel, waiting for her reaction.

"He's buying," she says with a shrug. Lucas skips along, no worse for the wear after the bullying incident, and as I take in the way Rachel watches her son with love and concern, my gut tightens. There's no doubt the kid needs a guy in his life. Someone to teach him how to stand up for himself, and be there for when he can't. That guy just isn't me.

We step into the bakery and delicious scents bombard me. Evelyn takes one look at me, her grandson's hand in mine, and surprise moves over her face. Who can blame her.

"Tavish?"

"Hi Evelyn," I say, and Rachel stands there shocked, her gaze going back and forth between the two of us.

"You know my mom?"

"She bought rocking chairs from me. Delivery is tomorrow."

Evelyn beams. "You do such beautiful work. Remember me telling you about the chairs, Rachel?"

"Actually, I kind of forgot. I remember now. I didn't realize... Brodie said you were good with your hands. I didn't put it together." A pink flush moves into her cheeks as she glances at my hands. Jesus, what is going through her head, and if it's the same thing going through mine, I should walk out the door. I'm all about a fast hook-up, but I'm not going to get involved with a woman with a kid. I'm not the guy she needs in her life. "I had no idea you lived near me or that you were the guy Mom bought the chairs from."

"Can we get some sticky buns, Nan?" Lucas asks.

I turn to investigate the near empty display as Evelyn frowns. "I'm sorry, hon, we're all sold out."

"I have an idea," Rachels says. "Why don't you come for dinner tonight? A little thank you for helping Lucas and I'll make some sticky buns."

It's not a good idea and that's exactly what I'm going to tell her.

"What do you think?" she asks.

"What can I bring?"

Shite.

I rush around the house, pausing briefly when I hear something in the wall. I want to press my ear to it, but I'm too fearful that whatever is scurrying around in there might jump through and eat my face off. Perhaps I watch too many scary movies.

Fighting off a shiver, I pick up the empty wine glass from the coffee table, and the can of fizzy water I'd drank last night while watching yet another rom com that reminded me my love life was in the toilet.

Is that why you invited Mr. Hot Scot in a Kilt for dinner, Rachel?

No, absolutely not.

I am simply thanking him for helping Lucas out.

With sticky buns?

Okay, fine but they're not *my* sticky buns, which are not at all sticky. Speaking of buns, I hurry to the kitchen and bend down to check on the tray rising in the oven. The delicious scents of cinnamon fill the air and I breathe them in. I hope Tavish likes them.

"Do you think this looks okay?" I turn and spot Lucas in the doorway, swishing left and right, to flare the skirt around his knees. My heart squeezes in my chest. I want my son to be happy and healthy and to be able to dress the way he desires. It hurts my soul when he gets picked on, but I don't want to prevent him from being who he wants to be. One of the psychologists I was seeing told me he liked skirts because I was his only role model. I'm not sure if I believe that, in fact I don't, and honestly, I don't know the answers. I do know that a male role model wouldn't be a bad thing.

"I think it looks great," I tell him, and cross the room to adjust it on his tiny hips.

His smile widens. "Do you think Tavish will wear a skirt tonight?"

"I really don't know. He wears it for work. It's called a kilt. It's a Scottish tradition. You can ask him about it if you like."

He nods and snatches his iPad from the table. "I'm going to go look it up."

"You should." He disappears and I smile after him before turning to see my bag on the counter, where I'd stuffed the contract Brodie gave me. Maybe I should sign up for Dad for Hire. The timer goes off and I pull the buns from the oven, setting them on a rack to cool. The icing is made and I decided to order pizza since the invite was a late one and I wouldn't have much time to cook after baking. As the buns cool, I hurry to my bedroom and pull open my closet. I stare at my wardrobe, which consists mostly of work clothes.

Why am I so nervous?

Stop being so ridiculous, Rachel!

Since it's a warm night and I don't have air conditioning, I opt for a sundress. I tug it on, and sit at my makeup table. The heat is doing nothing for my hair, so I clip it up and pull a few tendrils to frame my face. In the other room, Lucas is talking to himself, reciting fascinating facts about Scotland, and it warms my heart. I put on a light lip gloss and the door-bell rings just as I stand up.

I grab the edge of my makeup table, suddenly lightheaded, and I wish it was from rising quickly. The man downstairs is the only reason my blood pressure is going whacky.

What would be wrong with a brief hook-up, Rachel?

Oh, nothing other than the fact that he's my neighbor, a hot, muscular tattooed MMA fighter—yes, I did my research after kneading my buns—and I can't risk falling for a guy coveted by thousands of women. Been there done that, and well, look at how that all turned out. The fact of the matter is, I might be lonely, but Lucas is my main concern. I can't just bring random men into my life.

Didn't you just invite Tavish to dinner?

Oh, shut the hell up, inner voice.

"He's here, he's here," Lucas screams, running to the stairs and my chest tightens as I watch him fly down the steps. Wow, it didn't take him long to get attached, which is a fast reminder that I can't get involved. If I want Tavish as a friend, and he seems to be pretty good for Lucas, any sort of relationship would only mess that up, and right now my son has to come first. Not only that, who says he's even inter-ested in me? I've put on weight since having Lucas seven years ago—my ex constantly reminded me of that when we were together, and honestly, it did a number on my self-esteem.

The hinges creek as the door swings open. "Hi Tavish."

"Hey mate." The sound of palms smacking in greeting reaches my ears.

"You didn't wear your kilt?" My heart clenches at the disappointment in my son's voice. Until I was a mother, I never knew someone else's pain could be my own.

"Nae, thought I'd wear my trousers tonight. That okay with you, mate?"

"Trousers. That's a weird thing to call jeans."

"It's what we call them in Scotland."

"I know lots of facts about Scotland." I grin, loving how my little boy can bounce back so easily. I hope he never loses his happy go lucky nature. His father used to be easy going, until he started playing for the NHL. All the fame and glory went to his head, and when the stresses came, he liked to take them out on me.

"Oh aye, why don't you tell me."

As Lucas starts listing off random facts, I hurry down the rest of the steps, not wanting my son to bore Tavish to death. He comes into view and oh my... If I thought he was hot in a kilt, it's nothing compared to Tavish in jeans that showcase muscular thighs and a big package.

Big package?

Good lord, who am I?

Tavish's head lifts as I reach the bottom step and as his gaze sweeps me from head to toe, and back up again—it's okay,

I'm doing it too. Did someone just strap an Acme rocket to my libido, because I swear to God, everything in the way Tavish is checking me out has sent it straight into orbit. Perhaps I watch too much Looney Tunes with Lucas.

"Hi," is all he says but that one word holds more punch—especially with his Scottish accent—than a jab to the gut by an MMA fighter. Not that I know what that really feels like.

"Hi," I manage to push out past a tongue gone thick as I take in his short sleeve button down shirt. The man has more art than the Guggenheim.

He breathes in deep. "It smells amazing in here."

Lucas inhales deeply, mimicking Tavish. "That's Mom's buns. They always smell amazing."

Tavish's lips quirk as I no doubt turn about one hundred different shades of pink. I know Lucas is talking about my baking, but I'm sure I spotted something dark and hungry in Tavish's eyes. Is he thinking of *my* buns?

"I bet they taste just as good," Tavish finally replies.

Lucas rubs his belly. "I think they might be better than Nan's, but don't tell her I said that."

"Get," I laugh. "I know you're just saying that so I'll give you extra screen time tonight." I point to the bathroom. "Go wash up for dinner."

He's about to leave, and Tavish says, "Does he get it?"

"When he sweet talks me like that, sure," I say, and Lucas pumps his fist as Tavish and I laugh.

Tavish scrubs his freshly shaved face. "I'll have to remember that."

Wait, what did he just say?

Lucas bolts to the bathroom, and since I'm too much of a chickenshit to ask for clarification, I nod toward the kitchen. "Beer?"

"Sounds about right."

In the kitchen, I walk to the fridge. "I picked up some Newcastle. I've never had it before, but you're Scottish, so I thought..." His footsteps stop at the kitchen entranceway, and I turn to take in his expression. Is that disdain? Confusion? Lust...oh, of course it's not lust. "Oh, you don't like Newcastle."

"Newcastle is from England. Dinna you hear, the Scots hate the English."

My stomach twists. Oh, Damn, maybe I should have done my research. "I'm sorry. I didn't realize. I can run to the—"

"I'm just messing with you, lassie." He steps up to me, crowding me in the most mind-boggling way, takes the beer from my hand and twists the cap off. I'm not even sure it was a twist off. He holds it out to me. "Ladies first." I let him press it to my lips and I take a swallow as he lifts it. He pulls it away and I twist my lips. "Not a fan?"

I laugh. "Not really."

"Good, that's an insult to the English." He takes a big swallow. "Bastards do make a good beer, though."

I stand there and watch his throat work, my gaze going to his mouth as he wipes the moisture from his lips with the back of his hand in that manly way I never knew made me lusty until this very moment. Honest to God, I've never been around a man who exuded testosterone quite like Tavish.

"What are you having, lassie?" he asks.

Oh, a tall glass of Tavish, thank you very much.

He arches his brow, and I realize he's waiting for an answer. I gesture to the bottle of red on the counter. "I...uh, was going to have a glass of wine."

"I'll get it for you."

"You're my guest, and you do enough serving at the pub as it is." I reach for the bottle and his big hand closes over mine, pushing it away and I try not to flush from the touch.

Too late.

"You did all this work on the sticky buns," he says, eyeing the buns cooling on the rack. "The least I could do is pour you a glass of wine, and what the hell is crawling around inside your wall?"

I blink once, and then twice, my brain trying to keep up to speed as he picks up the wine, reads the label and points to the top drawer, his brow arched.

"Yes," I answer, assuming he's wondering where I keep the corkscrew. He pulls open the drawer and as he produces it, I continue with, "As far as the wall, I'm not sure. I was thinking mouse, or squirrel, but it sounds a lot bigger. Racoon, maybe. Pizza okay?" I ask, my thoughts running a million miles an hour. "I thought I'd order in."

I try not to stare at his arms as he makes fast work of the cork. "Aye, pizza is fine." I reach for a wine glass and hand it to him. He pours a generous amount and slides it across the counter.

"Just like being at the pub," he says.

"At the pub, I would have gotten half this amount." I grin at him. "Are you trying to get me tipsy?"

He winks and...now I'm pregnant.

"Aye lassie, you're on to me. Get you tipsy so you won't protest when I take care of your big problem."

Oh good God, is he talking about my dry spell as of late, or rather the last couple years?

"My what?" I take a sip of wine, a big one.

He puts the bottle to his lips and takes a swig. "Brodie tells me you don't like asking anyone for help."

"I...no...that's not entirely true. I mean, I just don't like to put anyone out." Does this mean the two were talking about me after I left, and perhaps Brodie had been telling him I don't have a man around to help with the things I sometimes need a man for...like sex?

OMG.

He raises his bottle. "I don't mind putting out."

Dear God, is there a language barrier here? Do the Scots have a different way of saying things, or is he talking about...

He tips his bottle toward the wall. "If we don't take care of that big problem, it could lead to bigger problems, like chewed wires, damaged pipes, insulation."

"Oh, that big problem," I say as I exhale.

"What big problem did you think I was talking about?"

"That," I answer and take a big drink, almost draining my glass. "That, for sure," I add for good measure, wanting to make it perfectly clear that I didn't think he was referring to sex. "I um, should ice my buns."

His brow knits together. "You want to ice your buns?"

"My sticky buns. The icing." I grab the bowl, and a piping bag and start spooning the icing sugar into it. Now it's my turn to ask. "What did you think I meant?"

"I'm an MMA fighter, so naturally I thought..." His gaze drops, and unlike me, who tried to cover up what I really thought, he nods toward my backside. "...you injured your arse and needed to ice it."

I laugh at his honesty, and the simple way he drew conclusions based on what he did for a living.

"Nope, my arse is just fine," I assure him.

"Yeah, it sure is," he mumbles.

Wait, what did he just say?

4

TAVISH

As the buzzer goes off and the nose lights up, I cringe. "This is impossible," I blurt out and throw the tweezers onto the game as Lucas laughs. "I hate this game."

I glance up from the kitchen table and catch Rachel's smirk. Damn, she's pretty, and the way that dress hugs her breasts. Bollocks. I shouldn't be thinking dirty thoughts about her while playing a children's game with her son.

She pipes more icing onto the sticky buns, licking a bit from her finger, and I try to stifle a groan as she says, "I can't believe you never played Operation as a kid."

I stare at her. No, I never played Operation, because the people who ran the foster homes were motherfuckers and in it for the money. "I might not have played Operation but that doesn't mean I didn't play doctor."

Am I flirting? What the hell am I doing flirting?

"Oh," she says as Lucas pays us no attention, instead trying to remove something that looks like a toilet from the man's lower intestines.

Rachel goes back to piping icing. "I never played that game."

I'm about to tell her that we could play it later, but the doorbell saves me. Shite. I am not going to shag this woman—no matter how much my tadger is trying to convince me otherwise.

"Pizza," Lucas yells and bolts for the door. I stand, about to follow him. Rachel puts her hand on my arm to stop me, and when I glance down at it, she pulls it back fast.

"I got it," I tell her and pull my wallet from my pocket.

"You don't have to pay for the pizza." I note the way her chest is rising and falling quickly. "You're my guest."

"It's no big deal." She looks like she's about to protest, but stops herself. "I got this, Rachel." There's just something about this woman that makes me want to take care of her, even though she's a woman who can stand on her own two feet.

"It was my way of thanking you."

"You went out of your way to make me sticky buns. It doesn't get any better than that," I say and mean it. I can't remember the last time a woman did something like that for me. The women who followed me on the circuit wanted only one thing from me, and the women who influenced my life growing up didn't give two shits about the boy with a huge chip on his shoulder who continually wanted to prove he wasn't soft—like his mother.

I pay for the pizza, giving the young driver a generous tip, and carry the two boxes into the kitchen. Rachel is laying out plates and napkins and I set the boxes in the middle of the table.

We all sit and Rachel opens the boxes, sliding a slice onto Lucas' plate. He rubs his hands together, reminding me of myself after I received my first check from fighting. I'd spent it on all the food I always wanted but never received as a child.

Rachel then gives me a big slice and serves herself last. Something about that bothers me. I glance at her and sense there's a lot more to this woman than she shows the world. I guess I can understand that. There's a lot I keep hidden, too.

"Brodie tells me you're a pharmaceutical rep."

She nods as she bites into her slice, tugging it away and getting cheese all over her face. She chews, swallows and takes a sip of wine. "What else did Brodie tell you about me?"

"What did he say about me?" I ask in return.

"Not a whole lot. Just that he wouldn't be alive if it weren't for you." Her gaze moves over my face, curiosity lingering in her eyes.

I don't elaborate, or put that curiosity to rest with a truth that still haunts me—I might be more like my da then I want to be—instead, I redirect back to her. "He told me you might be signing up for his new business venture." She casts a quick glance at Lucas, and gives me a grateful smile for not coming right out and mentioning what that business is. Yeah, I can be smart like that sometimes. Reading people and knowing what to say, when to say it and how to say it, was a big part of not getting my ass beat every day growing up.

She puckers her lips. "I'm just not sure about it yet." I bite into my own pizza. "You're not interested in working the other end of the business?" she asks, being as careful in her wording, too.

"No thanks. Don't have the makings for a good one."

She shrugs like she doesn't believe that. Funny, she didn't look quite so sure of me at the pub earlier today when Brodie mentioned it. She looked downright horrified to think Brodie would recruit someone like me.

I finish my slice, and my beer. "I'll get you another," Rachel says.

"I'll get it." I stand, grab a beer from the fridge and refill her wine. She smiles at me, and I sit and turn to Lucas. "What do people do for fun around this town? I know it's not playing the piano. I haven't seen anyone using it yet."

Rachel laughs. "Be thankful for that. When they do play it, it's horrible."

"Good to know."

"We have a festival coming up at the end of the summer. It's fun."

I eye her, sensing our definition of fun might be different. "Define fun."

"There's an arm-wrestling competition. You might be interested in that." She flashes her bicep. "Not that you're going to take the championship trophy from me."

"No, you're right. I've seen your moves," I remind her, deadpan.

She laughs. "You're never going to let that go, are you?"

"Afraid not."

"Well, there's also mashed potato wrestling."

What the fuck? "Are you kidding me?"

"I wish." She laughs. "The mayor's wife is from Minnesota." I arch a brow, needing more of an explanation. "It's the potato capital." She holds her hands up. "It's weird, I know."

"It's probably not as weird as the clam on the water tower."

She covers her mouth to stifle a laugh. "So, it's not just me?"

"Afraid not. Americans are a strange bunch." I shake my head and ask, "You grew up right here, in Gloucester?"

"Yes, last year we moved back after..." Her words fall off and her gaze jerks to Lucas.

"After the divorce." Lucas fills the words in for her as he wipes sauce from his mouth with the back of his hand.

Rachel points to his napkin. "Use a napkin, Lucas."

He wipes his clean face with the napkin and Rachel rolls her eyes at me. "Do you play piano?" she asks.

"No, do you?"

"Not well. I took lessons as a child." A soft smile comes over her face. "Mom played, our house was always filled with music, until my father..." She snaps out of whatever daydream she was in. "Life changes. Mom got busy opening and running the bakery."

"You miss it," I state, meaning the music.

"Yeah." She holds her hands up in defeat. "What are you going to do? There's just no time anymore."

"There's a piano in your living room."

She grins at me. "You saw that, did you?"

"It's big, hard to miss."

"Mom downsized after I moved to the city. My place was bigger, so I took it with me. I couldn't bear for her to sell it." She once again looks nostalgic. The piano, the music brings back happy memories for her. "Mrs. Potter gave me lessons when I was young, then financially..." She pauses for a brief second. "...Anyway, she still gives them. She's well into her seventies now. She lives just two houses over. The cute blue bungalow."

Lucas plugs his nose and sounds like he'd just swallowed helium when he pipes in with, "She smells funny."

"Ohmigod, Lucas," Rachel blurts out and tries to stifle a laugh. "She just has a lot of animals."

"Cat lady? I heard about them over here."

"Bunnies, actually. She walks them like they're cats, though."

"Yeah, Americans are strange," I say again a teasing grin on my face.

She doesn't disagree. Instead, she says, "Have you seen the pet walking club? Dogs, cats, bunnies, and Mr. Peterson has a pot belly pig named Stanley. Now if you want to talk about strange."

I grin. "Maybe if we get that raccoon out of your wall—"

She holds her hands up. "Nope, no time for pets around this place. I'm run off my feet as it is."

"Same," I agree. Between work and my woodworking, I wouldn't be able to give a pet what it needed. There was a time though, long ago, that I would have killed for something to love—something to love me back. But it's that kind of thinking that would have gotten my head bashed in by Da. Today, well... today I don't have anything. I care for nothing or no one, and no one cares for me in return. When you're a kid and have everything, or everyone you ever tried to love taken away from you, you learn not to get too attached.

"Mom, I want a puppy."

I cringe, and mouth the word *sorry*. Rachel puts her hands on the table and pushes to her feet. "How about a sticky bun?"

Lucas licks his lips. "Yum."

Nice distraction trick. If I ever have kids, I'll have to remember that. Not that I'm ever having kids. Rachel goes to the sink to wash her hands and Lucas puts his arm out and checks his red elbow.

"You okay, mate?"

"Yeah, just banged up from those dickheads." My eyes go wide, and I glance at Rachel. Fortunately for Lucas, the water drowned out his words and prevented Rachel from hearing. For a second, I think about correcting him. I don't, partly because he's right. Those guys are dickheads, and partly because it's not my place to discipline.

"What do you do for fun?" I ask instead.

"I play soccer," he tells me.

"Did you know we call it football in Scotland?"

Lucas smiles. "I read that." He plunks his elbows on the table and rests his face in his hands. "Mr. Sutton is moving soon and we need a new coach."

I take in the sheer disappointment on the kids face. "That's tough, mate."

"Will you be our coach?" Lucas asks me, his eyes full of hope like he just solved world hunger or something.

"Nae, I'm not a coach."

Rachel puts a plate with a sticky bun in front of Lucas and me. "Lucas, Tavish is busy. I'm sure someone will step up."

"Mom, where were we on that puppy?"

She shakes her head, ignoring him.

"What happens if someone doesn't step up?"

Mind your business, Tavish, otherwise you're going to get yourself into something you want no part of.

"No soccer for the rest of the summer. I'd do it, but I don't know the first thing about soccer. I never played. I was a book nerd."

"I noticed the bookshelf in the living room." Her head jerks back a bit. She hadn't given me a tour of the place, but I always survey my surroundings. Not that I have to worry about anyone jumping out of the woodwork and pummeling me here in sleepy Gloucester, but old habits die hard. Although there could be a raccoon attack at any point tonight.

"Do you like to read?" Rachel asks.

"Aye."

She nods, somewhat surprised, and I get it. She's a girl who judges a book by the cover and by book, I'm talking about me, and by cover, I'm talking about my ink. I'm used to it.

"What brought you here? You're far away from home? Do you still have family there?"

"Aye, I am," is all I say to her three questions and bite into the sticky bun. I go quiet, my eyes closing as the flavor fills my mouth and dances on my tongue. "Shite," I say after a moment. "That is good."

"I'm so glad you like it."

Lucas bites into his, briefly closes his eyes and mumbles, "Shite."

Rachel gasps and after I swallow, I once again mouth the word *sorry*. If those last two apologies don't prove I'm not the best around kids, I don't know what will.

"You probably shouldn't say that, mate. I shouldn't either." Who knew kids were so impressionable?

"Is it a bad word?" he asks.

"Aye, it is." So is dickhead, but I leave that alone.

He frowns and glances down. "Oh, is it the same as shit? But in Scotland you say shite?"

I bite back a grin as Rachel stands. "On that note, I think dinner is over. Why don't you run upstairs and get into your pajamas, and you can watch some TV while I tidy up." Lucas pushes back from the chair and darts upstairs. Rachel shakes her head at me. "Out of the mouths of babes."

I carry a couple plates to the counter. "Sorry about that."

"Don't be. I'm sure he hears worse on the playground."

"He seems like a good kid, Rachel." I pause, not sure how to bring it up.

"But…" she adds, prompting me.

"His dad isn't in the picture?"

She rinses the plates and bends to put them in the dishwasher and I make it my mission not to stare at her arse.

Mission…impossible.

"He's on the road a lot." She shrugs like it's nothing but I'm guessing it's something. "He comes around when he can."

"What does he do?'

"He plays for the Boston Bucks."

"Hart," I mumble, searching my memory and trying to place him.

"No, that's my maiden name. I changed it back after the divorce. Lucas still goes by Anderson."

The last name brings instant recognition, and I stare at Rachel, having a hard time believing Jason was her type. Not that I know her all that well, and now look who's judging. "Jason Anderson, that's your ex?"

"Yup." She loads more dishes. "Heard of him, huh?"

"Yeah," is all I say. I don't want to tell her what I really think. But the guy is kind of an arse and recently made the news for some sex video and then caused such a scene when a server spilled beer on him, he made her cry and got her fired. Maybe he should pick on someone his own size. I wouldn't mind going a round or two with him in the cage—or even outside of it. Wait no, I don't fight with anger, or emotions. Not anymore, not after…

"He wasn't always like that," she says quietly, pulling my thoughts back, like she knows what I'm thinking. Her smile is strained as she tries to make me understand and I get it. She doesn't want to come off as a woman who chases after abusive assholes. "He can be really good with Lucas. He just doesn't always understand..."

"Why he wants to wear skirts?" She nods, and the second I see tears in her eyes, I fight not to pull her into my arms again. It felt too good last time. My thoughts go to Lucas wearing a skirt and the playground bullies. "Maybe Lucas should take some self defense courses."

She swallows, obviously struggling to pull herself together and I try to make light of things. "You watch Cobra Kai, and you looked like you had some killer moves on the playground. Maybe you could teach him."

A tortured laugh, or maybe it's a groan crawls out of her throat. "I am so embarrassed. I can't even believe...."

"Don't be. It was cute."

"I wasn't going for cute. I wanted to scare you."

"Sorry, Rachel. I don't scare easily and for what it's worth..." I nudge her chin with my fist. "Mama bear is a pretty great thing to be. We should all be so lucky." She angles her head, and for a second I think she's going to pick at old wounds, so I get ahead of it. "Thanks for dinner. I should check to see what's crawling inside your wall and then I need to go. I still have some work to do on your mother's rocking chairs."

Her gaze goes to my hands. "I can't wait to see them. Brodie told me you were handsy." She shakes her head. "I mean handy. I meant to say handy. Handy, yeah handy." I take in the color moving into her cheeks, the flustered way she's waving her hands, and my traitorous tadger twitches.

Does Rachel want me to be handsy? I saw her sweet ass earlier, and that's something Mr. Traitorous could get behind...literally.

Shite.

Walk the fuck away, mate.

What the hell is wrong with me?

Last night had been going well. I was having a great conversation with Tavish, getting to know him, somewhat. It's clear there are things he doesn't want to talk about and that's just fine by me. But how could I have stared at his hands like they were God's gift to women—and they likely are—and say he was handsy. I groan, and shake my head at my foolish girly behaviour.

"You okay, Mom?" Lucas asks from the back seat.

I glance at him in the rear-view mirror and smile as he tugs on the collar of his soccer jersey. His father wanted him to play hockey, naturally. He wasn't pleased when Lucas didn't have much skill with the stick and preferred soccer. "I am. Just complaining about the bad drivers."

"That's what Dad says you are."

My stomach twists. In the later years, Jason complained about everything I did. I used to think Lucas was too young to understand, or wasn't listening, but now I realized he heard and processed it all, and I really don't want him to turn out like his father.

I wink at him. "I'm not so bad."

"I think you're a good driver." My heart squeezes as tight as my throat.

"Thanks, hon."

I concentrate on the road ahead, happy to know Lucas still has a chance at being a decent human being. If I have anything to do with it, and I do, I'll make sure he treats others with kindness and respect.

I pull between two big SUVs in the parking lot, and Lucas opens his door and jumps out, running to the field. I hike my purse over my shoulder, grab my folding chair and Thermos of coffee and follow behind.

"Rachel," one of the other moms calls out and waves to me. Okay, that's strange. Most of the moms are all in a clique, turning their noses up at the divorcée who works, as opposed to hanging out all day with the stay-at-home moms. Why does there have to be a divide? Can't we all just support one another in whatever we decide is best for us and our kids?

I walk toward Tamara, and she has a curious look on her face. Oh, God, I think I know where this is going.

"So," she begins. "Bella says she saw that hot new Scottish guy in the neighbourhood coming from your place last night." She flicks her long dark hair over her shoulder and leans toward me, conspiratorial like. "I need all the deets."

First, why would I tell her anything, and second what I do with the hot Scot is none of her business. Then again, if I don't tell her, I'm sure they'll come up with something scandalous and starts spreading lies.

Maybe you should give them something scandalous to talk about, Rachel.

I shrug like it's nothing, because it isn't. "He helped Lucas out with a situation, and I invited him for pizza to thank him."

She frowns, disappointed in the answer, and taps her nail into the air "Oh, I thought maybe you were hitting that."

"Not hitting anything." I take a sip from my Thermos.

She moans. "If I were single…I'd climb that guy like a tree."

I nearly choke on my coffee. "Yeah, I'm not really in the market."

One of Tamara's other friends arrives, and she turns her attention to her, giving me a chance to walk away and set my chair up a little further down the field. I'm not a social misfit or anything, I just don't want to sit around gossiping about other people.

I check my phone, read through a few email messages, and when the coach blows his whistle, I turn my attention to the field. My heart warms as Coach bends to say something to Lucas and then ruffles his hair. Just then I hear, "Hurry Ben, we're late."

I turn and spot Sophie Potter, at least I think it's her, giving her son a nudge to send him to the field.

"I don't want to play," the child says.

"Just try it, and see. I bet you'll have fun."

The boy groans and saunters off, and I make eye contact with Sophie. But a noise behind her gains my attention and I turn, catching sight of a man on a motorcycle in a leather jacket parked on the street, watching the action on the field. Is that Tavish?

"Rachel," Sophie says with a squeal. "I thought that was you."

"Hey Sophie, how are you?"

She runs her fingers through her long blonde hair. "Running late as always."

"Did you move back?" I ask. Sophie was a couple of grades below me in school. She lived with her grandmother Mrs. Potter, the bunny lady. We weren't friends, but we weren't enemies, either. We just ran in different circles.

She looks out into the field. "Yeah, things didn't work out in California."

"I'm sorry."

She scans the sidelines. "Any hot single dads here?"

I laugh. "I really don't know."

Her mouth turns down. "Sorry to hear about you and Jason."

God, does the whole world know his antics? "Thanks," is all I say, not wanting to talk about his affair with a barely of age girl and the resulting video that was circulated. In the distance, the motorcycle revs, and Sophie turns. She tosses her hair over her shoulder.

"Who is that?"

"I have no idea," I answer.

She narrows her eyes. "Are you sure? I think he's staring at you." A small thrill goes through me. "Or maybe he's staring at me," she says with a grin, jutting her hip out as she turns back around. She giggles, not that Tavish can hear her, and what is he doing here anyway? A second later, he eases into traffic, taking my breath with him. "Do you think he's from around here?" she asks.

"No idea."

I turn my attention back to the field, and Sophie shades the sun from her eyes, and takes stock of the other parents sitting around. She tugs on her T-shirt, pulling it a bit lower to expose her very lovely cleavage. Damned if I don't feel a bit inadequate next to her. I quickly shut down that kind of thinking. After the years of insults from my ex—I could never live up to the puck bunnies who threw themselves at him—it's easy to slip into that negative thinking.

"I think I'll go say hello to the other parents," she says with a big smile. "I'll see you around, Rachel. Maybe we can get the boys together to play."

"I'm sure Lucas would love that." It'll be nice for my son to have a friend close by and with any luck, they'll hit it off and be in the same class come grade two. I smile as she walks away. I'm sure if there are single dads here, she'll have no trouble snagging one. The thoughts of her with Tavish, though, that kind of turns my stomach. Not that I want him for myself. I just...don't want her with him, and I really can't explain why. Seriously though, what was he doing here?

I work to get Tavish out of my brain and concentrate on watching the kids play a practice game. I really wish I knew more about soccer so I could help when the coach leaves. I suppose I could do a bit of research and figure out the rules. I pull out my phone and start reading and before I know it, practice is over.

Lucas comes running over, Ben tight on his heels, and I really love how he took the new kid under his wing. "Mom, this is Ben. Can he come for ice cream with us?"

"He'll have to check with his mother."

Ben takes off running to Sophie, and the next thing I know, Sophie is walking back with him, an almost sheepish look on her face. "Did you guys want to join us for ice cream?" I ask.

"Actually, if you don't mind, would it be okay if Ben went with you? I was just chatting with Derek over there. He's separated from his wife, and he's dropping his son off with her and we're going to grab a drink and get caught up."

Holy, fast work.

"Yeah sure. I guess." Lucas does a fist pump and that makes me smile.

Sophie wipes a smudge of dirt off Ben's face. "You can drop him off at my grandmother's afterward."

"Okay. Sure."

I pack up my chair and glance around, foolishly searching for Tavish's bike as we make our way to the car. Of course, he's long gone and I'm still not sure that was him. *Yeah, because there are a ton of leather wearing bikers living in your quiet neighborhood, Rachel.* Once the boys are buckled in, we head to the main street and get ice cream. We eat it at the park, and after we're done, I consider stopping at my mother's place to see if Tavish dropped off her new chairs, but I of course don't want him to think I'm stalking.

Maybe he was stalking me at the soccer field.

While that idea should be creepy, it kind of thrills me. I head home, but go a different way. Why? Oh, I don't know. Maybe

I want to drive by Tavish's place, catch a glimpse of him. I slow the car and try not to look like a creeper as I peer down his driveway, catching sight of his bike, but he's nowhere to be found.

"Mom, is that Tavish's bike?"

I gulp. Busted. "I don't know."

As I step on the gas, suddenly desperate not to get caught, Lucas starts telling Ben about Tavish and his kilt and facts about Scotland. I turn down our road, and frown when I see a big black truck in my driveway. What the hell?

Since I don't want to block in whoever's there, I park on the street, and the boys jump out and start kicking the soccer ball Lucas left on the lawn. I follow them and as I approach the truck, walking toward the driver's side, the door swings open, and my heart speeds up as Tavish steps out.

"Hey," he says.

"Tavish," Lucas yells, a smile on his face as he echoes my sentiments. "That's Tavish," he tells Ben. "The guy I was telling you about."

"What...what's going on?"

"This," he answers, reaching into the back of his truck to pull out what looks like a cage, a pinecone bouncing around inside it. But it's his biceps and the way they flex with the movement that's holding my attention. "It's time to catch ourselves a raccoon."

My heart misses a beat when I realize what he's done. "You didn't have to do that."

"Oh, okay then." There's a teasing grin on his face as he lifts the cage, pretending he's going to put it back, and I reach out and put my hand on his arm. A fine shiver goes through my body and I pray he's unaware.

"No, wait. I mean, since you're here, and you have a cage."

His grin widens. "You want it then?"

Oh, I want it, I want it so bad it's utterly ridiculous.

But that's not what he's talking about. I laugh to cover my inappropriate, and unwanted arousal. "Mr. Hot Scot in a Kilt, slayer of raccoons."

He angles his head. "Hot Scot?"

Good Lord, Rachel.

"Oh, I just mean...it rhymes."

"Rhyming is important here in America, is it?"

Heat flushes my face, and I wave my hand in front of it. "Yeah, something like that. "

"I'll have to remember that."

I nod toward the house. "Let's get out of the sun. I think I got overheated on the field."

I walk up the front walkway and fish my key from my pocket. "I'm going to need access to the attic," he says from behind me, his body close.

"I'm worried about what might attack you up there. Do you think I should call in a professional?"

"Nae, I got this. I'm going to need peanut butter, though?"

"Are you hungry? If you are, I can do better than peanut butter."

He laughs and pulls the pinecone from the cage. "No, I need to smear it on this to bait the raccoon."

"Ah...in the kitchen." We head to the kitchen where I grab the jar of peanut butter from the fridge and a spoon to dip into it.

"And a flashlight."

I root through the drawer for a flashlight as he scoops out a generous amount of peanut butter, smears it on the pinecone and uses his finger to spread it. I gulp as I watch him. That should not be turning me on. I'm clearly more desperate than I ever realized.

He finishes up and rinses his hand in the sink as I put the lid on the peanut butter and put it back in the fridge. The boys come running into the kitchen for a drink, and I walk him upstairs to my bedroom. He pauses at the door, his big body stiffening, and for the briefest of seconds, I consider what's going through his mind. Does he think I'm trying to get him between the sheets? "The hatch is in my closet."

"Right."

He continues to stand there, staring at something, and I nearly swallow my tongue when I turn to follow his gaze and find all my laundry on my bed, my black lace panties on the top of the pile. Dammit, I'd dumped the basket earlier, and didn't have time to put it away before soccer. How embarrassing.

"I uh, if you'll just point the way."

"Right." I hurry across the room, and swing open my closet door. "I think you'll need a ladder."

He sets the cage down. "Do you have one?"

My laugh comes out sounding strangled. "Actually, no."

"A chair will do." I turn to head back downstairs. "I'll get it," he says and I hurry to my bed to tuck my panties into my drawer as his boots sound on the stairs. I start folding the laundry and find myself smiling as he talks to Lucas and Ben in the living room. It's been a long time since a man has been in my house and I kind of like it.

He comes back with a chair and sets it below the hatch. I try not to stare at his big body as he climbs onto the chair and carefully pushes on the hatch to release it. He shines the light into the attic, and when he turns, I find myself face to face with his crotch. Dear God.

"Rachel, you've got a problem. A big one."

"Yeah, a big one," I mumble in response.

6

TAVISH

"What's that?" I bend, ducking out of the hatch, and find a flushed Rachel staring at me.

She blinks rapidly. "Huh?"

"You agreed when I said you had a big problem." I shine the light into the attic. "You know what's going on then?"

"No what?"

"Mama raccoon has a den up there." I turn the flashlight off. "You have a family of raccoons living in your attic."

Her brow pulls together. "Oh, that's bad."

"Yeah." I scrub my face. "I can lure the mother with the trap, and then carry the babies out once I have her secure. I think we need to take them to wildlife shelter. We probably won't catch the mother until tonight, when she's active. I can stay until we catch her if you'd like. I don't want to leave her in the cage all night, when she has babies to feed."

"I can't ask you to do that." She fidgets, like she's uncomfortable asking for help. "I can call someone."

"It's not a problem."

"I don't want to put you out."

I shrug. "Make me a peanut butter sandwich and we'll call it even."

She laughs. "I can do better than that."

"Let me get the trap set up, and I'll be right down." She nods and hesitates for a second. Is she worried mama racoon might attack me? Or maybe she's worried I'm going to go through her personal belongings, which I'd never do. I'm sure if you're judging a book by its cover, nothing about me screams trustworthy. Hell, if she knew the truth, there's no way she'd trust me either. "Don't worry. I'm a big boy. I got this."

Once again a light dusting of pink colors her cheeks. Was it something I said. "I uh...I have to walk Ben home. He's just two doors down, and then I was going to make a salad and put some steaks on the grill."

"You're my kind of girl," I joke, and I don't miss her quick intake of breath. "I'll just be a few minutes." I put the cage into the attic and hoist myself up. Not sure if she's still standing there or not, I position the cage, and climb back out to find her gone. I pick up the chair and step back into her room, my gaze going to the pile of laundry still on her bed. My tadger is happy that her panties are no longer visible. Speaking of my tadger, I adjust it in my pants. It sort of got out of place when it thickened earlier.

Downstairs, the door opens and closes and I take a moment to glance around the room. It lacks anything male, a telltale sign that no man lives here with her and her son. I spot a pink Thermos mug and an iPad on her nightstand. I'm tempted to open it to see what she likes to read before falling asleep. Instead, I take note of the pale blue walls, the quilt on her bed, and the open door, leading into a bathroom. Her house is old, but it has good bones, and unlike mine, it exudes warmth, much like Rachel herself.

I make my way downstairs and push the chair back under the kitchen table. My gaze strays to the papers Brodie had given her. Christ, she signed it. She's actually going to go with Dad for Hire. There's no doubt she could use a guy in her life, and Lucas would benefit from some male influence. Why then do I have a fucking knot in my stomach and what was it that changed her mind?

The door opens and Lucas comes barrelling into the kitchen, still in his soccer gear. "Why don't you head up and get a shower before dinner," Rachel says following him into the kitchen. She goes still when she sees me, standing over the papers. "Mom called when I was walking Ben home. She loves the chairs."

"Glad to hear it."

"I can't wait to see them." She walks around me, and picks the papers up, setting them on top of her microwave. "How did you get into woodworking?"

"At one of the schools I went to, the shop teacher, Mr. Phillips saw my interest and invited me to his home. He had a shop in his backyard. All equipped. But then..." I let my words fall off.

"One of the schools, huh?" she teases, keeping things light and I appreciate that. I don't need the reminder that I lose everyone I care about. He was my teacher. I was his student. Apparently, inviting a student to your home was frowned upon by the school board and that was the end of that. "You were at a lot of schools?" She pulls some vegetables from the fridge and sets them on the counter. "A troublemaker? Got kicked out a lot?"

I grin at the accuracy. "Something like that. I think Mr. Phillips wanted me to find something better to do with my hands." I hold my hands out and catching me by surprise she takes one between her palms and starts reading my tattoos.

She lightly traces the small lily. "This one is very delicate. Does it have meaning?"

"Lily was my mom's name."

She blinks up at me. "That's sweet."

I snort. "And that's why I got my ass kicked so many times." She frowns, and I slam a mental door on those old memories.

Her voice is low when she says, "You said was..."

I nod and glance at the vegetables. "Want some help?"

"You're good in the kitchen?" she asks, going along with the abrupt change in conversation.

"Probably not as good as you, but I've been cooking for myself for a very long time now."

"I'm sure women cook for you all the time," she teases. "Sophie would probably like to cook for you," she adds almost under her breath.

"Who?"

"Oh, uh..." She grabs a cutting board. "She's Ben's mother. Back in town. She was at the soccer field."

"The blonde you were talking to."

Her eyes go wide. "So that was you." I nod and she continues. "What were you doing there?"

I was driving by and saw your car. "Thought I'd see how hard it was to teach football to a bunch of kids."

"Are you kidding me?" Excitement moves over her face and it's like jumper cables to my heart. "Are you thinking of coaching?"

"I don't know." Fuck, I don't want to give her false hope. I wasn't really even sure why I'd stopped. Somewhere in the back of my mind, I thought I could give something to the community, but then I saw her signed papers. I'm sure her Dad for Hire will take on the job. "I just thought I'd check it out. What's this about Sophie?"

She chops into the lettuce, her gaze on me. "Why, are you interested?"

Whoa, is that jealousy?

"No."

Her next chop is with less intensity. "She was asking about you."

"What'd you tell her?"

She turns from me. "Nothing. I wasn't sure if it was you or not on the bike. It's not like you're the only tattooed big guy who drives around town on a motorcycle, you know."

"No, I never thought I was." I'm pretty sure I am. I've been in this small, picturesque town for a month now, and I haven't seen too many bikers. A few pass through, sure, but I don't think too many live here. I never thought this was the life for me, either. But I enjoy being out of the limelight. I never much liked it to begin with. It just came with the career. When I was really little, I liked being invisible. When you were invisible, you couldn't get hurt. That changed during puberty when I grew up and out. There was no hiding then, which meant I had to get good with my fists and fast.

"What can I do?" I ask, and rinse my hands.

She nods to the doors leading to the back deck. "How about getting the barbecue started?"

"I'm on it." I step outside and the warm breeze blows over me. Off in the distance, I hear a dog bark followed by clucking chickens.

I take the grill cover off the barbecue and turn the burner knobs until they light, hearing the click of the automatic starter. I close the cover and check out her big backyard as it heats up. A rooster crows and I shake my head. That son of a bitch has been waking me up early every morning. Rachel steps out with the steaks, and I take a deep breath as she smiles at me.

I lift the lid, and scrape down the grill. "Are you sure you wouldn't prefer rooster? If we cook it low and slow, it should be tender, enough."

She laughs. "He is so annoying."

"Tell me about it. Are we even allowed chickens and roosters in this neighborhood?"

"It's the mayor's wife who raises them."

"Maybe she needs to go back to Minnesota," I mumble.

Rachel laughs as I fork one steak and drop it onto the hot grill. "I'll get the sauce."

She disappears inside and I add all three steaks to the grill, and I have no idea why, but something about being here with Rachel and her son, this small family brings back long ago memories of my mom. Fuck, I never should have opened that door. I stare off into the backyard, the small shed that's a little off kilter—sort of like me right now—and take a couple fast breaths, working to push the memories down deep.

"Tavish."

I turn and find Rachel staring at me, a bottle of barbecue sauce in her hand.

"She died."

What the fuck are you doing, mate?

Confusion morphs into understanding as I lift my hand and show her the lily. She zeroes in on it, her face full of compassion. "I'm sorry."

I don't know why, and I don't normally like it when people direct compassion my way, but something in her face is very soothing. "It was a long time ago. I was a wee boy."

"Which makes it worse, in my opinion." My throat clogs, and I nod, but she doesn't know the half of it, nor will she. Silence hovers between us as I take the bottle from her and squirt sauce onto the steaks. She breaks the silence. "My dad didn't die, but he's not in my life. He hasn't been for a very long time."

I turn and eye her. "Is that a good thing or a bad thing?"

A line forms in her forehead as it wrinkles. "You know, no one has ever asked me that before."

"My da was in my life, for a while anyway, and it wasn't a good thing." Her hand lands on my arm, and my chest constricts as she gives a soft squeeze. "I grew up in foster homes." *Again, what the fuck are you doing, mate?* "That's how Brodie and I know each other." She stares at me, looking like she wants to ask me something but is almost afraid to. She doesn't have to voice what's in her head. I already know the question. "There was a kid in the house bullying him constantly and horribly, until I beat the shit out of him...badly."

"Wow."

A bolt of hot heat goes through me, still angry at myself for not having control. How was I any better than my father? "It wasn't good, Rachel." I swallow down the pain as those old memories haunt me. "I really hurt him."

"I'm sorry, Tavish. You were protecting a friend. I'm sure your heart was in a good place, and you didn't mean to really hurt him."

"No, I think I did. I worry I'm like my da." She stares at me, her eyes wide as they move over my face. Now that she knows who I am and what I'm capable of, is she having second thoughts about being my friend, having me in her house? I'm not going to put that on her, though. I close the lid on the barbecue and take a step back. "I should go."

"No," she blurts out quickly and I go still. "Did you see that salad? We can't eat that all on our own, and with the price of produce today, I don't want it to go to waste." I hesitate and she hurries out with, "And I have sticky buns left over. If you don't stay, I'll eat them all and hate myself. Plus...raccoon."

My shoulders relax. "Right. I really need to take care of that."

"How about a cold beer?"

"Sounds about perfect."

She goes inside and I turn the burners down as Lucas comes out, freshly showered. He has his football under his arm. "Wanna play?" he asks.

"Sure."

I take the three steps down and we start kicking the ball back and forth in the yard. "You're really good," Lucas tells me. He frowns. "Coach leaves next week."

"You really like playing?" He nods and I once again remember the signed papers. "I'm sure someone will step up."

"Yeah, maybe."

Rachel steps onto the deck and holds a beer up. "Come on, mate. Let's get a drink." I ruffle his hair and we jump back onto the deck. I take a sip of beer and turn my attention back to the steaks.

Lucas grabs his iPad and starts playing a game as the dog barks and rooster crows. "Mom," he calls out. "Where were we on getting a dog?"

"Not," Rachel says with an eye roll and sits. She gives me a grin and I turn back to the steaks. She looks like she has something on her mind when I glance back at her. Is she thinking about what I told her? Having second thoughts?

"Everything okay?"

Her smile is forced. "Work stuff."

"You like what you do?"

She takes a sip of wine. "Yes, but it's hard to get ahead." I eye her. "It's a boys' club."

"Aye," I respond.

"Single mom who doesn't get invited to play golf and make connections with the CEO. I was just passed over for a promotion. I thought..."

Her voice falls and she averts her gaze.

"Thought what?"

"It's probably stupid, but I thought maybe if I get a Dad for Hire, I could also get a guy to pretend to be my fiancé at the dreaded summer bonding retreat. It's not mandatory to attend, but it really is, you know. The guys at work have stay-at-home wives who take care of everything, so nothing inter-feres with their jobs. I thought if I could show I had support too..." She frowns and sighs. "I'm good at what I do...it's just...boys' club."

"I'm sure you are, but failing to get ahead isn't on you. It's the toxic culture."

She exhales, and stares off into the distance. "Jason went to the retreat once. He fit right in, and he made things worse for me."

My muscles clench. "How's that?"

"He comes from an old-fashioned family. His mom stayed home and his dad worked. None of them think I should be working. I grew up in a family with an absent father, and Mom always worked."

"There's nothing wrong with a woman working. This is the twenty-first century. If you want to work, you should work."

"There are times I do feel guilty and that I'm not doing the best job with Lucas."

I lean into her. "Lucas is an amazing kid. He's bright and funny and well-adjusted. You must know that."

She swallows, her eyes watery as she quietly says, "He gets...bullied."

"That's not on you, or him. Simply put, bullies are dickheads." I hold one hand up palm out. "Lucas's words, not mine."

"Ohmigod, what am I going to do with that kid."

I cringe. "I don't think I was supposed to tell you he said that."

"I won't say anything. I like that he's comfortable enough with you to say things like that. He needs someone like you. I don't want to mess that up for him." I'm not sure how she thinks she'll mess it up. If anyone is going to mess anything up, it'll be me. I'm about to tell her that, and go silent as she glances down, and says very quietly, "If Lucas...if he had a male role model, maybe—"

"I think Dad for Hire is a good thing," I tell her, my chest tight.

"Agreed," she says quickly and then as if wanting to end the conversation, she glances at the grill. "How are the steaks?"

"Done."

She heads inside and gets a plate for the steaks, and we all sit down like a family to enjoy a meal. Lucas tells us a funny story from camp and we all laugh. I like being around the table with this small family far too much, which bothers me. Lucas does need male influence, but Rachel doesn't need a guy like me in her life, not permanently, anyway. I don't know how to be a father, having been taken away from my own and tossed around. I can't get close; I won't let myself. Other than Brodie, whenever I get close to someone, poof, I do something to ruin it—or I don't do anything at all—and I still lose them. I'm better off not opening myself up and Rachel is better off not associating with a man who nearly beat a guy to death. I swore I'd never lose it like that again. But what if I do?

Once dinner is done and the dishes are cleared, Rachel gets Lucas settled in for a movie before bed. I gesture with a nod to the upstairs. "Should we check on the trap?"

"Yeah, sure." She nods rapidly. "Good idea. With any luck, we'll catch it while the wildlife shelters are still open. Otherwise I don't know what we'll do."

I grab a chair from the kitchen and we head up the stairs. With the sun setting outside, she flicks on the light and I press a finger to my lips. She nods and we tiptoe into the closet. I put the chair down but she's so close it lands on her toe.

She lets loose a squeal and starts hopping around. "I'm sorry," I whisper, and scoop her up. I set her on her bed, and drop to my knees. "How bad?" Another strange squealing sound catches in her throat, and when my gaze lands on hers and she takes a deep breath, sexual energy arcs between us.

Tap out, Tavish. Tap the fuck out.

I go up on my knees, my hands on her thighs, and she swallows as my gaze drops to her mouth. As I battle with myself, she wets her lips and the need inside me knocks my last ounces of willpower to the mat with a fatal blow.

I lean into her, my lips a breath away from hers when a loud clang, followed by a screeching sound, curls around us.

We both glance toward the closet, and her eyes go wide. "I think."

"Yeah, I think…"

I think I was just cock-blocked by a fucking racoon.

RACHEL

I can't believe I almost kissed Tavish. There's no denying I wanted it. I realize I haven't been touched in a long time and that could simply be it. But I think it has more to do with the fact that Tavish is big and hot and the sexiest man on the planet. It's so strange. I never thought I'd be attracted to a guy like him, one who exudes power and protectiveness and used to beat up people for a living. I'm a woman who hates violence, yet, I can't deny the attraction.

I did a bit of research on him after he left my place Saturday night. MMA fighter loved by all, and surrounded by gorgeous women. While he seems different from my ex, there are similarities too, with enough red flags that I could make a noose and hang myself with it.

So what? Have some fun and get out. It's not like you want to marry the man, Rachel.

True, and while the needy spot between my legs is encouraging me to jump his bones, after Saturday night, there's no reason for us to ever see each other again, except in passing.

He helped me with Lucas on the playground and the racoon problem in my attic, and I thanked him for everything with two meals and some sticky buns. I guess at the end of the day, it's a good thing we didn't end up kissing and getting into something that's probably not good for either of us.

I check myself in the rear-view mirror, smoothing my hand over my hair as I head to the pub to meet Brodie. I called him this morning from work to let him know I signed the papers and would be dropping them off. He offered to pick them up from my place tonight, but I told him it wasn't a problem to take them to him on my lunch hour, and no, it's not because I want to get a glimpse of Tavish—in his kilt.

Much.

When did I become so damn pathetic?

Downtown is busy this Monday morning and I struggle to find parking. I finally snag a spot, and put on a bit of lipstick —yes, my lips are chapped—before exiting the vehicle and walking into Kilting Around. It's lunch hour and it's busy, and I spot Brodie behind the bar. I hurry toward him and glance around. No, I'm not looking for Tavish.

Much.

As I approach the bar, I have a sudden bout of anxiety. Is hiring a dad for Lucas and a daddy for me a good idea? My steps slow even more, and the next thing I know, there's a big hand on my back.

"Keep moving or you're going to get run over."

"Oh," I say, a quiver going through me as the heat of Tavish's breath falls over my neck. It's ridiculous how happy I am to see him. I turn and his big body hovers over mine, and I suddenly forget how to walk. He nudges me again, and practically picks me up and sets me on the stool. He leans over me, and all I want to do is push up and finally see what it's like to kiss him.

"What can I do for you, Rachel?"

Talk about a loaded question.

"I uh…I'm actually here to see Brodie."

"Here I thought you were stalking me." I laugh lightly as his eyes leave mine to catch Brodie's gaze behind the counter. He puts his hand over my head and points down.

"Someone here to see you," he calls out.

He walks away and I'm not sure why his sudden departure hits like a punch to the gut. I stare after him for a second until he disappears into the crowd. Brodie puts a finger up and pours a beer. He puts it on a tray, wipes his hands on his apron, and walks my way. He's grinning. Did Tavish tell him that we've been eating together…that we nearly kissed? Oh, God, I hope not.

I pull the papers from my purse and set then on the counter. "Nice," he says and picks them up. "You won't regret this."

"I really hope not."

"I already found you a match."

My heart jumps not sure if it's from happiness or worry. "Can I see the file on him?"

"Yup, I'll email it to you later if that's okay." I nod, and try to tamp down my anxiety. "Do you want a drink, something to eat?"

"Water, but I'm hungry, so I'll order." He sets a glass of water in front of me and hands me a menu. I scan it and focus in on the traditional Scottish dishes. "I think I'll try something Scottish. Nothing too weird, though." I lift my head to find Brodie grinning. "What?"

"Nothing. I think you should try Scottish cock."

Blood drains to my toes. OMG, he knows. He knows how much I want to climb Tavish like a tree. "What?" I choke out, trying to play it cool.

He points to the menu. "Cock-a-leekie soup." He's still grinning, and I can only assume he knows something is up and is messing with me. "Scottish version of chicken soup. Nothing too weird."

"Yeah, sounds good."

"One Scottish cock coming up." His chuckle gets drowned out by the crowd as he leaves and my body nearly melts on the stool as Tavish comes back up to me and looks over my shoulder at the menu still in my hands.

"What are you having?"

"Scottish cock," I blurt out and his chuckle seeps under my skin and teases the arousal in me.

"Scottish cock is the best. I think you'll love it," he responds and I take a big drink of water, confident that he's right and that we might not be talking about the same thing. Or maybe we are.

He disappears again, and I suck in a breath. It's crazy what this man can do to me without even trying. I sip water and glance around. There are lots of business people in here today and most of them are with co-workers. Sucks that my co-workers are a bunch of assholes.

"Here you go."

Brodie comes back with the soup. "That was fast."

"You did just sign with Dad for Hire. That means you get preferential treatment, but don't tell anyone."

I pick up my spoon and smile. "I won't." He doesn't leave, instead he watches me take my first bite and the salty deliciousness dances on my tongue.

"Good, huh?"

"Delicious," I tell him. "I'm going to have to come here more often."

"For the soup or for the view?"

"What?" I ask as I spoon more soup into my mouth. His head lifts and I follow his gaze to Tavish. "I don't...I'm not..."

"He told me he took care of that pesky problem in your bedroom."

"Technically, it was in the attic off my bedroom. It was very nice of him."

"Tavish, nice..." He snort laughs. "Now that I'd like to see."

"He was nice."

"Maybe you bring something out in him others don't."

"You said he'd be a great Dad for Hire, and were trying to convince him. If you don't think he's nice, why would you want to bring him into your new business venture?"

He goes quiet, pensive for a second, and finally answers with, "Because I know him better than he knows himself."

Before I can ask exactly what that means, he tosses a rag over his shoulder and says, "Enjoy." A wink is followed up with, "The soup and the view."

"I am not..." I shake my head, not bothering to dispute it. Yeah, I've probably been blatantly staring. "I'm going to poison your next batch of sticky buns."

His laughter draws attention and I turn to spot Tavish staring at us. Heat floods my body and I go back to the soup, hoping I don't choke to death on it as my breathing quickens.

"I'll email you those papers." With that, Brodie goes back to work, and I work to tune everything out as I gobble up my soup. Once my bowl is empty, I catch Brodie's eye as I leave some bills on the bar. The place is still busy, with new customers coming in as I make my way to the door. I'm seconds from opening it when a big hand lands on it, just above my head, holding it closed.

"Were you going to leave without saying goodbye?"

Oh, God, does he have to always stand so close? I breathe in the smell of his soap, and can't help but think he'd recently showered. I will not, under any circumstance, picture him naked in his shower.

Okay, I'm picturing it.

I turn and put a smile on my face. "You were busy. I didn't want to put you out." God, I sound breathless. "I was in a hurry. Have to get back to work."

He pulls his hand back and opens the door for me. "Want me to come with you? Scare those assholes straight, and show them who's boss-girl?"

I laugh at that. "No, I got it." Will the new Dad for Hire be as intimidating as Tavish? I somehow doubt it. "Thanks again for all your help and uh, you were right, I did love the Scottish...uh." Oh, God, what am I doing.

He leans closer. "Cock."

"Yeah, that." I turn, embarssed. "I must run. See you around. Don't want to be late for my afternoon appointments." Out on the sidewalk, after the door shuts, I take a gulping breath. What the hell is wrong with me? A few people walk by, keeping a wide berth and I can't exactly blame them. I stand up straighter and pull myself together. I can't very well go to my next client's place of business looking like a hot mess.

Back in my car, I examine myself in the mirror and turn the air conditioning to full. I head to the physician's office, park, grab my briefcase full of samples and hurry inside. Maybe I should ask the doctor for something to curb my sexual appetite, which seems to have gone off kilter lately.

I head to the back, and I'm put in a room to wait for the doctor. I check my messages a few times, both excited and nervous about who Brodie set me up with. I suppose if I read through the information and don't feel like we'd be a good match, I could always swipe left. That makes me laugh. It's not a dating app, it's more about finding someone for Lucas and having a guy help me around the house with chores that are too hard. The last IKEA table I put together looks like it could topple at any moment. Honestly, I think Brodie is filling a niche needed in society.

Two physicians come into the room, and I push all my personal thoughts aside and step into professional mode. A half hour later, after a very successful meeting, I make my way to the car, checking my phone again. I guess Brodie must be too busy at the bar to send me the information. I'm getting anxious waiting, though.

Since I don't need to go back to the office and I have no more appointments, I head home, passing by Sophie and Ben on the street. They wave, and I wave back. I wonder if things worked out between her and Derek. While I don't know Sophie's story, I do know Derek is only recently separated. But why would he pass up a chance with someone who is as beautiful as Sophie?

That thought has me looking in the mirror and as old insecurities come rushing back in a whoosh, I grip the steering wheel harder. It's true, Jason did a number on my self-esteem, and months of therapy have helped, but I still have a lot of work to do.

Tavish makes you feel worthy.

Oh, God, I really need to stop thinking about him. I am not going to be seeing him anymore and I have no need to go back to the pub now that I signed the papers and handed them over to Brodie.

You could always go back for some cock, Rachel.

Lord, kill me now.

Since Lucas is still in day camp, I decide to take the next couple of hours to myself. Maybe I'll climb into the attic and clean up a bit. I think there's still some remnants of the nest still up there, and honestly, it all sounds like a horrible time.

I pull into my driveway, and decide to check my phone before heading in, and my heart leaps when I see a message from Brodie. I open the attachment, and nearly swallow my tongue when I read the name of the dad I hired: TAVISH FINDLAY.

What the ever-loving hell...

8

TAVISH

I'm tired after I finish my double shift at the pub, but my day isn't over yet. Now that I've taken on duties as a dad for Lucas and helper for Rachel, I need to get to work on the roof to ensure no more raccoons find their way in.

I hoist my backpack over one shoulder, step out onto the busy sidewalk and nod to those who are staring at me in my kilt. I get some strange looks but I don't care. At least no one is trying to pick a fight. Maybe as a dad figure to Lucas, I can teach him some self defense moves, if Rachel will let me. I get the sense that she doesn't like violence, and that's okay, but everyone should have a few moves up their sleeves, including Rachel. I could take them both to the gym and show them a few techniques.

I start the bike and the air is warm on my face as I head home. The sun sets on the horizon as I coast along the winding roads, my thoughts straying to Brodie and when I offered to be a Dad for Hire. Christ, the guy can read me like a book and no matter how many times I tried to play it cool,

I'm pretty sure he could see beneath the hard exterior, and see that I might want to be there for Rachel. The woman could use a break, that much I know.

I reach home, and drive past the park, checking to make sure Lucas isn't there and in trouble. Beneath the lights, I spot the woman, Sophie I think that's her name, with her son Ben—who is banging away on the underutilized piano—and her head lifts as I drive by. She gives a little wave and my head rears back a bit. Does she know who I am? Did Rachel tell her she knew me? Or is she teaching her son it's okay to wave to strangers?

I continue on, head home and change into a pair of jeans. I don't mind wearing a kilt, but jeans are more my speed. I grab a quick bite to eat, and as I sit alone, my mind wanders. What are Rachel and Lucas having for dinner tonight? Probably nothing Scottish. Maybe I should cook for them sometime. After shoving a sandwich down my throat, I grab my truck keys and head back outside. Since there is only one hardware store in town, I make my way there.

Half an hour later, after I get all the supplies I need, I turn the truck and make my way to Rachel's. As I approach, my stomach tightens. Is she going to veto the idea of me playing dad? Brodie told me she could refuse and choose someone different. It's possible she will after I nearly kissed her. While I tried to play it cool, like it didn't matter—and I wish to fuck it didn't—I kept trying to casually ask him if he heard back from her. He'd smirk, naturally, and I simply told him she needed her roof repaired ASAP, and I had no idea when that would happen if she decided I wasn't right for the role. We are, after all, good neighbors, and that's what being a good neighbor means. He didn't believe any of it. Bastard.

I ease into her driveway and hop from the truck. She doesn't have a ladder, which is why I bought one, and I pull it from the back of the truck as she comes out her front door, looking warm and sexy and maybe even a bit flustered.

"Hi," she says, almost cautiously, and I take a moment to admire her yoga pants and T-shirt.

"Evening," I respond with a tip of my head. "How was your day?"

She doesn't answer, instead she looks at all the supplies. "What...are you doing with that ladder?"

I point to the roof. "Racoons. That's how they got in. I need to assess the damage." I reach into the truck to pull out my toolbox and the next thing I know, Rachel is right there beside me. Fuck, she's gorgeous.

"Tavish," she begins, and her brow is tight. "I...you...this. You never wanted this."

She has no idea what I want. Fuck, what am I saying? I have no idea what I want or what I'm doing. I moved here a month ago, wanting a quiet life, and wanting to go incognito. Taking on the role of dad was not on my to-do list. But fuck, I like this woman and I like her son, and I have skills she can use.

In the bedroom.

Fuck.

"You told Brodie..."

I grab a piece of lumber. "Rach," I begin, but her hand on my arm stops me.

"I don't want..." She struggles for the right word.

"Charity?" I ask. Her frown deepens and I say, "This isn't charity. You're paying for my services. Brodie isn't running a non-profit."

That brings a small smile to her face. "No, he certainly isn't. It's just, you didn't want to do this, and I don't like anyone feeling sorry for me."

I drop the piece of lumber in my hand. "Maybe I just like being around you." Her eyes widen. "And Lucas," I add, not wanting her to think this is about sex. Yes, sure I'd like to have sex with her—and that can't happen now—but her son needs something from me. I grew up without a dad, much like him, and the father figures I did have were mostly assholes. I don't want that for the lad. I'll at least hang around until he learns to fight his battles. I never had anyone show me how, but Mr. Phillips took me under his wing in high school—for a little while anyway—and maybe I'd like to pay it forward.

"Hey Rachel," I hear and we both turn to see Sophie coming our way.

Rachel waves and I don't miss the way her body tightens. She puts on a smile. "Hey Sophie, hey Ben."

Sophie pushes her long blonde hair over her shoulder and meets us in the driveway.

"Is Lucas home?" Ben asks.

"He is, you can run in and say hello."

Ben runs to the front door. "Looks like the boys are becoming fast friends." Rachel nods and Sophie holds her hand out to me. "Speaking of friends, I don't think I've met yours, Rachel."

"Oh, Sophie, this is Tavish. Tavish, meet Sophie."

"Are you the guy who makes the rocking chairs?"

I nod. "That's me."

"I was chatting with your mother earlier, Rachel," she says, not taking her eyes off me. "She told me how good you were with your hands, Tavish." She casts Rachel a fast glance, her gaze somewhat accusatory. "I thought you said you didn't know the guy on the motorcycle when we were at soccer."

"I didn't know it was Tavish."

Looking somewhat skeptical with that answer, Sophie looks at the supply of lumber and roof shingles and asks, "How do you two know each other?"

"Oh...I we..."

As Rachel searches for an answer, I say, "Rachel hired me." Not a lie and I don't want any percentage of the money. I'm not about to tell her that though, or she won't agree to this situation. Sophie nods, and quickly examines the lumber. "Roof repair," I explain.

"You're just friends then?"

"Yes," Rachel answers.

"I'll be helping her out with some things around her house. These old heritage homes need a lot of upkeep."

"Oh, I do love a handyman. Speaking of..." She points to the house two over. Isn't that where Rachel said the bunny playing piano teacher lived? "I just moved back, and..." With her finger still aimed at her house, she points downward. "I really need to find a guy to help me with my downstairs." I stare at her. Wait, is she pointing to her girly parts? I'm not all familiar with American slang, and I'm not sure why I get the feeling—maybe it's the way Rachel's jaw just fell open—that the downstairs Sophie needs help with might not actually be the downstairs in her house.

"I'm going to be tied up here for a while with this project. I'm sure the local hardware store can recommend someone."

"Oh." She waves her hand. "It's not like I'm in a hurry. I'm sure you're worth the wait."

"I better get at it while there's light." I pick up the ladder and some wood and start around the back of the house, leaving them to chat and hoping I was wrong about Sophie's downstairs.

The ladder bangs against the back of the house and I grin as I hear Lucas and Ben inside playing video games. Sometimes in life you really only need that one good friend. I never knew that until Brodie. No matter what, we always had and still have each other's best interests at heart, and I swear to God, he needs to stop trying to pay me back for saving his ass all those years ago. He's done enough for me, and we're damn well even.

I head up the ladder to check the damage and Rachel's voice reaches my ears as she enters the house. The front door bangs shut, and I hear her tell Lucas it's shower time. I move up the ladder until I hit a window. I glance in and can see into her walk-in closet. To the right, there is a door that is open, allowing me to see her bedroom. The light flicks on and fuck me, I'm no peeping Tom, but I can't help but take a fast glance inside.

The second I spot her, punching something into her phone, guilt races through me, and I tear my gaze away, but the next thing I know, she's opening her window and peeking her head out.

"How's it going out there?"

I inch back to see her. "Good, how's it going in there?" She laughs.

Her smirk is all kinds of accusing. "You mean you don't know?"

I'm pretty goddamn sure I've never blushed in my life. "I wasn't...you know."

"I know, I'm kidding. I'm just getting Lucas in the shower, and then I'm headed *downstairs*."

I stop and stare at her and when her lips twitch, I shake my head. "Was that for real?"

"She likes men, and she's blatant, and I guess there's nothing wrong with that."

"I guess, but I'm not interested in her...*downstairs*."

She laughs. "Are you interested in mine?" As soon as the words leave her mouth, her face turns beet red. "I mean, I'm headed downstairs, and I was going to pour a glass of wine and I have some coffee cake Mom made, and uh...we could perhaps go over the rules of this Dad for Hire stuff. I'm sure it doesn't involve roof repairs, and you have to let me know the costs of all these things, and—"

"Great idea." I cut off her rambling, even though it's adorable.

"My downstairs is actually haunted."

My head rears back and I nearly topple off the ladder. "Haunted, you say."

She laughs. "Yeah, well actually, there's a suit down there that's haunted."

Okay, this is getting better and better. I grip the ladder, needing to hear more. "And..."

"This house is old." We both obviously know that, but what does that have to do with a haunted suit, as if such a thing exists. She leans toward me, and her voice is low when she whispers, "I think people have died in it."

"The house or the suit?"

"Both." Her voice remains low when she adds, "The suit though, that's creepy." She looks over her shoulders, like she's afraid she might have offended these spirits. I cover my mouth to hide a laugh. "Tavish, it's true."

"Does it move around or something, like a walking suit, no body?"

"Not exactly. It just...I don't know, I get this weird feeling when I go near it. It moved once too. The arm lifted, not like it was going to hurt me or anything. I think it's benevolent."

Unable to hide my smirk, I say, "As long as it's benevolent."

She folds her arms. "Are you making fun of me?"

"Yes."

She juts one arm out, like she's going to push the ladder away from the house. "I can reach this ladder, you know. Maybe not from here, but I can from the closet."

I laugh. "Then who's going to take care of your roof, and your haunted suit...downstairs."

Her lips purse and her chin inches up. "You're not touching it."

I eye her. Is she talking about the suit, or her...downstairs? Because there's only one I want to touch. The other, I'll have to deal with, in time.

"It's been there since I moved in, and...and..." As I stand there, no doubt skepticism all over my face, her shoulders fall. "I'm going to pour a glass of wine."

"What, I want to hear more."

"Bite me, Tavish." I burst out laughing. Honestly, she wouldn't be saying that to me if she knew what was going through my mind.

"I'll meet you for a drink once I'm done up here." She's about to walk away, and I say, "I guess that means I am interested in your downstairs."

I shake my head. *What the hell are you doing, mate?* I really don't know, but I couldn't help myself. I'm not one to purposely embarrass a woman or make her blush, but there's just something so fucking hot, innocent and alluring—all the things I shouldn't be teasing to life—about Rachel when her cheeks turn that pretty shade of pink.

She groans and slams the window shut so hard, it rattles the ladder and I hang on for dear life until it stops. I am such an arse. I climb to the roof, and spend the next hour assessing the damage. It's getting late, and I'm only able to pound down a few boards as a temporary fix. I'll have to tear into it on the weekend when I have more time.

I climb back down and set the ladder on the ground. Can't risk Lucas climbing it and playing around on the roof—which is totally something I would have done as a kid. Debris falls from my hair and I brush old leaves from my clothes.

Once clean, I'm about to walk back around to the front of the house when the back patio door opens. "How bad is it?" Rachel asks.

"Nothing a few new boards and shingles can't fix. Shite, I left my hammer up there." I shrug. "I'll get it in a minute."

Her smile is soft and sincere as she hands me a beer, and sits. "I really appreciate you helping out like this. I'm not sure it's part of Dad for Hire."

"Keeps me busy."

She angles her head like she doesn't really believe me. "Aren't you busy enough with the rocking chairs and the pub?"

I shrug it off. "I like to stay busy. I used to train from sunup until sundown. This is just a different kind of busy."

"Do you miss it?" She takes a sip of wine, real curiosity in her eyes, and unlike other women in my life, I sense she's interested in me, the man outside of the cage. "The life, the limelight?"

"Not really."

"Not even all the women?" she asks with a raised brow.

I chuckle and take a sip of beer. "Nope."

Her gaze rakes the length of my body. "You must still train."

"I do." I scrub my face and since she gave me an opening, I ask, "Have you ever thought about self defense lessons for Lucas, and maybe even yourself? A single woman in this neighborhood," I tease. I glance around her quiet backyard. It's a nice safe neighborhood, but a woman should always have a few moves up her sleeve. "You never know who you'll get for a neighbor."

She chuckles. "Yeah, I'm always worried about some tatted up, bad-ass motorcycle dude moving in. That kind of guy has trouble written all over him."

She's not wrong. "All the more reason for self defense lessons."

She cringes but there's something else there, a story she's not telling me, and my entire body stiffens. "I don't like violence of any sort."

"I can show you things, easy things simply to protect yourself. Nothing about the moves are violent and I think this is part of what I'm supposed to do as a Dad for Hire." Skepticism dances in her eyes as I put my beer down and reach for her hand. She stares at it for a second before accepting it. I pull her to her feet.

"Now, I know your Cobra Kai moves are excellent, but if you don't see someone coming at you, say they come from behind..." I turn her, and she lets me move her around, and my damn mind strays. Would she be this pliable in the bedroom? Fuck, if I got her between the sheets, I'd take extra care with a woman like her. "If a guy grabs you and locks your arms like this," I do as I'm describing. "And he picks you up, what do you do?"

"Call out for you," she says.

I laugh. "Yes, you do, but if I'm at work, here's what you can do." I show her some moves, a punch to the nuts, a kick to the shins, and once I'm done, I turn her to face me. "I can show Lucas some moves to protect himself from getting shoved to the ground. Nothing violent and nothing that is going to injure his bully." My stomach knots as my thoughts go back to that day I protected Brodie. I damn near fucking killed the guy. Fighting in the cage is one thing, but what happened that day was pure rage, and I never want to experience it again. I can't—otherwise a cage is where I belong. A locked one.

"I don't want him to get hurt, but I don't want him hurting anyone either." I'm not sure what it is, but there's something in her voice that tugs at my gut, and I always listen to my gut. It saved my ass numerous times.

I scrub my face, and since I'm not sure how to ask, I blurt out. "Did...Jason hurt you?" She looks away fast, breaking from my hold, and I put my hand on her hip, bringing her back to me. "Did he?"

"No, but he scared me. He became increasingly verbally abusive, always picking on everything I did and my baby weight. I don't know what happened to him. He wasn't always like that. I used to think he was using drugs, but I never had any proof."

"When Lucas sees him, are they alone?"

"I try to supervise, but sometimes I can't. He mostly takes him to his parents' place. They don't live to far from here."

"You must run into them." That must be so awkward for her.

She nods. "They blame me for everything."

I put my hands on her arms and rub up and down, offering warmth and comfort. She's clearly been through a lot, and I'm so happy I signed up to be her daddy, or rather Lucas's dad. "Of course, they do."

Her eyes brighten. "They're very good to Lucas though, and he really loves them and that makes me happy."

"Good." I dip my head, not missing the quiver in her lips. But when she wets them, I'm not exactly sure it's from dragging up painful memories.

"Don't worry, Rachel. I'm not going to let Jason hurt you or Lucas. You have my word on that."

She glances up at me, and the pure trust I see shining there pierces my heart. Brodie is the only person who's ever trusted me like that, "Yeah?"

"I'm going to take care of you, lassie. I promise."

"I know you are," she answers, and the next thing I know she's on her tiptoes, her lips on mine. Every instinct tells me this is a bad idea. Why then am I wrapping my arms around her and dragging her close? Fuck, her body feels good next to mine. My cock thickens, and I hug her tighter, ready to pick her up and take her to her bedroom and show her how a woman like her should be treated.

"Mom, I'm ready for bed," Lucas hollers out.

Rachel breaks from my arms and backs up, her eyes big, her chest rising and falling as she stares up at me. "I...Lucas..." I nod as she disappears inside. Once she's gone, I shake my damn head. Why does this shit keep happening to me?

Obviously, it's a sign from the universe and I should listen to it.

Are you going to, though, mate?

9

RACHEL

I'm breathless when I reach Lucas' room, but it has nothing to do with running up a flight of stairs. Okay, it might have a little to do with that, but it has more to do with initiating a kiss with Tavish. What was I thinking? But seriously, he was being so sweet and kind and gentle, and it's been a long time since anyone has been any of those things to me. I realize I'm a woman with a child and acting like a silly schoolgirl, but Tavish makes me 'feel' again. Until him, I had no idea I'd been walking around in a state of numbness.

"Hey kiddo." I turn on his white noise sleep machine, which I bought him a couple years ago when Jason and I would fight every night, and sit on the edge of his bed. I pull the covers up to his neck.

"Why is Tavish on the roof?"

My stupid body quivers just hearing his name. "He's helping out." He nods, and I ask, "Do you like Tavish?"

"He's nice, Mom."

"Yeah, he is."

"Do you like him?"

"I do. He's going to be helping us around the house. You'll probably be seeing a lot more of him. Is that okay with you?" I lean down and kiss his forehead when he yawns.

"Yup. Ben's mom is looking for a new dad for him."

My heart seizes. "He told you this?"

He rolls to his side, looking so sleepy. "At camp today. I know I have a dad..." This time my throat tightens. "Ben has a dad too. Can he have another one?"

"If his mom marries again, the man would be Ben's stepdad. You can have a biological dad, and you can have a stepdad."

"What's a biological dad?"

Oh boy, this is a deep discussion for a Monday night. "He's the dad who made you. You come from me and your dad, but if I remarried, you'd have a stepdad."

"Are you going to remarry?"

"Right now, I just want to be your mom, Lucas."

"I'd like a stepdad. Do you think I can get a stepdad, Mom?"

"I don't know, kiddo. Right now, it's time for sleep."

"Mom," he says seriously as his eyes grow heavy. "Where are we again on getting a dog?"

I laugh at his antics and push his hair back, and as his eyes fall shut, I sit there for a moment until he falls asleep. I give him another kiss and I'm about to head back downstairs, to Tavish—if he's still even here. He might have bolted after that kiss. If he didn't, what do I even say to him? I feel like such a fool. Then again, when he pulled me close, I did feel his reaction—between his legs—and it wasn't like he was opposed to me jumping his bones. Not that a kiss could be considered jumping his bones. That was about to come next, until my son called me.

I stop at the sound of footsteps on the roof. I head to my bedroom and glance out my window. He must have gone back up to get the hammer. I step into my closet, and flick the light on to see the ladder right outside the window. The second I hear his footsteps on the top rung, I turn my back to the window and tug off my T-shirt and bra.

Are you really doing this, Rachel?

Yes, yes I am. His footsteps continue down the ladder, and I take a moment to pull myself together, hoping I do this right. Zero sound rings out from outside, which means, he's stopped outside my window. My heart speeds up. My God, I've never seduced a man before, especially not a hot, tattooed guy like Tavish. Will this work, or will he think he accidently stumbled upon me changing and be a gentleman and turn the other way—which is the opposite of what I want him to do?

I'm not at all looking for a stepdad for my son, it's the furthest thing from my mind, and the last thing I want in life. Right now, I just want to feel Tavish's hands on my body, his mouth on mine. I slide my hands to the elastic on my yoga pants and tug. What if he doesn't like what he sees? My ex's cruel words come back to haunt me and I use all my power to push then back.

Here goes nothing.

I wiggle my backside as I slide the tight pants down my legs. Leaving my panties on, I kick them away, and reach for my frilly pink robe. I hum silently to myself, even though the sounds come out strained, garbled…aroused. I slip the robe on and turn to stand before my long dressing mirror. I angle my body, and catch Tavish's eyes in the reflection. He's gone completely still, and as our gazes lock and I spot the sheer heat in his eyes, I give him the smallest smile, turn the closet light out, and make my way to my bedroom.

I take a few deep breaths as I stand at the foot of my bed. Did I just make a huge mistake, or—.

My head jerks to my door as boots sound on my stairs and the second his big body comes into view, eating up my entire doorway, air leaves my lungs in a whoosh. His body is tight, everything about him intense, and I swear to God, I have never in my entire life seen a man look at me with such sheer hunger.

"Hi," I manage to get out.

I expect him to say hi back but he doesn't. Instead, he enters my room and shuts my door behind him, twisting the lock to keep the world out. My heart jumps into my throat as he takes two big steps toward me, closing the gap in seconds and as my body screams yes, my mind can't help but think I've bitten off more than I can chew.

What was I thinking?

Before I can run and tuck my head into my pillow, hiding like a foolish ostrich, he says, "Hi." The tenderness in his voice, the sheer sweetness and softness, curls through my body and my anxiety ebbs.

"Hi," I say again, and it brings a smile to his face, which relaxes me even more. He touches my robe, and his big hands toy with the belt.

"I like the view."

"Thanks," I manage to say. I mean, what does one really say to something like that? Although I can't give that any further thought. Not when my entire body is burning from his touch. His eyes never leave mine as his big fingers work the knot free. Once he has it undone, he doesn't remove the robe. Instead, he dips his head, his lips close to mine as his fingers go to the fluffy collar. He rubs the material, and ever so slightly pulls it open, just enough to expose a hint of my cleavage. His groan might as well be a caress to my swollen clit.

"It had me wondering, though," he whispers into my mouth.

Oh God, oh God, oh God. I love the roughness in his voice, the way everything in his eyes tells me he's going to take really good care of me. "About?"

"What this view would be like?" He pushes the cotton from my shoulders and my robe falls to my feet. He exhales sharply as he glances down to take me in, and I gasp as his warm breath falls over my naked flesh. My nipples peak under his careful inspection and his appreciative moan eases the last of my worries.

"Do you like it?" I find the courage to ask.

"Aye, Rachel. I like it." He takes my hand and puts it on his cock, and for some strange reason, a giggle catches in my throat.

I give him a squeeze and he groans, his eyes briefly closing. "You like it a lot."

"I like it a lot," he agrees.

His hands move to the outer edges of my breasts, and he lightly caresses me as his lips find mine. I whimper and push against him, encouraging him to just take me already, but he clearly plans to take things slow, and I have to say, while I'm desperate to feel his touch, to feel him inside me, it's been a while and I do appreciate his gentleness.

"You are so beautiful," he murmurs, and turns me. He walks backward to the bed, drops down onto the mattress and pulls me between his spread legs. Big hands brush my hair from my shoulders, giving him a full, unobstructed view of my breasts. His mouth is right there, inches away from my nipples and I arch my back.

He grins up at me, and takes my breasts into his hands. He gives a gentle squeeze, leaning in to take my nipple into his mouth. "God, yes," I moan, and run my fingers through his hair. His tongue is warm and soft on my aching nipple and I push my body against him. One hand leaves my breast and travels down my back, cupping my ass cheek, to hold my sex against his stomach. I move against him, a new desperation overcoming me.

His hand leaves my ass, and he grips my hip and inches me away from his body. I'm about to protest, until he slides his big hand between my legs, the rough pad of his thumb sliding into my panties, and going to my clit. Oh yes, the man knows exactly what I need and he's not going to make me wait for it.

"You're so wet, lassie."

He's not wrong and his finger slicks around easily as his hungry mouth goes to my other aching nipple, giving it the same glorious tongue treatment as the first. I arch more, and move my body, as pleasure fills my core. I'm so aroused, I'm sure I'm going to explode before he even gets started. He slides a thick finger into my channel, and I whimper and move my hips towards him. I don't ever remember a finger feeling this good. I'm sure I'm going to blast off when he puts his cock in me.

He's going to put his cock in me, right?

My thoughts die an abrupt death as he moves his finger in and out of me. His other hand joins the first and pays extra attention to my clit. The trifecta, two hands between my legs and a mouth on my nipple, sends me catapulting over the moon. I take deep panting breaths, reveling in every second as my pleasure peaks.

"Tavish," I moan, and put my hands on his broad shoulders, loving the way his muscles flex beneath my touch. I rock into him, my head rolling back and my eyes falling shut as nothing but ecstasy fills my brain and soul.

God, it's been far too long since I've been touched. *Have you ever been touched like this though, Rachel?* Like you're the center of a man's universe? Like you're the most cherished possession he's ever put his hands on? It's crazy, because I'm the one always doing for others, always putting others' needs first, especially as a parent, but right now, in this moment in time, someone else is showering me with all the attention, and I like it.

I grow wetter, my core tightening as a climax grips my entire body and while I want to hang on and make this moment last, I simply can't.

"Yeah, lassie," he murmurs around one nipple, my body trembling from head to toe as a keening cry catches in my throat.

My body breaks around his fingers, and my hot juices drip down my thighs, and I grip my breasts, holding them as he alternates between nipples, sucking, licking and nibbling as I ride out each glorious pulse.

He tears his mouth away from my nipple, and his breathing is deep and laboured and I'm not sure what it is, but seeing this man a little frayed raises my arousal and my confidence to new heights. I step back an inch, and his hands fall from between my legs. I squeeze my thighs together, missing his fingers. His gaze is dark, intense as it holds mine, and his breathing ragged and fast as I retreat. He angles his head, confused, and I'm sure he must be thinking bedroom time is over.

Oh, he is so wrong.

I remove my damp panties, extend my arm and shove him. He falls back on the bed, and before he can get a word out, I bunch my robe on the floor and sink to my knees.

"Fuck," he murmurs, and I grin, because that's the plan—right after I taste him, of course. I catch his gaze and hold it as I release the button on his jeans and pull down the zipper. His hand snakes out and grips my hair. My entire body quakes. He wraps my long strands around his fingers and lifts his hips as I tug his jeans down to give myself better access.

His gorgeous, hard cock springs free, and I whimper as I tug it forward and wrap my mouth around his crown, drinking in his tangy pre-cum. His hips come off the bed, and he slides deeper into my mouth, nearly choking me. I move back and grip his cock to control the depth and rhythm, and he groans and collapses back onto the bed.

"Rach, lassie." I steal a glance at him and he puts one arm over his head like he's in complete agony and I love everything I see before me. I work my hand up and down the long length of him, my body quivering, aching to feel his hardness inside me. My thighs are sticky and wet as I squeeze them together, working to find a way to soothe my aching clit. It simply arouses me more. I shift until I have one of his legs between mine, and I rub myself against him as I take him deep.

The second I begin to ride his leg, he goes still...and silent. His cock thickens more in my mouth as I grind, and he goes up on his elbows, his eyes wide, deeply hungry—watching me intently—as I blatantly work to get myself off again.

"Lassie," he murmurs quietly his face twisting in agony. He spurts more pre-cum into my mouth, and the muscles in his jaw clench. He's close, so very, very close, and while I want to feel his cock inside me, I don't believe that's going to happen.

I suck harder, working to milk his release, stopping as his fingers bite into my shoulder. Not hard enough to hurt, but with enough pressure to gain my attention. With his cock still in my mouth, I lift my head, and he groans at the sight. I grin around his cock, and I'm about to sink back down again, stopping when he shakes his head. He inches back, and his cock falls from my mouth.

"You don't like?" I ask, snaking my tongue out to lick his crown. I kind of like seeing this big tough guy come undone... because of me.

"I like it too much and that's the problem," he growls.

"Oh."

"I'm seconds from shooting my load down your throat, lassie."

I shrug. "I'm okay with that."

"I'm not." I lightly run my fingers up and down his legs. "I want my cock inside your sweet pussy."

My chest rises and falls quickly. "I want that too." I try not to sound as desperate as I feel, but I think my attempts are futile.

"Stand up. Let me look at you."

I push to my feet, and while I know I'm not perfect, the way he gazes at me makes me feel like I'm the most beautiful woman he's ever set eyes on.

"You didn't get enough the first time?" I tease.

"No."

I stand there as he drinks me in. "See something you like?"

"Everything."

I chuckle, because this Tavish reminds me of the one I met at the bar, when Brodie said he only speaks when he has something to say.

He sits up, reaches over his back and tugs his shirt off. "Oh my," I murmur, unable to stop myself. I did a deep social dive on the man, and there are numerous pictures of him shirtless, but they don't compare to the real thing.

He holds his hand out to me. "Come here." Even though he's deeply aroused, his voice holds a measure of tenderness, and it's that tenderness I'm going to need to be careful with. I walk up to him, and he puts his hands on my waist, easily lifting me until my knees are on the bed and I'm straddling him.

My breasts are aligned with his mouth and he buries his face between them, breathing me in as I wiggle on his lap, trying to lift myself up so I can sink back down on his cock. Problem is, his big hands are holding me down and I quickly understand it's Tavish who is now controlling things. I try to move again, just to see if I can, despite that fact that I love the way his fingers are spanning my body.

His deep, animalistic groan vibrates through me and in a fast move, he shifts, and the next thing I know, I'm in the middle of my bed, his impressive weight holding me down. Damned if I don't like this. My sex quivers, and honest to God, I'm not sure it's ever quivered before.

He smooths my hair from my face, his gaze racing over me as his cock throbs between my legs. I lift, rubbing him, and he growls. "Keep that up and this will be over before it starts."

His words thrill me. "You barely touched me, Tavish and...." I snap my fingers.

"It's been a while, huh?"

Why does he seem happy to hear that? My laugh comes out heavy and aroused. "That's an understatement. Maybe though," I admit, almost sheepishly. "Maybe it's just you."

Something comes over him. A new kind of softness I've yet to see.

"I told you that...." His lips brush mine, and our moans mingle as our tongues tangle. "...I was going to take care of you, and I meant it."

"I had no idea you meant in the bedroom." I'd only been secretly hoping, even though I shouldn't be getting involved with the man I hired to be my son's stand-in dad.

"Now you do." I move my hips, my body desperate for his cock, and my heart...well, desperate for something it hasn't had in a long time, and I need to nip that in the bud right freaking now. I can't go there, not with Tavish.

His cock rubs against my pussy and he groans. "Condom," he murmurs. He shifts and I nod as he reaches for his pants and pulls a condom from his pocket. The tightness in my chest is absolutely insane. I shouldn't be feeling jealous just because he carries condoms. A guy like Tavish should carry condoms. I'm sure he's having sex every day, around every corner. He's not married. Not like Jason was. Maybe the odd jealousy stems from something more. Maybe it's because he makes me feel special, and the condom is a reminder that I'm not, that he sleeps with numerous women and probably makes them feel special too.

"Hey," he whispers, falling back over me. "Where did you go?"

I smile, and push down my foolishness. "I'm here."

"I'm here too." His gaze searches my face, and I pray he can't see the old demons that still exist below the surface. "I'm here with you, Rachel."

I nod. He's right. He is here with me, and I'll not let thoughts of other women—my ex's infidelity—ruin this moment.

"You good, lassie?"

"I am awesome," I tell him and it makes him smile. He goes back on his knees, tears into the condom, and I watch, my body aching with need as he rolls it down the long length of him.

Once sheathed, he falls over me and I wrap my legs around his back. His body is hard, the intensity on his face primal, and I expect him to power into me. My stupid heart misses a beat as he positions his hard cock, and ever so slowly eases into me, and I'm pretty sure this is some kind of strategy to make me lose my damn mind—and heart. Not that he's asking for the latter, and I don't want that either.

"Tavish," I murmur into his mouth as his lips find mine.

"Yeah, lassie?"

"It's good. So good."

"Aye, it is."

He kisses me with tenderness, his heartbeat strong against my breasts as his battered body moves against mine. For the briefest of seconds, I want to pinch myself. Am I really having sex with a bruised and scarred former MMA fighter, one who seems to know exactly what this divorcée needs between the sheets?

I groan as he slides in and out of me, and he shoves one hand under my backside, easily manipulating my body for pleasure as he lifts me too him. Oh, that is nice. The position allows him to hit my cervix at a different angle. Here I thought this new position was for him, but it's not, it's for me, and arousal hits like a punch.

"Ohhh...." I gulp out, and he grunts, pleased with my responses. I claw at his tattooed back and chant his name.

"I've got you lassie."

He's right, he's got me, and if I'm not careful, it will be in more ways than one.

"Yes," I cry out as my arousal sharpens and centers between my legs and in response he drives in deep, hitting the exact spot I need to push me over the edge again. I curl forward, my stomach clenching, and he puts his other arm around my back, holding me against him as my muscles grip his hips and clench hard. He buries his face in my neck and I close my eyes, wanting to concentrate on each hard pulse.

"Fuck, lassie. I'm right there."

I pant and gasp and he gently lays me back down, his hips picking up speed as he chases his climax and I open my eyes, surprised to find the profound way he's watching me. I put my hands around his head, my heart beating just a little faster, and bring his mouth to mine.

The second our lips touch, he groans into my mouth, and every muscle in his body—except the one inside me—goes still. His cock throbs with his release, and I love the carnal way he grunts with each hard pulse.

He collapses on top of me, shifting a bit so I don't suffocate, although I'm beginning to believe air is overrated. I run my fingers through his hair, and after a long moment, his head lifts, a small smile on his handsome face.

"So just to clarify," he begins, easing his cock out of my body. "You were purposely putting on a show in front of your window, right?"

I laugh. "I was."

"Then I didn't just break into your room and ravage you for no good reason."

"Oh, there was a good reason," I tell him. I move my body, rubbing his cock. "Actually, a big reason."

He grins. "Keep that up and we'll have a big reason again."

"That's the idea."

10

TAVISH

It's Tuesday, nearing three o'clock by the time the afternoon crowd dies down and I'm off before the dinner crowd starts piling in. My mind, of course, is still on last night...Rachel. After a second round of sex—I'll consider that the main course—we followed that up with sticky buns for dessert.

Christ, my tadger is thickening beneath my kilt, just thinking about how good she tasted and felt in my arms, beneath my body. I shift to adjust my kilt before it tents and alerts the staff and patrons to my aroused state. At least Brodie isn't here to razz me.

Speaking of Brodie.

In he walks, just as I finish adjusting myself. I untie my apron, and while I managed to get my cock under control, there's still nothing I can do to wipe away the ridiculous grin I've been wearing all day—a grin that advertises I shagged last night.

I put on my toughest game face, one I perfected in the cage fighting under the name of Tavish the Terror. "Hey," I grumble as he shoves his backpack under the counter, grabs his apron off the hook and ties it.

"How did it go with Rachel last night?"

I nearly flinch, and catch myself before I do. "I started on her roof, you know, as Dad for Hire. Got too dark. Have to do it this weekend." I pause and when he doesn't respond I lift my head and catch the knowing way he's looking at me. Bastard. "Did she say something to you?" I ask, trying to sound casual.

He grabs a cloth and starts polishing glasses. "You mean about me choosing you as her Dad for Hire?"

I glance away, and reach for my helmet under the counter. "Aye."

"I hadn't heard a word." He sets a glass into the tray and reaches for another. "She must have been too busy last night to respond."

I shrug. "Beats me."

"Can you do me a favor?"

"Depends," I answer, even though he knows I'd do just about anything for him. Hell, I even signed up to be a stand-in dad. Although maybe that had more to do with Rachel and Lucas.

"I signed the papers she sent to me and I need to give her a copy. You want to drop them to her tonight? Or, you might catch her at the office." Even though I hadn't agreed, he reaches into his backpack and pulls out a file. All signed by three parties now.

I take the papers from him, and look over the signatures. I note the address of her work, which isn't too far. I could drop them to her tonight, but maybe I could take them to her office and check out this boys' club she was talking about. Yeah, that's what I'll do, and it has nothing to do with wanting to see her again, and not wanting to wait until tonight.

"I probably won't see her tonight," I tell Brodie. "I'll just drop them to her at her office."

"Yeah, you should do that."

I take in his grin and resist the urge to smack it off. I just shake my head, shove the papers into my own backpack and hike it over my shoulders. Outside, the sky is a bit overcast, and I hope I make it home without getting soaked. I start my bike, and use my phone to check the fastest route to MedFlex, where Rachel works.

I pull up in front of the tall building and find a spot to park. I get a lot of stares as I head inside, dressed in my leather jacket and kilt. It's an odd combination, for sure. Security stops me and I tell them who I'm here to see. They make a phone call, exchange words that I can't hear, and then I'm directed to the elevators.

A woman stands beside me, clutching her purse as we wait for the elevator. It arrives and I step on, holding the door open for her. She blinks rapidly. "Oh, I'll catch the next one." She reaches into her purse and pulls out her silent phone. "I have a call."

"Suit yourself." I ride up to the tenth floor, and it's weird. I'm not usually afraid of anything, yet as I approach her floor, strange sensations knot my stomach. What if she's not happy about me showing up at her work? What if I'm not the kind of guy she wants to be associated with?

The doors ping open and I step off, and I'm greeted by a receptionist. Her eyes go wide. "You're here to see Rachel Hart?" I guess I must not look like her usual clientele.

"Yes."

"Just down the hall to the left. Her name is on the door." She picks up her phone. "I'll let her know you're coming."

I nod and start down the hall, glancing into the offices, taking in the guys on their phones, and computers making deals and appointments with their clients. I reach Rachel's office and her door is closed. I glance at her through blinds that go from her floor to ceiling. They're pulled closed, allowing only a small glimpse of her, and the glimpse I see—Rachel frowning as she holds her phone to her ear—tightens the knot in my stomach. Shite. I shouldn't have come here.

I'm about to back away until her head lifts and her gaze meets mine, and I note the sadness about her. I grip her doorknob and push it open. "Rachel," I say firmly, getting the sense this might not be about me at all. "What's going on?"

She stands and comes around to the other side of her desk. "What are you doing here?"

"I came to deliver these papers." I reach into my backpack and pull out the forms Brodie gave me. "Is everything okay?"

She scans the papers and then tosses them onto her desk. "Actually, no."

Maybe I'm wrong. Maybe this is about me. "I shouldn't have come. This is your workplace."

She puts her hand on my chest and her warmth curls around my body. "No, it's not that. Seeing you is actually a bright spot in my day." Goddammit, I like that. Probably too much.

She gestures toward her phone. "Lucas' camp councillor, Miss Tammy, called. I was just trying to get a hold of his back up babysitter. She's not answering, and Mom is at work. I could call his other grandparents...I just...ugh."

Panic invades me. "Is Lucas okay?"

"He's not feeling well. Probably a stomach thing. He'll be fine." She turns to glance at a file on her desk. "I landed a big, important client today, just before the camp councillor called. I told Matthew—he's the CEO—that I wouldn't be able to put a portfolio together until tomorrow. The client wanted it by the end of closing today. Jakob overheard and he ever so kindly suggested he take over, as he could 'get right on it'." She does air quotes around those last three words.

"This client," I say, keeping my tone even when all I want to do is pummel this Jakob eegit. "This is important for your career."

She gives a humorless laugh that comes out more of a snort. "Oh, yeah."

"Jakob knew that?" She nods and a hard quake wracks my body as my dislike for the guy just jumped of few points on the Richter scale. Jakob the eegit is going down, because no one fucks with my girl.

"These are the kinds of things they hold against me. It's why I can't get ahead." She's about to turn and I put my hands on her shoulders to stop her. "I need to go get him, Tavish."

"I'll pick him up."

Her brow furrows. "I can't ask you to do that. He's not your responsibility." She bites her lip and my fingers clench. I'd like to show every guy in the office her worth with my fists.

You can't do that, Tavish.

Yeah, yeah, I know.

"Did you forget I'm his stand-in dad now and these are the things I'm supposed to do. I believe it's in the contract." She glances at the papers, and shakes her head.

"It's not. Not really."

I step up to her desk, grab a pen, and flip the papers over. I scribble on the back and hand them to her. "See."

She reads, "Pick Lucas up when he's sick and Rachel needs to work." Her head lifts and the smile on her face cuts off air to my lungs faster than the rear naked choke, an MMA signature submissive move.

"It's settled then. I'll take him home and put him in his bed. It'll give me time to check out this haunted suit."

Her shoulders slowly begin to relax. "You really don't mind?"

"Nae, lassie." She blushes. Is her mind going back to last night, to when I called her that when my cock was inside her? Fuck, now is not the time to be thinking about that.

"The suit really is haunted, Tavish. Don't say I didn't warn you." She walks around her desk, pulls her purse from the drawer, and pulls out a key. "I'll call the camp to let them know you're picking Lucas up." She takes one of the keys off the ring and hands it to me. "You can keep this. I have more at home."

"Does this mean we're going steady?" I ask, and she grins. "That's how they say it in America, isn't it?"

"No, it does not mean we're going steady. You should have a key now that you're my...well you know."

"Yeah, I know." I shove the key into my pocket. "Do you think Lucas will like a ride on the bike, if he's feeling up to it?" Her eyes go wide, and she opens her mouth, no doubt about to protest. I hold my hand up. "Back at the house, I have a helmet that will fit him, and I think he'll like it and I'll be extra careful. If you don't want me to, and prefer for me to pick him up in the truck, consider it done."

Her face softens, the worry leaving her eyes. "I think he'll love it, and I know you'll be careful. How can I ever thank you?"

"Fuck."

"What?" she asks quickly. "If you can't—"

"No, I was just thinking about all the ways I'd like for you to thank me, but helping out is in the contract, so that means you don't owe me a thing."

"What if I want to owe you a thing?" She laughs, goes up on her toes and kisses me. The door flies open, and we quickly break apart before we're caught. Rachel backs up an inch and shuffles some papers on her desk. "What can I do for you, Jakob?"

"Am I interrupting something?" His head, which is too big for his body, bobbles back and forth between the two of us.

What a twat. Of course, he's interrupting. He knows it and doesn't care.

"Jakob, this is Tavish. Tavish, this is Jakob, a colleague." I don't miss how she doesn't identify who I am, or what I am to her.

"Nice to meet you, Tavish." He holds his hands out and I don't want to shake it. I can't be rude to one of Rachel's colleagues, though, so I offer my hand and I don't miss the way he stares at my body, all the while trying not to.

"Tavish," he says, his face twisted. "You look familiar. Do I know you?"

"Maybe, I'm Rachel's boyfriend. Perhaps you've seen us together."

His beady eyes nearly bulge out of his head, and I probably shouldn't be taking so much enjoyment in it.

"You...and Rachel?"

"Aye." I fold my arms across my chest, and don't miss the way Rachel's lips quirk at the corners.

"I...well...ah, I guess we'll see you at the retreat next weekend," he says to me, almost like he's testing me.

"I'll be there." I can feel Rachel's eyes boring in the side of my head, but I continue to hold Jakob's gaze.

He lifts his arm and mimics a golf swing. "Don't suppose you play."

"Why's that, now?" I ask as he insults me. Sure, he looks at me like I'm a muscle head eegit, judging me because of my size and tattoos.

He drops his arm as I stare him down. "Oh, no reason. You just seem more like..." His gaze falls to my kilt, and he frowns. "Did you just come from a parade or something?"

"I work at Kilting Around."

"Oh, right. I should have put it together. I love that place." He turns to Rachel and holds out his hand. "I'll be taking on that new client," he says a rather smug grin on his rat face. "If you want to hand over the file."

I take a step forward, half blocking Rachel. "Looks like you're getting off easy today, mate. I'll be picking up Lucas. No need for Rachel to rush home, which means she can take care of *her* client herself."

He swallows, and tugs on his tie. "Matthew...he said...."

"I'm sure now that the circumstances have changed, Matthew wouldn't want to put the burden of a new client on you. You can take that up with him, though. I have to run, and Rachel has work to do." He stands there, unsure, fidgeting like a goddamn cornered rat. "Close the door on the way out. I need a moment alone with Rachel."

Jakob turns, and the door closes with a click. I snort as I turn to Rachel. "Do you think he's running to Matthew to tattle?"

"Likely." She shakes her head. "You didn't have to do that."

"Do what?"

"Tell him you were my boyfriend, and then intimidate him."

"Oh, but I did, Rachel. I really did." I step closer, and pull her soft body against mine. She gasps and her lips part as I lower my head. "Now, where do I go to take golf lessons and buy a pair of plaid shorts?"

11

RACHEL

Fortunately, Matthew let me keep my client after Tavish came to my rescue and I was able to put a portfolio together by closing. The fact that Tavish stood up to Jakob and helped me out when I was desperate means more to me than he'll ever know. Although he'll know soon enough because I plan to show him just how grateful I am.

The thoughts of him in my bed again bring a smile to my face. I stand and stretch my arms out, as Matthew pokes his head in. "I hear you have a new male friend."

Oh, is that what he's calling Tavish. "Yes, his name is Tavish Findlay. You'll meet him at the retreat, if not sooner." I honestly can't believe Tavish agreed to go. While I like the idea of having him there, I'm not so sure I would have asked. A weekend retreat away with the boys' club. That's going above and beyond in my book.

He chuckles. "Seems like you have a type."

What the hell?

I close the file on my desk, trying not to take offense. "Excuse me?"

"Big sports guys, handsome."

Okay it's true both Tavish and Jason are big and both are handsome. That does not mean I have a type. "At least Patty said Tavish was handsome," he clarifies.

Patty at reception is talking about me? Really, am I that surprised? From what I've seen, she upholds the boys' club culture.

"I don't think they're alike at all," I say, my body tightening. Brodie never would have set me up with a man who wasn't a stand-up guy. We're friends, and we care about each other's well-being.

He didn't set you up romantically, Rachel. Tavish is a Dad for Hire. At that reminder, I say, "All is good, Matthew."

"Let's hope so." His smile falls, all teasing gone from his tone. "We all know what happened last time."

Last time, my husband fooled around and broke my heart and there were many days that I had to leave work, to attend to Lucas, my mental health, and of course the divorce and moving. What I'm really wondering here, though, is if Matthew is worried about my mental health or if he's warning me about my job. I can't lose this job. Jason's child support helps, but I need to work too, which is why I didn't go straight to human resources after I was passed up for promotion. Matthew could probably find some reason to fire me, and he was generous with me when I had to take time off after Jason and I split.

I glance at my watch. "It's getting late. I should get home to check on Lucas."

"How is he?"

Wow, I'm surprised he's asking. "He's good. Probably just caught a bug at camp. You know how germs get passed around at camp."

"I don't much remember those days." I nod. Of course, he doesn't. His wife was home to take care of the kids. He taps my door frame. "Safe travels and see you tomorrow. Great work today."

I nod and he disappears, and I stand there for a second, needing to pull myself together after his words picked at old scars. Maybe I should start looking for another job. I like what I do here, I love sales and I love my clients. It's the boys' club culture that gets to me, but I've been in sales since I graduated college. It's all I've ever known. I have a marketing degree, and Boston is a big city. Maybe I really should start looking around. I hate the thought of these guys thinking they pushed me out, or that they'd broken me. It makes me want to stand up to them all the more, but am I wasting energy? Is pushing back futile?

I gather up my things, and once the sound of Matthew's footsteps fade, I leave my office and head home. I pass Jakob, who gives me the evil eye as I glance into his office, keep my head high and step onto the elevator. It did kind of feel good to put him in his place today.

I reach the lobby and head to the back parking lot. As I walk, I pull my phone from my purse and call Tavish. He answers on the second ring and it's crazy what it does to my wobbly heart.

"Hey," I say, hugging my phone to my face and using my fob to unlock the car.

"Hey lassie," he responds and my smile widens.

"How's Lucas?"

"In his room playing video games. I hope that's okay. I'm not sure about the protocol for sick days and this whole stand-in dad is new to me."

My heart squeezes for the boy who lost his mother and was taken from his father. "It's perfectly fine and I really appreciate you being there for us. I'm headed home now, so we won't keep you much longer."

"I don't mind, lassie. Did you get your work done?"

I slide into the driver's seat and start the car, putting Tavish on speaker. "Yes, you saved the day."

Glancing around, I pull out of my spot and into traffic. "Glad to hear it."

"How was your afternoon?" I asked, wanting to hear his voice a little longer, and he doesn't seem to be in a hurry to hang up either.

"While Lucas was playing, I was able to do some work on the roof."

My heart skips a beat. "That's great, Tavish. Why don't you let me cook you dinner tonight, to thank you for your help?"

"I don't think so."

"Right, you probably already have plans." Disappointment floods my body. "Okay, no worries. I'll be home as fast as I can, then you can take off." I glance at the clock. "If you need to go now, I could call my mom. She'll be closing up soon and can head over. I don't mind—"

"Lassie," he begins, cutting me off. "My plans include you."

The deepness in his voice curls through my blood. "Oh."

"We're having dinner together," he states, his tone full of innuendos. "But what I meant was that's not how I want to be thanked."

"Ah, I see." I take a turn and pull onto the highway. "What a coincidence. That's not how I really want to thank you anyway."

His deep growl curls through me. "Get your arse home, as fast and safe as you can."

He ends the call and as my car accelerates, so does my heart. I can't remember the last time I smiled like this, or looked forward to something. Tavish is fun, and I don't care what Matthew says, I'm not going to get my heart broken with him. Unlike my life with Jason, I'm going into this wide-eyed, knowing what to expect and what not to. I'm not some ingénue looking at life through rose-colored glasses. Nope, those days are gone.

I focus on the road, and consider what I can make for dinner. I was in such a rush this morning, I didn't take anything out. With Lucas not feeling well, I should opt for something quick and easy. That will allow Tavish and I to get to dessert faster. Flicking the radio louder, I sing along, my heart lighter than it has been in a long time.

I spot Sophie and Ben in their yard as I pull in behind Tavish's motorcycle, and I jump from my car and bolt inside, not wanting to answer questions from Sophie. I have no doubt Ben told her Tavish picked Lucas up from camp.

The second I enter, the smell of food reaches my nose. Tavish cooked? He comes from the kitchen, my apron around his kilt. My heart leaps as he walks up to me, bends and presses his lips to mine, like any couple would.

You're not a couple, Rachel. You're just playing house with a man you hired.

"You cooked?"

"Aye lassie, I did. I hope you don't mind."

"No that's the second-best thing I've heard all day." He narrows his eyes. "Make that the third." I laugh as he stands there waiting for an explanation. I hold my finger out. "First was you offering to pick up Lucas." I add a second finger to the first. "Second was that you didn't want a meal as a thank you." He grins at that. I hold out a third finger. "Third is you made dinner."

"I found haddock in your freezer. Cooked a traditional haddock chowder."

I briefly close my eyes. "Sounds divine. How is Lucas?"

"Hi Mom," Lucas calls out at the sound of his name.

"I'll go check on him." I put my hand on Tavish's arm. "Thank you."

"Aye lassie. Go check on your son, and I'll scoop him up some chowder and bring it on up to him." I nod as he walks back to the kitchen, my gaze on his backside as he disappears. A sigh escapes my lips. This guy is too good to be true.

And you know what they say about that, Rachel.

Matthew's warning words come back in a flash and I push them down. I am not going to get emotionally mixed up with a guy like Tavish. With that, I head upstairs and step into Lucas' room. He drops the iPad beside him.

"Hey kiddo. How are you feeling?" I drop down onto his mattress and put my hand on his forehead. He's warm but not feverish.

"Better. Tavish wore a kilt when he came to get me," he rushes out quickly, his eyes full of life. "Some of the guys laughed at first. I didn't like that. Tavish explained his heritage to them, and how Scottish warriors wore kilts in battle. After that, they all thought it was cool and wanted to wear one. Do you think I could get a kilt?" I'm about to answer, and he hurries out with, "Miss Tammy really loved his kilt." He pauses and frowns. "She got really red in the face when she was talking to Tavish, though." He rubs his stomach. "I think she might be getting sick too."

I bite back a smile and push down the unwanted jealousy. "Let's hope not. Do you feel like eating something? Tavish made haddock stew. It's a traditional Scottish recipe." I expect him to make a face, as he's not a huge lover of haddock.

He nods excitedly. "I want to try everything Scottish." I smile, because I get it. I do too, just in a little bit of a different way. "I really liked riding on the motorcycle with Tavish. It was so much fun. You should do it, Mom. You'd love it." He holds his hands out and makes revving sounds as he pretends to twist the handles.

I ruffle his hair. "I bet I would and I'm so glad you had fun."

He looks past my shoulder and a huge smile spreads across his face. I turn to see Tavish standing there, a tray in his hands. Tavish is good at this dad stuff, despite what he thinks. It's easy to see how much Lucas adores him, and that's a good reminder that I can't mess up their relationship by falling for the man closing the distance between us. Good God, his mere presence messes with my body. I want him to stay in Lucas' life—my son has had enough loss—and any emotional entanglement that could result in a bad breakup is absolutely out of the question.

I stand and Lucas sits up a bit straighter. "Thanks, Tavish."

"I hope you like it, mate." Tavish sets the tray on Lucas's little lap. "Careful, it's hot."

Lucas snatches up the spoon and takes a big bite. "Mmm, this is delicious."

"Glad you like it, mate." Tavish ruffles his hair and Lucas beams up at him. "I'll come collect the tray later." We leave the room and I can't stop smirking. "What?" Tavish asks.

"You got Lucas to eat haddock stew. You're not a Dad for Hire, you're a miracle worker."

He laughs as we head down the stairs. "Nae, I just make a mean stew."

"I have no doubt, Tavish. I think you're good at everything you do. I still haven't seen these rocking chairs of yours. I have got to get to my mother's place."

"Or you could come to mine."

Did he just invite me to his house?

"I could show Lucas my tools. I think he'd like that."

In the kitchen, he gestures to the table, and while it's my inclination to head to the stove and serve up dinner, I sit. A minute later, a big steaming bowl of stew is placed in front of me and I breathe in the delicious aroma.

"Wow, this smells amazing."

He winks at me. "Wait until you taste it." I pick up my spoon and wait until he's seated across from me with his own bowl. I dig in and the delicious flavor dances on my tongue. "Oh my God, this is so good. Where did you learn to cook like this?" As soon as the words leave my mouth, I instantly regret them. He learned out of necessity. Unlike me, he didn't have a mother to teach him.

He shrugs. "Picked things up here and there." He rubs his very muscular stomach. "Plus, I like food."

I grin. "Me too." I take another spoonful. "I'm sorry you didn't get a chance to change out of your kilt."

"No worries. I might have frightened a few squirrels climbing back down the ladder, I'm afraid."

"Oh no." The visual of Tavish on the ladder in a kilt makes me laugh.

"Yeah, I think they were laughing too."

"At you or with you?" I ask.

He grins. "Sophie stopped by. I think I might have flashed her too. I didn't know she was in the yard until I reached the ground. I think the sight of my bits dangling might have shocked her into silence." He laughs and takes a bite of stew, and I sit waiting to hear more as he chews. He glances at me. "I don't mean to go around frightening your neighbors or wildlife."

"I'm sure she wasn't shocked silent because you weren't wearing boxers." I know what he's packing.

"What?"

"Nothing."

"She brought up her downstairs again."

"How could she not after getting a glimpse of yours?"

"Cheeky, Rachel."

I set my spoon in my bowl. "She's still after you to take a look at her downstairs, then?"

"Apparently, her grandmother has a leak in her laundry room, which actually is downstairs. Plumbers are expensive and I think money is a little tight for them. I told her I'd take a look at it when I had the chance."

"That's nice of you." I pick my spoon up, trying not to appear jealous. "If you want to get out of the kilt, you can put the suit on."

With the spoon halfway to his mouth, he stops and asks, "The haunted suit?"

"Yes, that one."

"If you want me in a suit..." He drops his spoon and his eyes darken with hunger. "I'd rather slip into my birthday suit, lassie."

12

TAVISH

I'm sweeping the floor by the time Rachel comes back from tucking Lucas in for the night and having a shower to wash away her day. At the sound of her footsteps, I turn and find her standing in the doorway. My gaze drops to take in her comfy yoga pants that showcase her sweet curves and drive me nuts, and the thin T-shirt that does little to hide the black lacy bra beneath. Is she messing with me on purpose? My gaze lifts and my muscles tighten when I catch the slackness in her jaw along with her wide-eyed stare.

"Everything okay?" I ask.

"You're...sweeping..."

I glance at the broom in my hand. "Aye, but the broom is doing the heavy lifting." I expect to get a grin from that, but I don't. "You've never seen a man sweep before, lassie?" I bend, and put the dirt into the dustpan, dumping it into the garbage. I straighten and find her still standing there, staring at me.

She snaps her fingers, and her voice is quiet, dazed like, when she says, "Boom, pregnant."

"What?"

She blinks, snapping herself back to the present, and a flush crawls up her neck and spreads across her cheeks as her gaze finds mine. "A man in a kilt sweeping... It's just..." She pauses and waves her hand in front of her face. "...It's hot."

I lean on the broom. "Oh yeah?"

"Uh huh."

"I had no idea." I glance at the red handle on the broom. "I guess I'll have to sweep more often."

Her eyes dim as her gaze moves down my body. "Or you could put the broom away and get into your birthday suit."

Like she has to ask me twice. I toss the broom aside, quickly cross the floor and lift her, putting my hands under her ass to hold her against me. She gasps as her legs wrap around my waist, her arms linking behind my neck. "I want you in yours, too."

"It's not my birthday."

"It's going to feel like it," I promise her, keeping my voice low as I hurry up the stairs. I step into her room, shut the bedroom door, and lock it behind us.

"On my birthday, I usually blow out candles."

Fuck me twice.

"You want something to blow, Rachel?" I ask, my voice deep and hoarse as arousal grips me by the balls.

She blinks innocently. "I can't consider it a birthday if I don't have something to blow, Tavish."

"I don't think that's going to be a problem, and believe me, you might be the one blowing but I'm the one getting the present." She slides from my body and sinks to her knees, lifting my kilt and making a little *oooh* sound when she finds me in my birthday suit.

"Lifelong mystery solved, and those squirrels had nothing to laugh about." I chuckle but it turns to a groan as she takes me into her mouth and sucks. I grip her hair and move my hips forward, sinking into her warm wetness.

"Happy fucking birthday to me," I murmur. She makes joyous little moaning sounds as she pleasures me, and I clench down on the inside of my cheek to keep myself from spurting down her throat. She rocks into me, taking me deeper than she did the first time, and everything in the way my cock disappears into her mouth, coming out slick and wet, is enough to turn a sane man crazy.

"Lassie," I murmur. "I'm rock hard."

"Uh huh," she mumbles around a mouthful of cock, and I harden even more.

As my tadger throbs, I move my leg, rubbing her sweet pussy through her yoga pants. "I want to taste you. I want you on my face," I blatantly tell her.

An excited little gasp rumbles in her throat, and I move her off my dick before I lose it. I wipe the corners of her mouth with my thumb, and pull her to her feet. The scent of her vanilla soap fills my senses as I grip her T-shirt and tug it off, taking a moment to admire her lacy bra.

"Did you wear this for me?" I ask."

Her grin is cheeky. "Well, you did say you wanted to get into your birthday suit and I wanted to give a nice wrapping to your present."

"Best wrapping, ever." I lightly touch the lace, my dick throbbing at the sexy sight. Rachel moans as I slide my finger inside the soft cup, lightly stroking her hard nipple. "I normally like to rip into the packaging, but I'm going to want to see you in this again." I slide my hand around her back and with a quick flick, unhook her bra and toss it onto the bed. "Mmm."

I cup her perfect breasts and squeeze them in my palms and her little sigh rumbles around me as I bend forward to take her nipple into my mouth. She moves her hips, her body as desperate as mine, and I'm not going to make her wait too long. My mouth simply needs its fill of her pussy before I put my cock in her.

"What about downstairs?" I tease. "Any chance you're wearing those sexy panties I saw in your laundry?"

She blinks her eyelashes, and purses her gorgeous kissable lips. "You'll have to unwrap me and find out for yourself."

I kiss her sweet mouth and drop to my knees. Hands on her hips, I pull her to me, and press hot, open-mouthed kisses to her stomach, breathing in her sweet scent. Fuck, I love the warm softness of her skin. She whimpers as I grab the band on her yoga pants and gently tug, just to expose the lace hugging her hips.

I glance up at her and smile, my heart racing, knowing she did this for me. "It really is like my birthday." After dragging her yoga pants to her ankles, she lifts one leg and then another, allowing me to get rid of them all together.

I test the lace, running it between my fingers. "Are these replaceable?"

She angles her head, suspicion in her eyes. "Yes."

"I'll replace them," I inform her, and growl as I take in the gorgeous woman before me, who went out of her way to wear sexy lace panties—for me. Only problem is, while I love them on her, they need to come off and fast. I lean into her, bury my face between her legs, and with my body burning hot, need and hunger making me a little delirious, I grip the thin lace, and in one quick tug, I tear her panties from her hips.

"Oh, God, Tavish," she cries out, her eyes glazed with lust when I glance up at her. Her chest is rising and falling fast as her hands go to my hair, everything about her wild and on fire, just the way I want her.

I grin up at her. "Sorry, but sometimes, when the gift is this good..." I lightly run my fingers over her slit, parting her to glimpse her pretty pink flesh. "...A guy just has to find the fastest way to get to it."

"Yes, I think that was a good idea."

I chuckle at her enthusiasm, the way her cheeks are turning the same color as her gorgeous pussy. With a flick of my tongue, I taste her from bottom to top, and her flavor rockets through me as I spend an extra moment on her clit.

She groans and I grin, inching back, only for her to scramble forward, trying to rub against my face. "I want you on my face, like this..." I tug off my shirt, and release the belt on my kilt. My clothes pool on the floor as I slide onto the bed, flat out on my back. "Come ride me, Rachel."

"Oh my God," she murmurs, and stands there, staring at me. I crook my finger, desperate to get my mouth and hands on her.

"Get your arse over here," I growl, my voice lacking any kind of patience.

She climbs onto the bed and straddles my waist. I tug her until her sweet pussy is hovering over my hungry mouth, mine for the tasting. She's dripping wet as I breathe in her aroused scent and drag her down, settling her hot cunt on my mouth. I kiss her wet lips, and slide my tongue all over her, wanting every drop of juice on my tongue.

Her little whimpering sounds turn me on even more as I devour her, and I love how she's soaking my face as she slides around, taking exactly what she needs from my mouth. I let her have her way for a while, then grip her hips to control the movement and her whimpers grow louder, a good indication that she loves when I take control.

I eat at her, devour her gorgeous pussy as she rides my face with wild abandonment. This is what she needs, simply to let go and enjoy and I like being the guy she feels free enough to do it with. I reach up and cup her full breasts, and my cock throbs as I explore her pert nubs. She bends forward, placing her hands on the headboard for leverage and rides me harder. I suck and lick and she rubs wildly, until her orgasm hits. Soft moans spill from her throat and her liquid heat is dripping into my hungry mouth and down my chin.

She whimpers and I slide my tongue over her, softly this time as her body grows more sensitive. I grip her hips again, and hold her to me until her spasms slow. Her breathing is ragged as I move her down my body, setting her on my chest. She leans forward, her hair framing her face, her eyes half-lidded.

"Tavish..." she murmurs, and my heart thumps. "Tavish," she says again, her voice low and rough and I laugh. She shimmies down and lifts her body, about to impale herself on my raging cock. I grip her hips hard to stop her.

"Condom." She shakes her head no, and I swallow against a tight throat. "Rachel, condom." She's clearly not thinking straight.

"It's been a long time since I've been with anyone, Tavish. I'm clean and I'm on the pill."

I stare at her. Is she thinking straight? Before I can answer, she shifts between my legs, takes my cock into her hand and licks it. "I want you inside me." Her laugh is edgy and broken. "This isn't something I do often, or ever. I want to make the most of it." She arches a brow. "I want to feel you."

"I want to feel you too," I say, damn near losing my mind as she laps at my crown like it's a damn ice cream cone.

"I just assumed you were clean. You carry condoms."

"I always use condoms," I tell her,

She blinks, and a line forms in her forehead. "Of course. I'm being silly. I don't know—"

"Rachel. I want to feel you," I explain quickly. "No condom, and I'm clean, I promise."

She nods, and my heart thumps. I don't think she trusts easily and it's insane how much faith she puts in me. She knows a bit about my past, my life, my struggles and what I'm capable of. I wouldn't hurt her purposely, ever, but am I really a guy she should trust so easily?

She sits back up and I pull her onto my waist, lifting her until she's poised over my steel cock. Her moans mingle with my grunts as I tug her down, burying every inch of my cock inside her, until she's pressed against my pelvis. She wiggles and whimpers and my cock throbs inside her warm wet heat, wanting to take up residency until tomorrow morning, but I have to be out of here long before then. We have Lucas to think about and can't give him the wrong idea.

Her soft palms land on my chest, and she moves her hips. I grunt and it brings a smile to her face. The little lassie likes making a mess of me. My fingers span her hips and I easily lift her, moving her body up and down my cock. Her hot muscles spasm around me, and when she sits up a bit straighter and puts a hand between her legs to spread herself, giving me a gorgeous view of my cock sliding in and out of her, I know I'm a goner.

"You are so beautiful," I murmur.

Her gaze races over my tatted body. "Your body is a work of art, and I'm not just talking about your tattoos."

I take a deep breath, moisture breaking out on my skin as I shag her, no barriers keeping our flesh apart. "You know you got me right there, don't you?"

She nibbles her bottom lip. "I do?"

"Fuck, lassie."

She lifts herself up and comes down on me, everything in her eyes indicating this pleasure is all for me. "I want your cum in me, Tavish."

"Aye, that's going to happen. What about you though, lassie?" I ask, and run the back of my knuckles over her face. Her eyes soften and my chest expands as she leans into my touch, a new kind of warmth about her.

"I just came all over your face, Tavish." I grin at the way she says that.

"Aye, you did."

"You feel so good inside me."

She lifts up and as she comes down, I slide into the depths of her and groan. While I'd like to make her come again, she's making this all about me, and there isn't a damn thing I can do about it. Not at the moment anyway, but the night is still young.

She cups her breasts and squeezes as she rides me, her sweet pussy massaging my cock and milking my release, until I can't even think with clarity. Sex with a condom is good. Sex without one is fucking mindblowing. Would it be like that with any other woman?

I pant, and gasp and can't seem to fill my lungs as she moves over my cock, giving me no reprieve. My orgasm builds, expands, and I pull her down, and hold her to me as I let go, spurting my seed high inside her.

"I feel you," she whimpers, her head rolling back, and as I gaze at her, it's her body, her reactions that are art in its truest form. I pull her to me, her chest against mine, and slide my hands around her back, holding her small frame to mine as I fill her. Soft moans of contentment and fulfillment seep under my skin and weave their way around my heart.

Fuck, I really like this woman.

Careful there, mate. You're not cut out for this kind of life.

I hold her for a long time, until my cock grows flaccid. I roll her off me, and her eyes are closed. "Hey Rach," I whisper.

"Mmmm."

She's so tired, I'm not going to wake her. I make a quick trip to the bathroom, and wash up, bringing a cloth back to wipe her down. Once we're both clean, I tuck her in and stand there for a second.

I should go. I reach for my clothes.

"Tavish," she murmurs and reaches for me. I guess one more second holding her isn't going to hurt. Besides, I don't want to shag and leave.

Why not, mate? That's what you always used to do.

Yeah, but none of those women were Rachel. She's tough as nails—as a single mom she has to be—but there's a vulnerability about her too. She hides it and dammit, I want to be the guy who's there for her. Just for a little while, anyway.

"I'm here." I crawl back in next to her and pull her warm body to mine. I'll just close my eyes for a minute and then get out of here. My bike is still in her driveway and if it's there all night, I'm sure we'll be the talk of the neighborhood. I don't much give a shit what people say about me. Rachel though, she grew up here, and doesn't need anyone talking trash about her. As I consider that, my lids fall shut, and my body shuts down.

"Mom," Lucas calls out, and my eyes fly open.

I rub the blur and that's when Rachel's room comes into view. "Fuck." I hadn't meant to stay the night. I turn as Rachel stirs. Lucas calls again and her eyes go wide.

"Shit." She scrambles for the blankets.

"Sorry, Rachel."

"It's okay." She jumps up and pulls on a robe. "I'd better go check on him."

I hurry from the bed, and tug on my kilt and shirt from last night. I open the door, fully intending to tiptoe to the front door. Christ, I can't remember the last time I had to sneak from a woman's bed.

"It's okay. I'll call in sick."

I stop at the top of the stairs as the worry in Rachel's voice pounds against my chest.

"Maybe Tavish could stay with me."

"You're not pretending to be sick so you can hang out with Tavish today, are you?"

"Nooooo…"

I turn, knowing I could be making a huge mistake, and walk to Lucas' door. "Hey mate, I just got here." I point up as Rachel's worried eyes meet mine. "More work to do on the roof. Heard you say you weren't feeling well." Rachel relaxes as Lucas' eyes light up and their reactions mess with me in strange ways.

"I don't feel great," he moans.

"I'm going to call in," Rachel says, worry once again brimming in her eyes.

"Nae, I got this. I'm off today so my mate and I can hang out."

13

RACHEL

I finish my last meeting of the day, guilt tugging at me as I make my way to the car. I'm pretty sure Lucas was faking it this morning, wanting to hang out with Tavish instead of going to camp. I owe Tavish big time for stepping up to help me like that. My shoes tap the busy city sidewalk and I nearly crash into someone who has their head in their phone instead of looking where they're going.

Dodging around them, I pull my own phone from my bag, and hold it until I'm inside my car. I shoot Tavish a text. Not the first of the day either. I don't know what it is, I just like messaging him.

Me: Any changes in Lucas?

Three dots appear quickly and it's ridiculous how happy that makes me.

Tavish: Nope, he's the same. Happy and no fever. I've been showing him how the tools work in my shop and we had some ice cream for a snack earlier.

Me: Don't make the day too good for him. He'll fake sick for the rest of the summer. I'm on my way home now. I'm going to grab some things for dinner. Anything you feel like?

Maybe I shouldn't be so presumptuous. He could have dinner plans of his own, and I'd be wise to remember we're simply playing house.

Tavish: Yes, but I probably shouldn't put it in writing.

I giggle, like a silly little girl. It feels good inside, and I haven't felt this good in a long time, so I just go with it and let his teasing fill my soul.

Me: See you soon.

I toss my phone aside, and instead of heading to the grocery store to pick up groceries, another idea hits and I go through my contacts and make a couple more calls. Once I finish, I pull onto the highway and head to Gloucester. I sing along to the radio and the closer and closer I get to Tavish's place, the more excited I find myself.

By the time I make it home, it's nearing dinner time, and I ease into Tavish's driveway. The garage is open and I peer in to find him and Lucas sanding a piece of wood. My heart wobbles a bit in my chest. This is exactly what Lucas needs in his life, and honestly, I'm pretty sure it's what Tavish needs too, whether he knows it or not.

I turn my car off and step into the sunshine. Lucas beams when he sees me.

"Mom, Mom, look at what we did today," he yells and jumps up, running up to some big piece of machinery to show me stacks of lumber. "This looks like wood right now, but we ran them through the planer, and we're going to make rocking chairs out of them." I turn and my heart jumps into my throat as Tavish stands there, tapping a piece of wood against his muscular thigh, his other hand holding sandpaper. His mere presence throws me off and completely overwhelms me. Of course, it could also be the hunger in his eyes and the way they're undressing me that's turning my legs to rubber.

"I'm impressed," I say, and walk over to where there are two rocking chairs sitting. I push one gently and it glides back and forth. A lot of care went into this chair. "These are gorgeous, Tavish."

"They still need to be stained. You can sit in one if you like."

I drop into the chair, and it's nice to get off my feet. I push back and forth and let loose a contented sigh. "I can see why Mom loves hers so much." Tavish and Lucas exchange a glance, like they know something I don't.

"What?" I ask and stand as Lucas works to hide a grin.

"Nothing," they both say, and I guess if they want to have a secret they're allowed. I think their bonding is kind of cute.

Tavish walks up to me and his rough knuckles brush mine. "How was work?"

"It was good."

He studies my face. "The guys give you any trouble?"

"Nothing I can't handle."

He grins and lightly nudges my chin with his fist. "That's my girl. That one lesson is paying off."

I laugh. "I didn't have to knee anyone in the groin." I brush sawdust from his shoulder. "You're kind of a mess."

He runs his fingers through his hair, and more sawdust falls to the floor. "I could use a shower."

I turn toward Lucas. "I should get him home and cleaned up. Tomorrow, he doesn't get to play hooky."

"I work a long shift tomorrow. Do you have a backup sitter?"

"Mom helps when she can, and I do have his other set of grandparents." He nods, and I hold my hand out to my son. "Come on, Lucas. You need to shower before dinner."

Tavish steps closer, and his warm scent combined with the sawdust swirls around me, makes me dizzy. "He can shower here. You both can."

While I think that idea is fun, the logistical side of me kicks in. "He needs clean clothes and so do I."

"I don't want to go, Mom."

"Do as your mom says, Lucas. You can come back another day."

Lucas grumbles as he walks to the car and jumps in. "So firm, I like that."

His eyes darken. "You don't know the half of it."

"Why don't you shower here, and meet me at my place? Oh, and we're going out. I called a sitter for Lucas."

His eyes narrow. "Where are we going?"

"It's a surprise. To thank you for today."

"That's not how I want to be thanked," he growls into my ear.

"I know." I turn and put an extra swing to my hips as I walk to my car.

"Is there a dress code?"

"Anything but a birthday suit." I steal a glance at him over my shoulder, and find him shaking his head. "Whatever you're most comfortable in. Nothing fancy."

His growl follows and I slide into the passenger seat.

"Is Tavish growling?"

"I think he got some sawdust stuck in his throat." I look at Lucas and he pulls the skin on his throat and starts growling too. I resist the urge to laugh. It never fails to surprise me how impressionable kids his age are, and I don't think I made a bad decision bringing Tavish into his life. I just need to be careful I keep him there.

"What's a birthday suit?"

Oh God. Instead of answering, I redirect the conversation by pointing as I drive past the dog/pig/cat/bunny walking club and wave as I slow and move to the side to give them a wide berth. "Looks like Mrs. Potter has a new bunny."

Lucas stops clearing his throat and sits up a bit straighter to see the animals. A few in the group wave back, but the strange stares I'm getting are a little disconcerting. A burst of anxiety moves through me. Am I the new topic of conversation for the club? The desperate divorcée and the former MMA fighter. I really don't want that. I can't even imagine the rumors. Actually, maybe I can and none of them are good.

Turning my attention back to Lucas, I say, "You sound like you're feeling better." I know my son well enough to know what was really going on today.

"I guess."

"Camp tomorrow, then?"

"But—"

"Tavish works, so he won't be able to take care of you. We got lucky today. Isn't tomorrow beach day? That's fun, right?"

"Yeah, that's fun. Can we get a dog?"

I pull into our driveway. What brought that on? Oh right, the dog walking club. "I don't think now is the right time."

"What about a bunny? I played with the bunnies today."

My body stiffens. "You were at Mrs. Potter's?

"Yeah, Ben was at camp, and Mrs. Potter was out. Sophie gave me a bunny to play with while she showed Tavish her downstairs." I nearly choke on my tongue. What the ever-loving hell? "Apparently, there's a plumbing problem. She needs a pipe."

Oh, my dear God!

"How...did she come looking for Tavish?"

"Yeah, we were locking up and getting ready to go to his place, and she came running over when she saw us."

I swallow. Did she see his bike here all night?

"What time was that?"

He shrugs. "I don't know. She thought it was odd that he was at our place early, but he told her I was sick and he was watching me."

Lucas exits the car and I hit the fob and lock it. I'm a grown woman and I'm entitled to grown-up sleepovers if I want. I just don't want to be the talk of the town—again. Lord knows I was on everyone's lips after the divorce and oddly enough, even after Jason's scandal. For some reason, I was the one given the strange looks, like it was somehow my fault. I just want a simple quiet life now, which is why we moved back here. Nothing, however, is proving to be simple or quiet with Tavish.

I glance around, half expecting Sophie to come running over to find out why Tavish was really at my house so early. But what happens between Tavish and me is no one's business but our own. I take a step toward the house and my phone pings. Half expecting it to be Tavish, I fish it from my purse and my stomach tightens when I read the message from Jason.

Maybe I was wrong.

What happens between Tavish and me likely isn't going to stay between Tavish and me, not when Jason has so many fans, and people in this community like to gossip. I read the message as Lucas runs up the steps and I follow behind him to unlock the door.

"Emma is coming to watch you tonight. How does pizza sound? Unless you want me to see if there is any leftover fish chowder in the fridge."

"Pizza is good," he yells back as he races up the stairs. I laugh and drop my purse and turn my attention back to my phone. Jason is home and looking to see Lucas this weekend. It's been a while, and even though he has rights to see his son, it still makes me uneasy. Sometimes I'm sure I'm just overprotective, and of course he'll be taking Lucas to his grandparents' house. I shoot back a message that he can pick him up either Friday after school, or Saturday after breakfast.

I wait for him to message back and when he doesn't, I head upstairs, shut my bedroom door and strip off. It's nice to get out of my dress clothes and into something casual. I shower, wash my hair and tug on a pair of jeans and a blouse. I check myself in my closet mirror. The blouse is probably too fancy for what I have in mind. I leave it, wanting to look nice for Tavish.

I finish up, and head to Lucas' room. He's dressed in his pajamas and naturally he's on his iPad. Emma will be here any minute.

"Where are you going?

I cross the room and sit. "I was going to show Tavish around. He's new here in town, remember?"

"Can I come?"

"Not tonight. Another time, though." I smooth his hair back. "Your dad just messaged me. He's going to come by to get you this weekend." I brace myself. I'm not sure what to expect. Lucas is always a mess of emotions after his father comes around.

"Tavish said he'd take me for a ride on his bike this weekend."

I swallow against a tight throat. I want Lucas to have a healthy relationship with his father, and that's hard to do when Jason only fits him in when it's convenient. Lucas is getting older, and he's starting to figure these things out. If Lucas doesn't go, Jason will blame it on me, I'm sure. I've never said one bad word about him to his son, and that's not something I ever plan on doing. Jason and I had our troubles, but they were ours.

"I'm sure he can take you another day. It's been a while since you've seen your dad. You must be excited about that." He stares at his iPad and shrugs. "I bet Buster will go crazy when he sees you."

His face lights up. Buster is his grandparents' black lab, and Lucas' favorite animal. "Can we get him those treats he likes?"

"You bet we can. We can stop at the pet store on the way home from camp tomorrow." The doorbell rings and he tosses his iPad down.

"Emma likes extra cheese on her pizza, just like me."

I exhale and smile, pushing down my unease as he darts down the stairs and lets Emma in. I head to my room to put on a light dusting of makeup. I listen to Lucas chat up Emma and honestly, it's not a surprise that he'd rather spend time with Tavish. I can't imagine how Jason would react to that, though. It's his own fault, really. He's the one who barely comes around, which is why I signed up for Dad for Hire in the first place. It's probably not something I want Jason to know about, but with the rumor mill in this town, he'll find out about Tavish soon enough. Will he kick up a stink that a man like Tavish is in Lucas' life? Lucas is his son, sure. I still don't think he has a right to say who I allow into his life. It's not like Tavish murdered anyone.

By the time I descend the stairs, I glance up to see Tavish at my door, his hand raised, ready to knock. I wave him in and when he enters and fills the doorway, it momentarily takes my breath away. Without any shame, I blatantly let my gaze move down his body, take in his buttoned-up shirt and jeans that hug his body to perfection.

My God, the man cleans up nice. Why again did I tell him not to wear his birthday suit? Oh right. I remember, because we're going out in public. Later though, I'll have to see what I can do about getting him out of them.

"Something on your mind?" he asks with a grin.

●14

TAVISH

"Take a left up here," Rachel says, and I steal a glance at her as I drive out of town, leaving the dinner hour traffic behind.

I follow along the coastal road, enjoying the water and the lighthouses. There's no doubt that I'm a long way from home, and not missing it one little bit. "It would probably be easier if you told me where we were going."

She playfully wags her brow. "Even if I told you where we were going, you wouldn't know how to get there." Her phone pings and she ignores it. "You're new around here."

"I cruise a lot on my bike. I'm sure if you told me, I'd know how to find it. I think you just like telling me where to go."

She laughs at that. "I could have driven. Then you wouldn't be asking a million questions."

"I wanted to drive you and if I wasn't asking a million questions, we probably would still be in the driveway or on our way to Florida."

She whacks me and a strand of hair falls across her eyes. She blows it away and shoots back, "Hey, I give good directions."

I take her hand and kiss it as I admire the open buttons on her blouse and the hint of lace I'm hoping she wore for me. "Did I tell you how nice you looked tonight?"

Her face softens. "Thanks. You look good too."

"It's no kilt."

"It's not the kilt I like, it's what's beneath it," she teases with a smirk.

"I knew it, you're after me for my body." Although I'm joking, there's a part of me—that wee boy who was never wanted until he started fighting—that still exists. Then, that wee boy grew up and got noticed for his fists. Then, everyone wanted a part of him. It was the fighter they wanted, not the real me.

Her phone pings again and I glance at her bag at her feet. "Are you going to get that?"

She fidgets, rubbing her hands on her pants. "I don't want to be rude."

Okay, what the hell is really going on here? Is someone pestering her, and if so, I'd be happy to deal with them. "I don't mind. What if it's the babysitter?"

"It's not," she says with a nervous certainty that raises the hair on my neck.

"It's someone you don't want to talk to." I take in her features as I state the obvious.

She exhales, her blue eyes narrow as she reluctantly pulls her phone from her purse. "It's my ex."

My fingers tighten on the steering wheel. Okay, now that I wasn't expecting. "Is everything okay?" I steal a glance at her and take in her frown.

"It is." Okay, her words are saying one thing, her body language, however, is telling an entirely different story. Hey, if she doesn't want to tell me she doesn't have to. What right do I have to know what's going on with her and her ex? I concentrate on the road and try not to feel offended—which I have no right to feel. Maybe I'm getting in a little deeper here than I should. How much involvement is a stand in Dad for Hire supposed to have anyway? Perhaps I should have clarified that with Brodie. Still, I probably shouldn't be getting involved.

After a long moment, she breaks the silence. "He's asking to see Lucas on the weekend."

"You don't want him to?" I ask. So much for not getting involved.

"It's not that." She glances at her phone and drops it back into her bag. "It's hard, you know. He shows up when he feels like it, hangs out and plays great dad mostly, and then he disappears. It's not easy on Lucas."

I reach over and take her hand, giving it a squeeze. "It's pretty shitty." She turns my way. "Sorry," I say quickly. "It's not my right to judge."

"It's okay. Lucas wasn't actually all that enthused when I told him. When he goes, he does have fun. It's just...he's older now and needs a little more stability."

"I totally understand that."

A warm sincerity comes over her and she puts her hand on top of mine. "I know you do."

My heart squeezes tight, and wow, what the fuck is going on with me? Words don't usually affect me, yet something in hers —it's not pity, but more like understanding—curls around me and oddly enough soothes the demons deep inside me. It's been a long time—okay, never—since a woman offered me real softness and compassion. As a child, I was a nuisance in the home, as an adult, an MMA fighter, I was good for a shag and nothing more. I take a couple of deep breaths to pull myself together.

"Lucas is a tough little guy, Rachel. I saw that in him today."

"He bounces back fast, doesn't he?"

"Yeah, he really does. I do understand he's at a vulnerable age and you have every right to be worried about his father coming and going. Nothing about that is easy." She squeezes my hand, once again letting me know she understands the damage done to me during my childhood. "If I were him, I would never have fucked up what I had with you and Lucas. He had a great family and couldn't even see that."

Her gaze rakes over my face and I shift. "You want a family, Tavish?"

"No," I say quickly and give a humorless laugh. The truth is, I'd like to have a family of my own. I just worry that my father was wrong, and I have more of him in me than Mom and I'd end up fucking things up and hurting others. I don't want to hurt anyone. MMA was one thing. It was a job, zero emotions in the cage. Real life is complicated and messy and I nearly killed a guy protecting Brodie. Getting out of control like that was fucking scary. "I'm not cut out for that."

"I don't know about that," she says quietly.

"Do you want a family, Rachel? Another child, another marriage, a father for Lucas?"

She glances down, a new kind of sadness about her. "I don't think I want to go down that road again, and Lucas does have a father."

Yeah, just a shitty one, but that doesn't mean I could or would be a good one for him. Wait, why is that thought even going through my head?

"I'll do what I can for you and Lucas. I can be a stand-in for now." There's a sorrow about her as she nods, and it wraps around my battered soul. The truth is, I take this stand-in role seriously. Clearly, I was reluctant at first. I didn't want to get involved with a family. It scares the shit out of me. Now I can't bail.

While I'm not sure I'm the right role model—I was never convinced I was—I've made the commitment and the connection, and I have to follow through with it for the next six months. After that, who knows what's going to happen. We'll still be neighbors, and I can't see why Lucas and I can't still be mates. Hell, Rachel could change her mind on marriage by then, and have a new man in her life.

"Right here, take a left."

I slam on the brakes, and take the turn fast and the wheels spin a little as I hit the gravel road. I glance at Rachel to make sure she's okay. "Shite, lassie. How about a little warning next time?"

Rachel grips the dashboard. "Sorry, it just sort of crept up on me."

I swallow, totally understanding that. The strange things I'm feeling for this woman have sort of crept up on me too, and it kind of feels like I'm spinning out of control. I peer out the front window.

"Where the hell are we?"

A wide smile splits her lips. "Read the sign." She points and I follow the direction and the second understanding hits, I laugh.

"I got dressed up for this?"

"It's not like I asked you to wear a three-piece suit."

"Good. I hate formal." I step on the gas and head toward the mini putt. Dust kicks up as I drive the long road to the mini putt park. "Are we really doing this?'

"You wanted golf lessons, didn't you?"

"I don't think mini putt qualifies as golf lessons." I ease my truck between two cars and kill the ignition.

She arches a curious brow. "You've tried it, then?"

"No."

I glance around at the over-the-top animatronics. From what I can see in the parking lot, you have to walk through a big skull to get inside and the place has everything from pirate ships and talking pirates to a huge crow towering over waterfalls. It's kind of cool.

"What about dinner?" I ask, since the sandwiches Lucas and I had earlier are doing little to sustain me now.

"We're eating here." She unbuckles and opens the door and as soon as she does, the smell of carnival hot dogs and fries and grease swirls around me. "Best hot dogs on the planet."

"Doubt that." I step from the vehicle, and while mini putt and carnival dogs are the last thing I expected tonight, the wee boy in me might be a bit excited.

I walk around my truck, and she takes my hands and tugs. "Food first." We head inside and pay and the next thing I know we're standing at a kiosk and Rachel is ordering us hotdogs, fries and drinks. I gather the tray and we find a table.

"Fine dining at its best," she teases. "I bet these would go over really well at Kilting Around." She bites into a mustard package and coats her extra-long hot dog.

"I forgot hot dogs were traditional Scottish food," I tease, and cover mine in ketchup. She bites into hers and moans and I have to say, I do like the sounds she makes. When was the last time I ate a hot dog? When training, my diet was ridiculously strict, but I'm not on the circuit anymore and I'm not in Scotland. When in Rome.... "I can't believe you eat these."

Her jaw drops and she glares at me, like she's truly offended. "Says the guy who eats haggis."

I shrug. "Don't knock it until you try it, lassie."

"I'm never trying it." She practically snarls at me, and damn, she's adorable.

"Why not?" I run my finger along my hotdog to push it deeper into the bun, and smooth out the ketchup. Rachel watches as I lick my finger clean.

"It's disgusting, that's why."

"You've tried it then?" I bite into my hot dog.

"No."

"You can't say that unless you've tried it." I glance at the big pirate animatronics making an *arrgh* sound when someone gets a hole in one. "I think you'd like it."

"Want to bet?"

"Actually, I do." I glance around as I chew. "If I win, I make you haggis and you try it. If you win…" I pause to let her come up with her own reward.

She looks up and to the left. "Hmm, let me think on that." I chow down on my carnival dog, which is truly scrumptious, until she comes back with, "I don't think I'm too good at this game. You're already doing so much for us."

I don't think she realizes just how much I do want to do for her. "How about this? If you win, I coach Lucas' football." Her eyes go wide with excitement, and I don't bother telling her I'd already planned to do it.

"I'll help you," she rushes out excitedly. "I just don't know the rules."

"Don't get ahead of yourself, lassie. You haven't won yet."

"I do not plan to eat haggis, Tavish. So you'd better brush up on your soccer skills." I grin at her as she takes a big sip of her soda. I finish off my hot dog. "I'm going to have to find a way to work off those two billion calories."

"That's what the mini golf is for." Excitement lights her eyes and I love her childlike enthusiasm. When was the last time she did something just for her? Oh, yeah, I remember. Last night in her bed. There's definitely going to be more of that, because Rachel deserves to have a life outside of work and motherhood.

"All these years I was going to the gym to condition myself for the cage. No one told me all I had to do was play a round of mini golf."

She grins and gathers up our garbage, dumping it into the can. "Live and learn, Tavish."

I throw my arm around her, loving this easy way we are together as we walk over and pick out our clubs. "First up is Captain Jack's boat. We shoot through it."

We step up to what's supposed to be a derelict pirate's ship with a golf green running through it. Rachel lines up her ball. She takes a shot and comes close. "You'd better keep score. I don't know anything about golf."

She writes on the note paper and I line up my shot. I take a few practice swings and then proceed to sink the ball in one shot.

She eyes me. "What was that all about?"

"Beginner's luck, I think."

"You're not hustling me, are you?"

"Me? Hustle you?" She purses her lips and I bite back a grin. "I wouldn't even dream about pulling the wool over your eyes. You'd see through me in a minute."

She lifts her chin high as I retrieve my ball, and she lines up for her shot. "That's right I would." Her ball goes in on her second putt, and she writes on the paper.

"Am I winning?" I ask.

"Barely."

She snatches up her ball and we continue through the course, laughing and having a great time, and it's fun to see her competitive side. We finally reach the last green, the waterfall, and she misses her shot. The game is close. All I have to do is make this in one shot and I win.

I set my ball down. "Shoot," she mumbles and moves so she's hidden behind a post and I glance around. Who the hell is she hiding from?

"What?" I ask my voice low.

"It's Jack Robertson." She points to some spot to her left. "He's here with his grandson."

"Is he an axe murderer or something?"

"It's not that," She lowers her voice to match mine, even though there is no way Jack Robertson can overhear us. "He's the nosiest man in the neighborhood, and he likes to talk about everyone."

"You don't want to be seen out with me?" I'd never want to do anything to upset her, but since he can't see us, I step up to her, put my arm around her waist and pull her close. "Should we give him something to talk about?"

Her face flushes. "It's probably not wise."

"Aye, I get it. You just want to live a quiet life." I nod, totally understanding that. What I don't understand, however, is why I'm acting all caveman like, dragging her to me, like I want to lay claim and let every man in the universe know that she's mine—even though she's not. Maybe it has something to do with her ex, and the fact that he's coming around this weekend. "I moved here to get out of the limelight too, lassie."

She smiles and peeks around the post. "Okay, he's gone. Besides, I'm sure you've given him enough to talk about for one day."

I line up my shot and catch her grin. "How's that?"

"Going into Sophie's downstairs."

I burst out laughing, and shake my head. "I was wondering when you were going to bring that up."

"Someone had to. You clearly weren't going to tell me."

I drag her to me again, loving the way she feels against my body. "You sound like you're jealous, lassie."

"Me, pfft, not even a little bit."

"Ah, you're trying to throw me off my game then, are you? Wanting me to think about your downstairs."

"Are you?" she asks innocently.

"I've never stopped, and trust me, your downstairs is the only one I'm interested in. So why don't you let me finish this shot, win the game and get you home so I can have my way with you."

She's warm and flustered as I let her go and prepare for my shot. "You miss, I win."

"Right." I agree with her, not at all planning to miss. I take a shot, and the pirate growls *arrgh* as I sink the ball. "Looks like I won." She makes a whimpering sound, and I wrap her in my arms. "I guess we should get home. No worries though, the night is far from over."

"No?"

I run my finger over her bottom lip. "There's something we need to put in here."

Her face flushes and she moves against me. "Oh, and what exactly do you have in mind?"

"Haggis."

15

RACHEL

I check my watch as we pull into Tavish's driveway. I'm sure Lucas is long asleep by now and it's nice to have a free night. I can't stay out too long, though.

"Somewhere to be?" Tavish asks, and I glance at him.

"I don't want to keep Emma out too late." I crinkle my nose. "She works at the bookstore by Mom's café. It was nice of her to come last minute, and I don't want to take advantage of her generosity."

"I understand that." He turns off his truck and looks my way. "Speaking of taking advantage...How long do I have to take advantage of you?" he asks with a grin.

"About an hour."

"Let me see," he mumbles. "By the time I mix the ingredients for the haggis and get it boiling..."

"Tavish!" I yell and whack him.

Ignoring my protest, he frowns and shakes his head. "I'm afraid it's not going to be enough time tonight anyway, lassie. It takes a good three hours to boil."

I feign disappointment. "Oh no, and I was really looking forward to it." Lies, all lies. "Maybe there's something else Scottish that I could try."

"Aye, lassie, I think we can rustle something *up*."

My heart is light and happy as he circles the truck and I slide from the passenger side, and he takes my hand. I'm oddly looking forward to seeing the inside of his house. We step up to his front door, and in the distance a dog's bark penetrates the quiet of the night. Across the street, a door opens and closes and I step closer to Tavish. I don't want to get caught sneaking into his house under the cover of darkness.

I press against his strong body and breathe in his clean, soapy smell. He told me about his hard past, and the violence. While I'm sure it's still there, lurking beneath the surface, everything about him makes me feel safe and protected. Like nothing in the world can touch or hurt me when I'm with him.

He opens the door and moves to the side, putting his hand on the small of my back to guide me into his home. My entire body quivers at his touch and he stays close, his big frame hovering over mine as I enter. My eyes sting as he turns on the lights and I blink as they adjust to the brightness.

I'm not sure what I was expecting, maybe a messy bachelors' pad, but his place is anything but that. I glance into the living room which is just off the foyer, and it's neat and tidy and sparse. He hasn't collected many items over the years. Maybe that's because he moved around a lot on the MMA circuit, or maybe it's because he doesn't like to get attached to many things.

I glance up at him as I think about his hard childhood. How can a man who'd been tossed and kicked around be so good with me...with my son? My heart does some weird little flip and I'm suddenly breathless as his warmth curls around me.

"Drink?" he asks.

I nod, my throat tight and dry. He takes my hand in his, swallowing it whole, and leads me to the kitchen. "If you're not having a traditional Scottish meal, how about a traditional Scottish drink?" He reaches into his pantry and pulls out a bottle of whiskey.

"I'm not much of a whiskey drinker."

"That's a nae."

"That's an aye." I laugh. "I said that right, didn't I?"

Two tumblers clink together as he pulls them from his cupboard and sets them on the counter. "Aye, you did, lassie."

"Are you really going to make me eat haggis?"

"A bet's a bet," he tells me and pours our drinks. He hands me mine and holds his out for a salute. "To winning, and for the record, I'm still going to coach Lucas' football team."

I squeal. "Really? He's going to be so happy."

"I was going to do it no matter what. The haggis was just for fun."

"Fun? Haggis is not fun. It's cruel." He grins, and I eye him as we tap glasses. "You were hustling me, weren't you? You know how to play golf and have just been pretending."

He takes a drink of his whiskey and nods for me to do the same. "Maybe I'm just a natural athlete, and maybe I'm going to kick Jakob's arse at the retreat."

I laugh, my insides full of happiness. "He's really good."

"I bet I'm better."

"Where did you learn to play?"

"One of my trainers was into golf. He thought I'd be a natural at it. I think I just have good hand-eye coordination. Hey, I only won by one point tonight."

"Oh my God, you did that on purpose. You could have smoked me." I take another sip of whiskey. "You're good at everything you do, aren't you?"

He takes a big sip from his glass, sets it down, and pulls me close. His big hand goes around my neck and his fingers brush my hair from my neck. "I don't know, why don't you tell me if I'm good at this."

His wet lips, which taste like whiskey, land on mine, and I moan into his mouth as our tongues hungrily tangle. I go up on my toes as he tastes the depths of me and I close my eyes, the world around me spinning.

His kisses slow, become softer, and his breath is heavy against my face as he inches back. "Verdict?" he asks.

"Good," I mumble. "Good at that." He grins and picks me up, holding me in that familiar way he does, and I wrap my legs around his waist. "You're good at this too," I add.

He laughs, his rumbling chest vibrating through my body as he carries me upstairs, straight to his bedroom. He doesn't bother closing the door; we're the only two in the place. His bedroom is sparse too. A bed, a dresser and a single rocking chair. There are no pictures on his walls, or on his dresser, and I wouldn't exactly say it lacked warmth, it just lacks attachment. My heart once again hurts for the wee boy who'd been so damaged.

He sets me on the edge of his bed, and his eyes are dark and needy as he sinks to his knees. "Let's see if I'm good at this." With a quick flick of his wrist, he unbuttons my pants, and I fall back and lift my hips, making it easier for him to peel them down my legs. My panties follow, and as soon as he has me half naked, he buries his face between my legs.

"Oh, God yes." He licks at me, swirls his tongue over my clit, and I grow wetter with each purposeful flick of his tongue. I go up on my elbows, and lift my legs, putting my feet on the edge of the bed to cradle his head—and maybe lock him in place.

"So good, Tavish," I murmur, beyond grateful that he's a man of many talents. He stays between my legs, puts his hands on my knees and pushes on them until I'm spread wide, and holy hell that comes with its own pleasure. With my sex open, he feasts on me, and somewhere in my brain, I register that he's unzipping his pants. He grunts and I sit up a bit, watch him take his cock into his hand, and a flash of heat goes through me.

My muscles clench and I whimper, needing something hard and thick to grasp on to. "Tavish, more," I whimper, and he slides a thick finger into me. "Yes." I fall back onto the bed as he fingers me, sliding in and out of my slick core, taking me higher and higher.

I grip the bedding and tug, every cell in my body dancing with sheer pleasure. He tears his mouth from my sex. "Verdict?"

"Good. Great," I blurt out, wanting his face back between my legs. Except he has different plans. He leans over me, slides his hand around my waist and lifts me until I'm sitting up. He drags me to the edge of the bed, and lines my sex up with his rock-hard cock. He's going to take me just like this.

I lift my hips, my arms balancing me on the bed, and in one fast thrust he's deep inside me. "Tavish!" I cry out, not bothering to keep quiet. I let go, give myself over to him completely as he fucks me. I buck against him and our bodies slam together. He grunts louder and I moan and gasp and cry out as I scratch at his back with wild abandonment. I am sure I have never felt so reckless or indulgent.

I love this no condom thing, love the way his flesh feels against mine as he rides me hard. Big hands span my waist and hold me as he powers into me. I bend forward and run my teeth along a black butterfly tattoo, and he growls and shifts his body, pounding into me with a new kind of need.

I meet each thrust, and my gaze moves over his face as he watches me with care. The pleasure is so intense, I want to close my eyes and let it overcome me, but I can't tear my gaze away. There's pain in this man. Everything about him is captivating, and as we hold each other's gaze, my heart can't help but get involved. I really, really like this man, for more reasons than what he's currently doing to me.

He slides a hand between our bodies and a keening cry catches in my throat as he applies pressure to my clit, and boom, just like that, an explosion tears through me. His face softens as his gaze holds mine, taking in the pleasure spilling over my face and between my legs. He loves it when I orgasm. I love it when he brings me to orgasm. I guess we do have something in common.

As I clench around his cock and dig my fingers into his shoulders, his entire body tightens. He's right there, everything in his eyes tell me. "I want to feel you," I tell him.

He growls and captures my mouth, kissing me deeply as he lets go and spills his seed inside me. A warmth travels through my body, nourishing parts that have long ago been closed off and something new, something I hadn't felt in a long time blossoms inside me.

Happiness.

A soft laugh bubbles out of my throat, and he inches back, smiling as he checks in on me and smooths my hair back. "I'm pretty sure I know the verdict," he whispers with a laugh. He stares at me for a second. "I like hearing you laugh, Rach. You should do it more often."

"I think it might take mind-blowing orgasms every day." I arch a brow. "Are you up for that?"

"Maybe in five minutes."

I laugh again as he inches out of me, and I whimper with the loss of the fullness and warmth. It's short-lived as he stands, pulls me up and wraps his arms around me, holding so tight I think he might be using some MMA move to restrict my breathing. He lets go and drops the softest kiss onto my mouth.

"How are we doing for time?"

I check my watch, loving that he's conscientious of my sitter's time. "A few more minutes."

He nods, disappears into his bathroom and comes back with a cloth to wipe me down. I love the way he takes care of me after sex.

"Sorry I didn't even get my pants off."

"It's okay. We were on a time crunch." I tug on my jeans and he slides his hand around the back of my neck and holds me. "One of these nights, there's going to be no hurry."

"This weekend," I remind him. "It's the retreat. Mom was supposed to watch Lucas for the weekend. I always hate asking too much of her. Now, though, he'll be with his father."

He scratches at his face. "The retreat is a weekend thing. Not just a day event."

My heart sinks. "I'm sorry. I don't know why I thought you knew that." I start buttoning up my blouse. "Of course, you wouldn't know that. I understand if you're busy. I can't expect you to just spend your whole weekend with me. You have work, and your rocking—"

He puts his finger to my lip. "Rachel." I blink up at him. "Of course, I'm coming. I just thought it was a day. I cleared Saturday. I'll just get Brodie to cover for me Sunday. It's not a problem."

"If you're sure."

"A weekend away with you, and shoving a win down Jakob's throat? Why wouldn't I be sure?"

"Play nice. I have to work with these guys."

He kisses my forehead. "I know you do. Come on, I'll show you around and then get you home before you turn into a pumpkin."

He takes my hand and shows me the two other bedrooms upstairs. They're pretty empty, just a bed in each. "Do you have company?"

"Not yet. I have friends from my fighting days and they're always welcome to stay if they make it this way."

Downstairs, we walk through his living room, and dining room, and kitchen. Even though he's a big guy and it's not a big house, it's somehow perfect for him. "There's a really nice backyard."

He slides open the patio door and the warm night air falls over us. I take in his fenced yard. "Great place for a dog."

"When you get one, I'll get one," he answers with a laugh.

"I wish I could. I just don't have the time."

He peers into the dark. "What was that?"

I follow his gaze and spot something hopping. Tavish disappears inside and comes back with a flashlight. He shines it across his yard, coming to stop on what looks like a bunny. "Shite. Looks like one of Mrs. Potter's bunnies got loose." His feet stomp on the stairs as he makes his way to the yard, and scoops the bunny up. "We need to take him back."

I nod and we head outside to his truck. "We could walk, but the bunny is squirming, and I don't want him getting loose. Can you hold him while I drive?"

I jump in the passenger seat and he carefully puts the fluffy bunny on my lap. "I wonder how he got loose." We drive the short distance to Mrs. Potter's place and find one light on in the living room. "Looks like she's awake."

We hurry to the door and knock, and I listen to the sound of feet shuffling on the other side. The door swings open, and Mrs. Potter stands there, surprise on her face when she sees us. "What do we have here?"

"I think you lost one of your bunnies," Tavish says and she frowns.

She pulls her glasses down her nose, and eyes the bunny. Her lips purse as she inspects the brown fluff in my hand.

"Nope, he's not one of mine."

"Are you sure?" I ask. Honestly, how would she even know one was missing?

"Positive. My babies are all tucked in and accounted for." She pets the bunny, smoothing her hand over his groomed fur. "He's very handsome and well cared for." She pushes her glasses back up. "Where did you find him?"

"My backyard." He holds the bunny out. "Do you...want him?"

"No, my luv. I have a full house right now. You best find the owners or care for him yourself." Tavish is about to protest when she disappears and comes back with a brown bag. "Here are some pellets, they'll get you through until morning."

"But—"

"It's getting late. Good night now." She closes the door, and we stand there on the stoop staring at each other.

"What now?" Tavish asks.

I throw my arms up. "You could always take her advice."

"What the hell am I supposed to do with a bunny?"

"I don't know, take care of it."

"I'm not keeping a bunny, Rachel."

"Maybe you can take him to the shelter, you know, the one we took the racoons too."

"Yeah, good idea." He holds the bunny out and examines it. "Or I could make a rabbit stew."

I whack him. "Tavish!"

"Kidding," he says. "I think this is someone's pet."

"Are you on our neighbourhood app?"

"What's a neighbourhood app?"

I explain it to him, and ask for his phone. "Let me download it for you and you can post and see if someone lost their pet. If no one claims him, maybe Lucas and I can make posters and you could care for him until someone finally claims him. If you take him to the shelter, who knows what might happen." I download the app, and take a picture of the bunny. "Post the pic of him. I'm sure by morning he'll be back with his owners."

"I'm sure he'll be fine at the shelter tonight. Better than he will be with me."

"I think you should give it one night. It will be a lot easier for someone in the neighborhood to pick him up at your place versus the shelter." I'm really not sure why. I just think the bunny might be good company for him. He says he doesn't want a family, that he's not cut out for it. Maybe if he starts small, with a tiny pet, he'll see he's made of the right stuff.

Why exactly do you want him to see that, Rachel.

No reason. No reason at all. Heck, it's not like I'm thinking our fake relationship could one day blossom into more...much more.

Oh boy.

"I don't know, Rach…" The bunny, like he knows exactly what we're saying, and exactly how to soften the big man holding him, snuggles into Tavish and Tavish growls in response.

I bite back a laugh as the man with the tough exterior and soft interior shakes his head and curses. "Bollocks."

16

TAVISH

fter seeing Rachel safely home, I'm back in my truck staring at the bunny in my hands. "What do we do now, mate?"

He snuggles in and his soft hairs tickle my face and I fight back a sneeze. No need to scare the little guy. He looks frightened enough as it is. I drive the short distance back to my place, and the first thing I do is head to the garage to find a box to put him in. I can't have a bunny hopping all around my place and destroying things. Do bunnies destroy things? That's how little I know, which is why I am not the guy to be caring for anything or anyone but myself.

I find a big empty box, and as we head inside, I do a fast Google search on how to care for a bunny. I read quickly, and set him in the box, along with a small bowl of water and the pellets Mrs. Potter kindly gave me.

"Now where am I going to put you, mate?"

I walk around the house, and decide the master bath just off my bedroom is the best location. If he gets out, there's not much damage he can do in there. The second I walk into my room and take in my mussed sheets, I smile, my mind going back to an hour earlier and all the things I did with Rachel in that bed.

The bunny hops in the box and nearly spills the water. "Easy there, mate." I lightly pet his back. "You must have a name." He stares at me with amber eyes and it's possible I melt a little. "Don't be pulling that shite with me. Tomorrow, you go to the shelter, if your owner doesn't come for you." I set him on the bathroom floor and turn the lights out. He makes a small noise. "It's all right, mate, I'm just in the other room."

Shite. I'm trying to reason with a damn rabbit.

I strip off, climb into bed, and reach for my phone. I open the neighborhood app, figure out how to use the thing and send a picture of the bunny along with my address. My eyes grow heavy as I wait for a response, and when none comes, I drop my phone and close my eyes.

Next thing I know, a knock at my front door pulls me awake. I rub the sleep from my eyes and nearly have a fucking heart attack when I turn to see the clock and spot the rabbit on my pillow staring at me.

"What the fuck, mate? How the hell did you get up here?" He wiggles his nose at me, and I scoop him up, checking my bed for a mess and happy that there's none.

I tug on my jeans and head downstairs. "Looks like you're going home, little guy." I pull open my door and I'm seconds from passing the bunny over only to realize Rachel and Lucas are standing on my steps.

I wake fully, worry zinging through my body. I have no idea why I'm suddenly on high alert. Maybe it has something to do with Jason wanting to spend the weekend with Lucas. Did something happen? Did he show up early? Did he hurt them somehow? "What's going on?" I ask quickly. I look past Rachel's shoulder and check the street. "Is everything okay?"

Rachel puts her hand on my arm. "Tavish, everything is okay." She takes a step toward me. "Are you okay?"

"Yeah...just a bad dream or something." She looks like she's about to press, and I can't explain this uneasy feeling I have about her ex. Maybe it's simply jealousy. I don't know, there's just something in my gut, and I try to listen to my gut.

"Bunny," Lucas screams. "Can I hold him?"

"Sure." I hand the bunny over. "What's going on?" I ask. "Are you here for breakfast? Haggis, maybe?" I lower my voice so Lucas can't hear. "Rabbit stew." I grin, trying to lighten things, even though that knot remains in my stomach.

"Not funny." Rachel reaches into her briefcase. "Lucas and I made these this morning." I stare at the stack of papers, with the picture of the bunny, and my number. "I saw that you posted last night on the app, and no one responded. Lucas wanted to help you hang these before he went to camp. I'm sorry we're here so early." Lucas drops to the floor with the bunny. "How did he make out?"

"Just fine. I put him in a box in the bathroom, and woke up with him lounging on my pillow."

"What's his name?" Lucas asks.

"I don't know." Don't know and don't care.

"Can we name him?"

I harden myself. "No." I respond, my voice hard and firm, and Lucas tenses. Shite, I didn't mean to scare him. I'm just not going to name something I'm not going to keep. At many of the foster homes I was just a number in the system and I can understand that. Although, it's not like any of the foster parents feared they were going to grow to care for me. Rachel purses her lips, admonishment for me all over her face at my harshness and I grumble under my breath.

"Would it hurt?" she asks quietly.

The fight drains out of me. What is it about her that softens me? "Fine. You need to know though, he's not mine. He's someone's pet, so don't get too close."

I need to remind myself of that. Rachel and Lucas are not mine and I shouldn't be getting close.

"What do you think we should call him?" Rachel asks.

"How about Fluffy," Lucas suggests, and I groan.

"I have to go around calling the thing Fluffy," I grouch.

She shrugs. "It could have been worse. He could have suggested Bunnikins or Honey Bunny."

"When you put it that way." I shake my head. Here I thought moving to the 'burbs' would be simple and quiet. "Did you have breakfast?"

"I am not eating haggis." She pulls a stapler from her bag. "How about you and Lucas go hang these on the lampposts, and on the bulletin board at the community center, and I'll make you something to eat. Unless you have to get to work."

"I have the late shift. Five to midnight."

"That means you can keep Fluffy company all day."

"Yay," I say with zero enthusiasm and Rachel chuckles, goes up on her toes and presses her lips to my cheek.

"You're not so tough, Tavish," she whispers and I grumble some more. "Go hang the posters, Fluffy will help me in the kitchen."

Lucas jumps to his feet and Rachel scoops Fluffy into her arms. He snuggles into her and she rubs him against her face. I stare at the two. Great, now I'm jealous of the damn bunny. Rachel smiles and says, "Maybe we should have called him Snuggles."

I grumble some more as Lucas takes my hand and tugs. "Come on, Tavish."

"Can I at least put on a shirt? Or were you so enthralled with Fluffy..." Shite, do I really have to call him that? "You didn't even notice I wasn't wearing one."

"I noticed," Rachel whispers into my ear from beyond and presses her breasts against my back. I growl, and Lucas lets go of my hand.

"Hurry up, Tavish, it's beach day at camp and I don't want to be late."

My God, what has my life become? I turn and give Rachel a warning glare as she grins at me and I adjust my damn tadger in my pants as I hurry upstairs and tug on a shirt. Rachel is in the kitchen, and pots are clanging as Lucas waits, somewhat impatiently, at the door. This was his idea so he can't blame me for not being ready or even fully awake, and dammit, couldn't he have at least let me have a coffee first. I ruffle the kid's hair, unable to be mad at him. His eagerness is kind of cute and reminds me of his mother.

"I'm ready, I'm ready," I say and pick up the stapler Rachel left on the entranceway table.

"If no one comes for Fluffy, are you going to keep him?"

"I don't know." I stop myself from asking if he wants the bunny. Rachel might kill me for putting that idea into his head. I chuckle to myself as I picture her scolding me. Hell, maybe I might like it.

"What's funny?"

"Nothing." We step up to a lamppost. "How about this one?" Lucas takes a sheet of paper and holds it up for me to staple. "Good?" I ask standing back to look at it.

"Good." We start walking, and I note he's wearing shorts and a T-shirt. "Beach day, huh?"

"I love beach day."

"Those boys...on the playground. They bother you anymore?"

"I haven't seen them." He shrugs. "They're not in my camp. I don't think they're going to bother me. The older kids can be such dickheads."

I bite back a laugh, and yeah, he's right. "Don't let your mother hear you say that." I ruffle his hair. "You know, I could teach you some self defense moves, if you're interested in that kind of thing." He nods eagerly. "Not to hurt anyone, but to stop anyone from hurting you. I don't want you to ever purposely hurt anyone. Promise me you won't do that."

"I promise." He holds his hands out and mimics his mother that first day on the playground. "This move isn't going to cut it, huh?" A grin tugs at the corner of his mouth and I can't help but laugh. The kid is funny, and those older boys—dickheads—don't know what they're missing.

We hang a few more signs on the lampposts and mailboxes and cross the street to reach the community center. I pin one to the cork board and turn to Lucas. "What do you think?

Enough for today?" He nods. "Should we head back and see what your mom made us?"

"I already had cereal." He rubs his stomach. "I could eat again if it's something good." He shades the sun from his eyes as he glances up at me. "Did you have anything good in your fridge?"

"I had some eggs, and bacon."

"That sounds good. Mom packed me the last sticky bun for my afternoon snack."

"Nice."

He crinkles his nose. "I'm sorry I'm eating the last one. I could split it with you if you want. I know you really love Mom's buns."

The kid doesn't know the half of it.

"That's nice of you, Lucas. I'm good, though. Maybe we can convince your Mom to make another batch."

"We'll tell her Fluffy asked for some."

I laugh. "Yeah, good plan." We walk down the sidewalk, as the neighborhood comes alive. People leaving for work, or out tending to their lawns, or walking their animals. Shite. If I end up keeping Fluffy, does that mean I'll have to join the pet walking club? Removing my toenails with pliers sounds like a hell of a lot more fun. Hopefully by the time I get home, someone will recognize him from the signs and call.

Delicious smells come from the kitchen when we enter, and Lucas darts to the kitchen. "Just in time," Rachel calls out.

"Be right down." I run upstairs to check my phone. No calls. Bollocks. I head back to the kitchen. "Coffee," I mumble and zombie walk, which makes Lucas laugh. I glance at the food in the pan. "You didn't have to go through all the trouble."

"No trouble at all, now sit," Rachel says with a smile and it's all I can do not to kiss her. I do however, let my gaze rake over her professional pencil skirt and the way it hugs her ass. Lucas coos over Fluffy as Rachel plates the bacon and eggs. She hooks Lucas up with a couple pieces of bacon, and he half sits in the chair, wanting to be close to Fluffy as he eats.

Rachel sets a cup of coffee in front of me. "Thank you."

I take a much-needed sip and nearly shoot it out my nose as Lucas sits back in his chair and says, "I'll have a cup of coffee too, Mom."

She rolls her eyes and sits down across from me, helping herself to a piece of bacon from my plate. I kind of like sharing with her. I eat as she turns to Lucas and starts telling him about the plastic bag she packed for his wet clothes. I glance back and forth between the two of them. Their conversation is mundane, boring, everyday things and yet, I somehow love every second of it. It's strange really, sitting down to breakfast like this. Life in foster care was chaotic and loud. The kids all fighting for attention and food. When I left that behind, all I wanted was a quiet morning. Time to myself to prepare for the day. It's how I prefer things. Or at least it's how I thought I'd preferred things. Until now. This is actually kind of nice, and while I've always been alone, I never thought of myself as lonely.

Rachel checks her watch, pulling my thoughts back. "I need to get to the office."

Lucas is back on the floor with Fluffy. "I can drop him off at camp. It's on my way."

She takes a sip of her coffee. "I thought you didn't work until tonight and the camp is not on your way."

"I have to go to the pet store. Fluffy needs…things." I have no idea what things Fluffy needs. I'm sure they'll tell me at the pet store.

"Aww, you like him," Rachel teases.

I'm about to protest until I catch the way Lucas is watching me. "Of course, I like him. He's a big cuddly ball of fluff. What's not to like?" Lucas' smile wraps around my heart like a tight belt.

"Lucas, are you okay with Tavish driving you?" She drains her coffee and puts her cup in the dishwasher. I scratch my arm and Lucas stares at my ink.

"Maybe we can stop and get tattoos on the way," he suggests, so casually I can't tell if he's kidding or not.

"Ohmigod," Rachel says, and rolls her eyes. "No tattoos. You're too young."

He shrugs it off. "Can Fluffy come?"

I grin at Lucas. I think the kid is smart, and probably gifted. "You bet, mate."

"Be good," Rachel says and bends to give Lucas a kiss. I walk her to the door, wanting my own kiss. I glance over my shoulder, and with Lucas distracted in the kitchen, I tug her to me and plant a kiss on her mouth, wanting her to be thinking about me today. It's only fair, since I'll be counting down the minutes until I get her naked again. I think it's more than that, though. I like being with her, talking to her about nothing and everything.

Shite.

I break the kiss and run my hands up and down her arm as I stay close. "See you tonight?"

"You're working until midnight, aren't you?"

I playfully wag my brows. "I have a key."

Her grin is slow and sexy and my damn cock responds. "I'll leave the porch light on."

"No need. I can find my way around in the dark."

"Yeah, you can," she teases.

I see her off and get Lucas buckled into my truck, Fluffy in a box on his lap. Thirty minutes later, after getting Lucas to camp, I'm standing in the pet store, Fluffy in my arms, and no idea what I should even be looking for. Is that a toothbrush for dogs? I walk the aisles, baffled at the puzzles, the lounge chairs and wait...is that a bell for a dog to let you know when it needs to go potty?

Christ, back when I was a kid, a dog slept on the floor and got a bone once in a while. Will I have to pamper Fluffy like this? I am so not cut out for being a pet owner. Wait, is that huge, gated house contraption for bunnies? I check my phone, hoping the owner has come forward before I have to buy a bunny condo, which costs about as much as a real one.

"Oh, isn't he the cutest." I turn and spot a woman walking my way. "What's his name?"

"Fluffy."

"How long have you had him?"

"Found him in my yard. Do you work here? I really need some help." She has a purse over her shoulder, so I'm guessing she doesn't.

"Unfortunately, no, but if you need help at home, you can always give me a call." She pulls a piece of paper from her purse and writes her name on it.

"I used to have a bunny growing up," another woman says, hurrying up to me. "I can help you out." She flashes her eyelashes my way, and tosses her hair over her shoulder.

Is this a pet store or a pickup joint?

A few more women approach and give me their numbers. Who knew bunnies were chick magnets? Not that I ever plan on calling any of these women. Nope, the only woman on my mind, and the only woman I want in my bed is Rachel.

Shite...I wasn't supposed to fall for her.

17

RACHEL

It's Friday night, and Lucas has been a little rambunctious since I picked him up at camp. I can't seem to calm him down. He's been running around the house and knocking things over, and refusing to do anything I ask. I talked to my mother and she agrees with me, that he's likely anxious about seeing his father. Jason hasn't come around since Christmas. That's a long time in a child's life. And the fact is, Jason's season ended in April, and he couldn't come to see his son for three months?

I push that anger down. Lucas is pretty good at feeding off my emotions, and that could be another reason he's a little wild today. I take a few deep breaths and follow him upstairs. In his room, I grab his duffle bag and toss it on his bed.

"Are there any toys or books you want to bring?"

He grabs his favorite book off the shelf and drops it in the bag. "I'm going to miss Fluffy."

"Tavish is going to bring him by before you go, and he promised a short ride on his motorcycle."

"I wish Tavish was my father," he says, and the world fades a little around me. I sit on the bed, and take his hand in mine.

"I'm sorry your dad isn't here a lot, Lucas. He's busy with hockey, and—"

"I hate hockey."

"That's okay, you don't have to like it. You like soccer and Tavish is going to be your new coach. Isn't that great?"

He nods. "I like Tavish."

I like Tavish too.

"I bet your dad has fun things planned for you this weekend and you get to see Grandma and Grandpa Anderson, and of course, Buster."

He smiles. "I love Buster. He's going to love the bone we got him." He tugs open his dresser drawer and grabs a bunch of clothes, including his favorite skirt and my chest tightens. I stare at the skirt, not knowing what to say. If Jason sees it, he'll have lots to say and none of it will be good. I don't want this weekend to be bad for Lucas. Should I just secretly take it out?

A bike revs outside, and Lucas runs to his window. "Tavish is here." He waves and heads to the door.

I put my hands on my hips. "What about your packing?"

"Can I do it when I get back?"

"I can finish it, if you like?"

"Thanks, Mom." He goes down the stairs so fast, I'm sure he's going to crash land. The front door swings open and their voices rise up from outside. I step up to the window and wave to Tavish, who's climbing from his bike and pulling Fluffy from the chest carrier he bought at the pet store, along with a million other things, including an elaborate bunny condo.

At this point if someone claims Fluffy, I'm afraid it will devastate Tavish, as much as he grumbles about caring for the thing. Turning my attention to the suitcase, I pick up the skirt and mentally struggle with what to do. In the end, I put it back in. I don't want to give Lucas mixed messages, yet I don't want his father to give him grief. I can only hope no occasions arise where Lucas wants to wear it.

I take his bag to the bathroom, and toss in his toothbrush and toothpaste. Once done, I go to the front door. Lucas is cooing as he pets Fluffy. Tavish isn't the only one who's going to miss the bunny if his owners come for him. My heart jumps a little as Tavish lifts his gaze and meets mine. You'd think by now I wouldn't still be acting like a love-struck schoolgirl every time he glances my way.

I check my watch. "You guys better get that ride in. Your dad will be here in an hour Lucas."

"We'll just go up and down a few streets." Tavish picks up Fluffy, and drops a kiss onto his forehead, like it's the most natural thing in the world to do, before handing him over to me. My heart turns to goo in my chest. Could this man be any sweeter? "Don't worry," he adds, "I'll be gone before his father gets here."

"You don't—" He arches a brow and I stop talking. "Thanks." I'm allowed to have men in my life, and men in Lucas' life. I've been divorced for just over a year now. I just don't want an interrogation from Jason or his parents. Even though it's not their business, that won't stop them from a cross-examination. I have my work 'bonding' retreat this weekend, and I can't take on any more stress than that. I suspect Lucas will bring Tavish up at some point with his father, and I'll deal with that after the weekend.

Lucas puts his helmet on, and Tavish double checks the clasp. I grab Lucas' boots and jacket. Even though it's hot, safety first. Once he's bundled, I wave them off and head inside with Fluffy. I grab a few of Lucas' favorite granola bars and snacks and add them to his bag, when I hear heavy footsteps coming up the front stoop.

"Back so soon." I zip the bag and head to the door. "Did you forget…" I stop dead in my tracks as I come eye to eye with Jason. My gaze flies to the clock on the wall. "You're early," I blurt out, speaking to him through the screen door.

"I was out and figured it was easier to pick him up now then come back."

"Oh…" I lift the bag. "I just finished packing."

Jason puts his hands in his pocket, and I stand here like an idiot staring at him. He looks good. Healthy and fit. His hair is a bit longer than it was at Christmas. There was a time I loved everything about this man, or at least the man he was when we met. Fame changed him, and it changed me too. I'm definitely not the doe-eyed ingenue I used to be.

"Can I come in?" he finally asks.

I shake my head to pull myself together. "Yes, of course." He pulls the door open and I step back a bit, setting Lucas' bag on the floor.

"Where's Lucas?"

"Oh, actually he just went out for a bike ride with a friend."

He runs an agitated hand through his hair. "Why would you let him do that when you knew I was coming?"

"You weren't supposed to be here for another hour."

He sneezes and jumps back as Fluffy comes hopping into the room. "What the hell is that?"

I pick up Fluffy. "This is my friend's pet." Jason sneezes again. "I think you might be allergic."

"Can you put it outside or something?"

"Sorry, no. I can't." Stomach tight, I look over Jason's shoulders and onto the street. "Lucas will be back any second now. Did you want to sit and wait?"

"I'll wait outside." He doesn't budge. Instead, he lets his gaze move down the length of me, and I shift uncomfortably under his inspection. "You look...different."

"Different?"

"Yeah, different. You changed, somehow."

Yeah, I have and it's probably because I've moved on from this man and found someone who puts my needs first. I wasn't in a great place mentally last Christmas when he came to see Lucas. I was still trying to deal with the loss of my marriage, selling our house in Boston, and finding a new place here in Gloucester. It was stress overload to say the least. I'm stronger and in a much better place now, which is better for my son as well.

Could that be what he sees?

He frowns, like he doesn't like this new version of me. He's such a narcissist, perhaps he doesn't like that I'm not still pining over him, or the loss of our marriage.

"Are you still working?" he asks.

"Yes." I don't want to get into this with him. It never ends well. "I landed a big client the other day," is all I say and redirect the conversation. "What are your plans with Lucas this weekend?"

"Hang out, swim, barbecue." He pauses for a brief moment and my heart jumps into my throat as Tavish's bike revs on the street. "You can come by if you want. Unless you have plans." His words are followed up with an eye roll, like me having plans would be ludicrous.

Up until Tavish, it might have been ludicrous, but over the last year I've grown, changed, become my own person with a new life. Honestly, I don't think Jason expected any of that. In fact, I think he thought with a snap of his fingers he could have me back and that I might be excited, grateful even, for the invitation.

"I actually do have plans."

His demeanor changes, something in his eyes hardening. "Yeah, what?"

I am not his possession anymore, and my whereabouts are not his business. I don't want to start a fight of any sort here —by nature I'm a peacekeeper—so I tell him, "Work retreat."

His body relaxes. "Oh yeah, I remember those." He mimics a golf swing. "Jakob still kicking ass?"

"He is."

"One of these days someone will knock that asshole off his pedestal."

I think that day might be coming. I don't say that, though.

"Did you—" Boots on the stoop draw Jason's attention and he turns, his body stiffening as Tavish stands on the other side of the door. "Yeah?" Jason asks.

I step past him and push the door open. "Sorry, I didn't realize you had company," Tavish says. "Can I grab Fluffy?"

I give Fluffy a kiss and hold him out.

Jason snorts. "He's the guy who owns the bunny?"

"Yes," is all Tavish says as I hand Fluffy over.

Jason moves in close behind me, and an unpleasant shiver travels down my spine. That's when I catch the murderous look in Tavish's eyes. Jason spots Lucas on the sidewalk, buckling his helmet to the bike.

"What the fuck." He steps back and I turn to him. "That's the bike Lucas was on?"

"Yeah, uh…" I hold the door open as Tavish tucks Fluffy into his chest carrier. "Jason, this is my friend Tavish. He lives down the street. Tavish, this is Lucas' father, Jason." I stand there, as the two men stare and size each other up. Jason stands a bit taller, and I relax a bit as Tavish makes the first move and does the polite thing by holding his hand out for a shake.

"Jason," he says, his voice low and deep.

"Tavish," Jason says in response. "You two are friends?"

I'm about to open my mouth, stopping when Tavish speaks first. "I moved in last month, and Rachel's been showing me around, and in return I've been helping her fix some things in her house."

Suspicion brews in Jason's eyes, and my entire body tenses. "You take Lucas for rides on your bike?"

"Yeah, he likes it."

"How safe is that?"

Tavish folds his barrel arms across his barrel chest. "Safe."

Lucas comes running up the steps. "Dad," he says. "Did you see me on the bike?" He holds his hands out like he's revving the grips. "I want to get a bike when I get bigger."

Jason turns to me. "We'll talk more about this when I drop him off on Sunday." He snatches Lucas' bag from the floor and pushes past me. Tavish, however, doesn't budge, forcing Jason to move around him.

I bend and hold my arms out. "Give me a kiss, Lucas." Lucas throws himself into my arms. "I put Buster's bone in the bag. You have fun, okay? And I'll see you Sunday."

"Bye, Mom." He breaks the hug and before he joins his father in the driveway, he throws his arms around Tavish's waist. "Bye, Tavish."

Tavish ruffles his hair. "Have fun, kiddo."

I ignore the way Jason glares at me as I step onto the steps and stand there waving to Lucas as they pull away. I exhale loudly and let my shoulders drop. "That went well."

"Sorry, Rachel. I didn't realize that was his car on the street."

"It's okay. My life is no longer his business."

"Yeah, but Lucas' is."

"If he wants more of a say, then he should spend more time with his son."

"Agreed."

I don't want to talk about Jason, or the inquisition I'm going to receive Sunday. I pet Fluffy. "Brodie doesn't mind watching him for the weekend?"

"Nope, I'm taking him to him now." He leans in and kisses me. "Afterward, you and I are starting our weekend." The retreat starts tomorrow, but I booked a room early, wanting a quiet night in with Tavish.

"Give me an hour. I have a few things to do before we head out." He stomps down the steps, gets on his bike and waves as he heads out. I stand there, pushing my exchange with Jason to the back of my brain, not wanting anything to ruin this weekend. I normally hate these retreats. I don't fit in with the men, and their stay-at-home wives look down their noses at me. It's a lose-lose situation, really. This year, with my pretend boyfriend by my side, it doesn't feel quite as awkward or intimidating. Jason was right about one thing. I am a changed woman.

I walk to the yard and gather up the soccer ball that Lucas had been kicking around. A dog barks and I glance up to see the pet walking club. I wave and Jack Robertson slows and picks up his poodle. He exchanges a look with the others, and lifts his head as he comes toward me.

Oh God, what is going on?

"Afternoon, Rachel."

"Afternoon, Jack."

His cloudy eyes narrow. "Saw you out with that guy." He shakes his thumb over his shoulder.

"Tavish, you mean."

"Yeah, that guy. You need to be careful, missy."

"Why is that now?"

"Heard he murdered a guy a few years back." He glances over his shoulder like he's worried someone is listening. He lowers his voice and adds, "It happened in Scotland, and he might be here on the lam."

On the lam?

I bite back a grin. "Did you now?"

Mr. Petersen removes the leash from around his pot belly pig's leg and asks, "Where did you hear that?"

"I hear things," Jack says and runs his hand down his yappy toy poodle's back as it snarls at me.

"Are you going to turn him in?" I ask.

Jack holds one hand out and waves the suggestion off. "Not getting myself involved in any of that."

"Tell her about the women," Ruthie says. I glance at Ruthie as she smooths a strand of white hair from her face.

"Women?" I ask.

"Has a string of wives, Rachel. Eight, I believe." She waves her finger. "You best not be getting involved." She makes a tsking sound.

"He does make nice rocking chairs," Belinda says, and I smile at her. I've always liked her. Maybe she doesn't believe everything she hears, either.

Ruthie points to Mrs. Potter's place. "He's been coming and going all hours from Gladys' house. I think he's in there doing scandalous things with that granddaughter of hers."

My stomach clenches as old painful memories grip me. I quickly remind myself Tavish is not Jason, and I'm not committed to Tavish. There were no vows of fidelity exchanged and if he is with Sophie, which I don't believe he is, he's not broken any promises. I hired the guy to be a stand-in dad for God's sake, and a fake boyfriend.

"I believe he's fixing some pipes," I counter.

"Oh, is that what they're calling non-marital fornication these days," Ruthie says with a tipped chin.

Non-marital fornication?

Did I somehow wake up in the eighteenth century?

Jack fixes his ballcap. "Thought it was called Netflix and chill."

I bite the inside of my lip to keep myself from laughing. The man truly looks perplexed by today's slang. Honestly, I don't want to be rude, even if they're all spreading ridiculous rumors, so I don't laugh or correct them.

Maxie, who's been quiet up until now, waves a dismissive hand toward a baffled Jack. "That's last year's news, Jack." Her cute dog, Peanut—a Chinese crested—barks, like he's in full agreement with Maxie. Come to think of it, the two look a bit alike. I think they have the same hair style.

"Your flower beds are looking a bit neglected," Linda kindly points out as her cat Sylvester circles her legs.

I look at the weed bed. "Yes, thanks for pointing that out. I should let you all be on your way." I glance at Mr. Petersen's snorting pot belly pig. "Stanley is looking rather anxious to get on with his walk." I turn and start down my driveway.

"You be careful, missy," Jack warns. "That guy has trouble written all over him."

He has a lot of things written all over his body and while trouble isn't one of the words, it should be, considering how much I'm growing to like him.

18

TAVISH

"Things are going good with Rachel and Lucas?" Brodie asks as I hand a squirming Fluffy over to him and run my hand down his back to soothe him. He's been through a lot this week, and while I hate to leave him after he's getting used to me and my place, I can't take him to Rachel's event.

"Yeah." I head outside and pull Fluffy's condo from the back of my truck.

"What the hell is that?" Brodie asks moving to the side so I can get into his living room.

"It's his condo." It takes me a minute to get it all set up and I stand back to check my work.

Brodie snorts. "That's bigger than some of the homes we stayed in when we were kids."

"You're not wrong." I pull instructions from my pocket. "This is his feeding schedule, and instructions and if you have any problems just text me." I eye my best friend. "Are you sure you've got this?"

"Fluffy and I are going to have a great time. Aren't we, mate?"

"You need to talk to him and play with him."

"We'll go to the park, and I'll take him to my favorite restaurant and get him carrot cake for dessert." He holds Fluffy up to his face. "How does that sound?" Fluffy wiggles his nose.

I point to the paper. "Don't feed him anything that's not on the list. He has a sensitive stomach."

"How long are you keeping him, anyway?"

"I'll give it another week for someone to claim him. Then it's off to the shelter. I can't take care of him forever."

I can, and I will.

"Right," Brodie says, seeing right through me. "So, you and Rachel are headed to a work bonding retreat, huh? You're really taking this stand-in role seriously."

"You know I don't do anything half-assed."

"That's why you were the best MMA fighter in Scotland."

I grunt my response and take Fluffy. "You be good for Brodie." I turn my back to my friend, give Fluffy a kiss on the head and hand him back. I check the time and walk to the door.

Brodie follows me and there's a seriousness about him when he says, "Rachel seems happier than I've ever seen her, Tavish."

I grunt. I'm not interested in talking about all the ways I've been putting a smile on her face, and vice versa. "I'm helping her out. Lightening her load. It's not easy being a single mom."

"That's why she signed up for Dad for Hire."

I nod. Brodie is a good guy with a big heart—even though he doesn't put said heart out there—he's always helping out where he can. He deserves to find someone nice...someone like Rachel. He can't have her, though. She's mine.

Shite. I've got it bad.

"I'll be back Sunday."

"Have fun. Fluffy is in good hands." I jump into my truck and he takes one of Fluffy's paws and waves it at me. I make my way toward Rachel's just as Sophie comes running out of her house, her phone in her hand as she waves at me to pull into her driveway. Instead, I slow on the street and roll my window down.

"Tavish," she calls out. "I was just about to text you." I'd given her my number for emergencies last time I was in her downstairs. "Can you help out? The washer sprung a leak." While I'm anxious to get to Rachel, I can't leave Sophie or her grandmother with a leaky washer. I pull into her driveway, and she slides her arm around mine when I jump from the truck. "Thank you so much." She looks me over, her gaze on my buttoned-down shirt. "You look nice."

"Thanks."

"Are you going somewhere?"

"Yes." She blinks up at me, waiting for more, and I nod toward her house. "Let's check it out."

She keeps her arm in mine. "Are you going on a date?"

"Helping a friend out." The front door creaks as we enter, and I spot Ben in the living room on his iPad. "Hey, Ben."

He smiles up at me. "Hi, Tavish. Lucas said you're going to be our new soccer coach."

"Aye, I am, mate."

"Down here," Sophie says, leading me downstairs to the laundry room, even though I already know where it is. "The floor is wet so be careful." She flicks the light on and tugs her T-shirt away from her body. It draws my attention as it makes a sucking sound. She chuckles. "I'm all wet, too. Water was spraying everywhere." As she tugs on her shirt, it exposes her lacy bra and ample cleavage. Yeah, she'd win a wet T-shirt contest and another time I might have been interested.

I check the pipes behind the washer, run my hand along them until I spot the problem. "Looks like the hose clamp came loose."

"How would that have happened?"

"It's an old machine and it probably shakes a lot. It just needs to be tightened. Can you grab me a wrench?" The toolbox is still down here from the last time I did some pipe work. She hands over a wrench and I'm careful not to get my shirt dirty as I tighten the clasp. "This should fix it."

I drop the wrench back in the toolbox. "Thank God you were here, Tavish. What can I do to thank you?"

"No worries. It's all good." I start toward the stairs, anxious to get to Rachel.

"The festival is coming up, let me buy you a beer. It's the least I could do for all the help you've been giving us."

"Yeah, sure." I don't need her to repay me, but maybe it's important to her, and what can it hurt. "Actually, I have another idea," I say. Her eyes light up, and she gives me a seductive smile.

She tugs on her T-shirt again. "Anything. Just name it."

My phone pings, and it's Rachel letting me know she's ready. "I have to run, but I'll text you later. See you on the field next weekend, Ben." Ben waves to me and I head outside. Sophie follows, and I don't miss the way the neighbor across the street is watching us. I think her name is Belinda and from what I know, Rachel likes her, so she's probably not one of the gossiping types.

"Thanks again, Tavish. I look forward to your text."

I jump in my truck and head two houses over to Rachel's, pulling into her driveway. She comes outside, looking happy and relaxed in a pretty blue dress with daisies on it. She hikes the overnight bag over her shoulder, and I jump from the truck, quickly close the distance and take it from her. It's all I can do to keep myself from kissing her. Mr. Peterson is walking home with his pig and I don't need to give him something to talk about.

"You look gorgeous," I tell her as I shoulder the bag.

"You clean up pretty nice yourself." Her lips are curled in delight as she lets her gaze move over me. "Wait, are you wet?" She touches the side of my shirt.

"Shite. I was just helping Sophie with her washing machine. The hose let go. I have another shirt. I can change."

"I'm sure this will dry by the time we get to the resort." I toss her bag into the back seat of the truck, and she slides in. "She's having a lot of trouble over there, is she?"

"Yeah, she came running out when she saw me. She was completely soaked." I circle the vehicle, climb in and put my hand on her thigh. That's when I notice the hint of worry in her eyes. "Everything okay?"

She waves her hand and laughs it off. "Oh, the pet walking club are telling stories." She grins at me. "I didn't know you had eight wives, Tavish."

I back out of the driveway. "Aye, eight wives." I rub my brow. "Or is it nine? I can never keep track." I shake my head as I head toward the highway. "Where do they come up with these things?"

"Don't know, but they've been noticing you coming and going from Mrs. Potter's quite a bit. And…" I eye her. "Apparently, you murdered a man back in Scotland. You're here on the lam." My gaze jerks to hers and she holds her hands up and laughs. "Jack's words, not mine."

I frown at that as old demons resurface and haunt me. I damn near did kill a guy. A song comes on the radio Rachel likes and as she sings along, it helps relax me. She dreads this retreat, and it's good to see her happy like this.

We drive along the water and head toward Oceans Stone Golf Resort. I've never been there, but according to Rachel it's a pretty nice place. "You packed your bathing suit, right?" Rachel asks, as she turns my way.

"Nope, thought I'd swim in my birthday suit."

She laughs. "I'm sorry. I'm so used to double checking Lucas' bag."

"I'm not Lucas, and you don't have to take care of me," I tell her. "In fact." I give her thigh a squeeze. "I plan on taking care of you all weekend."

"Oh, do tell," she says and sinks back in the seat, her face relaxing.

"Nae, I'd rather show you, lassie."

She chuckles and goes quiet, and I keep my hand on her leg, as an easy silence falls over us. After a while she asks, "Do you miss Scotland?"

"Sometimes, I guess. Beautiful scenery."

"It's a place I've always wanted to visit."

"Let me guess. You're an Outlander fan. Hoping to run into Jamie."

That brings on a laugh. "Mate," she jokes. "Jamie is a fine Scotsman..." She gives me a playful wink and blatantly looks my body over. My cock jumps at her seductive gaze. "But mine is even better."

I squeeze her leg. "Maybe I should have packed a kilt."

"Nae, you don't need it."

"You've really wanted to visit Scotland?"

"I'd love to see the castles and mountains, and the Highlands. It looks so gorgeous."

"Can I tell you a secret?"

"Ooh, yes please."

"I actually still have a place in Scotland."

"Are you serious?"

I nod. "Aye, I thought about selling it when I came here, but it was the first home I bought with my first big paycheck, and I don't know. I couldn't bring myself to sell it."

"It represented something to you. That you made it in life...despite..."

She lets her words fall off, and I take in her soft, sympathetic smile. "Yeah, despite," I say.

"Is it a castle?" she asks jokingly.

"Not everyone in Scotland lives in a castle."

She stares at me, and then suddenly her eyes widen. "Ohmigod, it's a castle, isn't it?"

"Aye, it's a castle."

"Ohmigod, Tavish." She whacks my chest. "I can't believe you own a castle. I can't believe I know someone who owns a castle. Why would you ever leave Scotland and come to Massachusetts if you lived in a castle?"

"It was just a castle, Rach. Big, drafty...I needed a change, needed to get away from the limelight and Brodie was here. Someday though, if you really wanted to visit, maybe we could. I don't know."

Yeah, I really don't know—what the hell I'm doing or saying anymore.

"Yeah, sure sounds fun." Her voice is laced with skepticism. It's not like she can up and leave and go on elaborate vacations. She's a working mom, just trying to do her best and Scotland is likely a bucket list dream for her. For me, Scotland doesn't hold the best memories. Maybe if she came with me, we could make new ones and they'd help push back the bad. Could that be why I suggested it? I'm not sure. I only know I like being with her.

"I love how you and Brodie remained such great friends over the years. He's a really good guy. He's helped me out a lot in the last year." She gives a little laugh. "I'm probably the reason he started Dad for Hire. Is he the only friend you have here?"

"I had lots of people I'd call acquaintances over the years. They weren't friends. I was an MMA champion and they always wanted something from me, you know? Women, men, everyone wanted a piece of me, and I grew tired of it all. Brodie is the only guy I ever trusted, or ever called friend. I love him like a brother and would do anything for him."

Even nearly kill a guy.

"I'm so sorry, Tavish." Her hand closes over mine and she glances down. "Trust is hard, I know. After Jason...the cheating...it's just hard."

"And me with eight wives," I respond with a snort, not wanting to make light of her suffering, but this is a weekend away for her, and I want to put a smile back on her face.

"Right," she agrees and tosses her hands in the air. "How do you keep them straight? For me, one husband was more than enough. I can't imagine taking on any more than that." Her head goes back and forth, reminding me of the bobble head one of my foster parents had on their dashboard. "Hell to the no."

I laugh with her, and we fall into an easy conversation about Scotland, and she talks about the places she'd like to see, and dammit, I've been to just about every one of them and would really like to be the guy to take her there.

"Is it true there are more sheep than people?"

"As far as I know. When I lived at Kilnrock castle, a neighbor's sheep used to wander onto the property all the time."

"Your castle has a name." I nod and she looks totally enthralled. "And sheep. Don't tell Lucas that. Next thing he'll either want to move there, or beg me for a pet sheep."

"A sheep would definitely add to the diversity of the pet walking club, and the neighborhood does have chickens and a rooster. A sheep would make a nice addition."

"Yeah, to living on a funny farm."

I grin at her, loving how easy she is to be with. Turning my attention back to the road ahead, I take a turn and we travel down a long road pathway with a canopy of weeping willow trees blocking the sun, and finally pull up to the castle-like resort. I take in the spectacular towering building over-looking a manicured golf course, the ocean in the near distance. Rachel rolls her window down and breathes in the fragrant scent of brine and foliage.

"It's something, isn't it? Does your castle look like that?" she asks.

I give her a sheepish grin. "No, mine's bigger."

Her eyes pop wide open. "Are you serious?"

I nod. "What can I say? The MMA paid well."

She stares at me like I might have taken one too many hits to the head and it's true, I have. "You're secretly Prince Charming, aren't you?" Her gaze drops to my biceps. "If Prince Charming was all tatted up and served food and drink in a kilt at Kilting Around, of course." She wags her brow seductively as she admires my body, and I like when she does that. Her brows suddenly flatline. "Wait, if you don't need to work, why do you work, and why at Kilting Around?"

"I need to do something with my time and my buddy needed a guy who could pull off a kilt."

"That you can," she agrees with a laugh. "That's nice of you," she continues, her voice a bit quieter, a little more reflective.

"What about you, Rachel? You obviously like pharmaceutical sales. The people you work with, not so much. Have you thought about applying elsewhere, or even doing something else?"

"Honestly, Tavish. Starting over again is hard and scary, and I have a son to think about. I'm not complaining here, I love my son. Doing it alone is hard."

"Starting over is hard. I don't have a kid to think about. I moved across the pond, though." She starts gathering up her things. "If you could do anything, if money and time and childcare were no issue, what would you do?"

She goes quiet, very quiet, and I can almost hear the internal struggle in her brain as I pull up in front of the resort. The automatic doors open and the valet walks out. Rachel opens her mouth, her gaze locked on mine like she's about to tell me a deep dark secret, until the valet comes to my side of the car, and knocks on the window.

Her demeanor changes, and she offers me a sexy, playful smile. "If I could do anything, it would be going straight to our room so you can show me what you meant when you said you wanted to take care of me."

19

RACHEL

"Everything good?" Tavish asks as he comes from the bathroom, completely naked as he towel dries his hair, his tattoos dancing over his hard muscles with the movement. Simply put, the man is built like a Scottish warrior.

"How am I supposed to think straight when you're walking around like that?"

"Who needs to think straight, Rach? We're at a gorgeous resort, on a much-needed vacation, and we should enjoy it."

"I need to think straight. I'm about to spend the day with my colleagues, and they don't respect me as it is."

He drops down onto the bed beside me, and his warm fingers brush my hair from my face. His touch sends shivers through me, and while I'd like to crawl back in bed with him—you'd think I'd be sated after he treated me like a princess last night, pleasuring every inch of my body—yet here I am, warming all over again. When it comes to Tavish, I can't seem to get enough.

He leans in and kisses me softly, and the tenderness in his touch wraps around my vulnerable heart. "You're not alone in this today. I'm a former MMA fighter and that's why I'm here, to fight for you. To show them you have someone in your corner and if they so much as try to push you out of their circle, they'll have me to deal with."

I exhale softly. The man does make me feel safe and cherished, and he did save my ass when he collected Lucas the day he was sick. Last week, when I was frustrated with the toxicity at work, I thought back to the appalled look on Jakob's face when Tavish shut him down. It still brings me joy. Does putting an underhanded snake in his place like that make me a bad person? Probably. Not that I was the one to personally admonish Jakob. Nope, Tavish did the talking. I was the one who not only allowed it, but encouraged it.

Guilt feathers through me, my mind going back to what Tavish said about everyone wanting something from him. Am I any different? He came here looking for peace and quiet. Was it my situation, and Brodie's pressure that made him fold? Also, if Brodie is the only guy he ever trusted, why did Brodie pressure him into Dad for Hire?

"It's not your fight—"

"Hey," he murmurs quietly and pulls me to him. "I fight for those I care about, Rachel. I think that's the one thing you might know about me." I swallow. Hard. I might know a lot more about him than he realizes, and everything I do know, I like. His arms tighten around my body and I sag against him. Hold it, is he saying he cares about me? Brodie is his only friend, the only one he loves...

He said he cared about you, Rachel. He didn't say he loved you.

"Thank you," is all I manage to push out from a tight throat as I try to rein in my stupid emotions.

His arms loosen and he inches back, going back to towel drying his hair, his face covered by the cotton. Why is there suddenly an emotional distance between us, as well as a physical one? "Any friend of Brodie's is a friend of mine," he informs me, his voice a bit tight.

"Right," I say, and square my shoulders. I stand and drop my phone, turning my body so he can't see the silly emotions in my eyes. I like Tavish, probably too much. He likes me too, he just said so. He also followed that up with a reminder that we're friends by association. He loves Brodie and would do anything for him, and I'm Brodie's cause. "I'd better hurry. Everyone will be meeting for breakfast and golf soon."

I stand and head to the bathroom. I was about to shower earlier, until Jason texted an update. I'm sort of surprised he did. He likes to keep me in the dark when he has Lucas. I think something—or everything—about Tavish spending time with our son threw him off.

"Lucas was good?"

I glance at Tavish over my shoulder, and find he's still sitting on the bed. The concern in his eyes touches me deeply. "He's great. He's having fun with the dog, and he watched a movie with his dad and grandparents last night."

"Good." Tavish stands and comes over to me. He tugs me against him. "Are you okay? You're tense."

"I need coffee," I say breezily, and he continues to hold me, his gaze assessing me. I shrug. "I'm a little worried about Lucas. He has fun while he's there, but it's afterward. Jason promises to call, or see him soon, and he never does. I'm the one left with the messy aftermath. When Lucas hurts, I hurt." He lightly brushes his hands up and down my arms, and it helps push back some of the cold inside me.

"I'll be around this time. I can find ways to help and distract him."

My chest expands as emotions flood me. What about when he's not here, though? Lucas is getting attached...so am I.

"And hanging out with the guys from work is never fun," I tell him, needing to focus on something else. I put my arms around him, go up on my toes and kiss him softly. "I'm really glad you're here, Tavish. Thank you."

He looks away quickly and the rustling sound of his morning beard as he scrubs his face tingles through me. "You don't need to thank me. It's all part of the job, lassie."

That stupid lump is back in my throat as he walks to the dresser and slides open a drawer. He pulls out his clothes and sets them on the bed. As I take in his stiff movements, I'm a little confused. What is going on with him? One minute he's all soft and tender, which makes me think there is something real here. The next, he's letting me know this is a job.

Do you want something more, Rachel?

God, I don't know. I never thought I did. Never thought I'd ever walk that road again. I haven't even known Tavish that long. Certainly not long enough to fall for him, right?

I really do need coffee.

I walk into the bathroom and turn on the shower. I step into the gorgeous, custom shower stall with more dials than I know what to do with—they've done some upgrades since I was here last. I tug on a couple knobs, and water falls from the rain shower above my head. Perfect. I let the water fall over my face and down my body, praying it will wash away these unwanted feelings blossoming inside me. I grab the soap, lather a cloth, and scrub my body hard. As I do, I remind myself what this is and what it isn't and especially drive home the fact that I can't ruin this relationship for my son.

I finish up, and have a new attitude by the time I wrap the towel around me and wipe the steam from the mirror, look myself in the eyes and recite that this is simply a hook-up. Neither Tavish nor I want more. End of story, and I won't do anything to allow what's happening between us to ruin what he has with my son.

I brush my damp hair and blow it dry. I'm nearly finished when I spot movement in the mirror. I turn. "How long have you been standing there?"

He grabs his crotch and shifts it. "Long enough. Sometimes a kilt is much easier when I'm around you."

I laugh at that and he holds his hand out. "Coffee."

"No way."

"I ran to the restaurant downstairs."

"Oh my God, Tavish, I love you." *What the hell, Rachel?* "I mean I love coffee, not you. That's such an American thing to say," I rush out quickly. "If we love something and someone gives it to us, we say we love them." I take a sip, and hope it works magic on my rambling mouth. "Ah, so good. Americans. Strange bunch," I add, mimicking something he once said to me. "It's perfect, just the way I take it." I take another sip and he lifts his paper cup in salute and takes a drink.

"I spotted Jakob downstairs."

My stomach knots at the reminder as to why I'm in this gorgeous hotel with a man that continually throws me off kilter. I mean look at him. Who has the right to look that good in a pair of khaki golf shorts and a polo? "Did he see you?

"No, he was busy chatting with a couple other people."

"We should get down there." He moves to the side so I can exit the bathroom, and I hurry to the dresser. I bend to pull out my white skirt and white polo with thick vertical pink stripes and palm trees on it.

Tavish growls and crosses the room. I catch his eye in the mirror. "Do we have to spend every moment of the day with them? I will if we have to, but..."

Warm heat goes through me as he gazes the length of me and that's when I realize I'm bent over in nothing but a towel, presenting him with my backside. "We eat, and golf and we'll have some quiet time to ourselves before a buffet dinner." I bite my lip, trying not to look tense. I really do dread this event and getting ignored and mansplained to all day long is quite exhausting.

"Good, we never did get to the pool last night and it's a gorgeous day."

Staring at him in the mirror, I shoot back, "I believe we didn't get to the pool because you didn't want to leave this room."

He slides his arm around me, a familiar move I've grown to love. With my back to his chest, I revel in the pounding of his heart, and the way his warm breath skitters over my skin as he puts his mouth to my ear and whispers, "I believe we didn't get to the pool because you wanted to get to this room so I could show you all the ways I wanted to take care of you. Is it my fault there were so many ways?"

He slides a hand up my thigh and under my towel. "Tavish," I murmur breathlessly and grab on to the dresser to hang on, knowing he's about to take me on a glorious ride. He growls as he slides a finger inside me, and my legs weaken. He holds me with his arm around my waist, and I grow ridiculously wet as he moves his finger inside me.

My entire body quakes and the world shuts down around me. Pleasure. That's it, that's all I can concentrate on and that's exactly what I'm about to do. He pushes his cock against my back, and I love how hard he is. He grinds, his deep guttural grunts, so animalistic and raw, bring me to new heights. He uses his palm to massage my clit, and I spread my legs wider, and rock against him.

Pleasure takes over and my body lets go, my heat running all over his hand and down my legs. I pant and gasp, and he holds me tight as I slowly come down. "Relaxed now?" he asks, his mouth near my ear.

"Yes," I murmur, my legs still rubbery. "What about you?"

"Lots of time for me later," he whispers.

"I think I'm going to need another shower."

He chuckles, disappears into the bathroom and comes back with a cloth to clean me up. When he finishes, he stands and looks me in the eyes. "Never let them know they're getting to you, lassie."

"Bullies—"

"You mean dickheads," he corrects.

I laugh as I take in his grin. "Yeah, dickheads."

"If they piss you off, keep your head high and think about all the things I'm going to do to you when I get you alone tonight. They're not worth stressing about."

"My own company," I say without thinking, my brain still buzzing from my orgasm.

"What's that?"

A hint of embarrassment grips me. "It's silly, I know. Last night when you asked." I smooth my hair back, and give a half-hearted snort. "What do I know about starting my own pharmaceutical company—"

"Hey, lassie," he interrupts, a warm, quiet strength in his voice that gives me a strange sense of confidence. "What you don't know, you learn, and with what's above your scope, you hire a consultant." He cups my cheeks. "This is what you want to do. What you were too afraid to tell me yesterday?"

"It's a silly—" He angles his head in warning. "Some days at work, I think about starting my own company, and filling it with strong women. Not just women though, men too, ones who don't believe in the boys' club culture." I briefly close my eyes, and happiness floods me as I picture it. "I have many connections and I have a good name in the industry. It's just the thoughts of doing this single-handedly."

Without saying a word, he steps away from me, his brow furrowed as he sits on the bed and reaches for his phone. My stomach tightens. Are you kidding me right now? I finally find the courage not only to vocalize my dream but to say it out loud and I've bored him to the point he's scrolling on his phone.

"Here," he says and extends his arm, showcasing something he just pulled up on Google. I'm too far away to read the words and I'm too afraid to let go of the dresser and fall on my face. My legs are still wobbly from the orgasm.

I tried to keep my voice stable. "What?"

He shakes his phone. "A whole article on how to start your own pharmaceutical company." He shrugs. "It's one of many. It could be a jumping off point, and you wouldn't have to do it single-handedly. I can help. I don't know anything about sales. I can support in other ways though, like helping more with Lucas."

My God, is this guy for real? A loud, almost sobbing cry rushes from my lips and my eyes flood. Trust is so hard for me. The thing is, I do trust Tavish. I wouldn't allow him to bond with my son if I didn't. Old demons and insecurities, though. God, they can creep up on you when you least expect them. I take a deep breath and turn to blink the tears away.

"Hey, lassie." He stands and pulls me to him. "What? Are you still stressed? Do you need a proper shagging? Maybe more coffee?"

"I just...You looked that up?"

"Aye." He thumbs the tears away from my cheeks. "If you're going to do it, I want to make sure you do it right."

"That's really nice, Tavish." I cup his face and kiss him. "It's a dream, though. I appreciate you doing a fast search to show your support. In reality, I don't think it can happen. I have a son, and a house and...responsibilities. Dreaming about my own company is a technique I use to get through the day when the men in the office are being particularly toxic."

"I know, lassie. When I was a wee boy, I dreamt about a lot of things. It's how I got through most days, even though they were big dreams and I never thought I could actually do it.

Brodie always believed in me, always pushed me. Maybe that's all you need. Someone in your corner." He lightly rubs his knuckles over my cheeks.

"Brodie is a good friend."

"Aye. You start small and go from there. I didn't win an MMA championship overnight. It took lots of backyard brawling to get me noticed and from there I trained in mixed martial arts, which helped get me where I needed to go. You're a fighter, like me." He lightly nudges my chin. "You might not think it, but we're not so different." I smile, my heart a lot lighter than it was a minute ago. "Just promise me you'll think about it."

"I'll think about it." Voices sound in the hall, and he bends and gives me a soft kiss.

"Good, now if you don't want to be late, get dressed before I toss you on that bed and give you a proper shagging that will bring more tears to your eyes."

I tap my chin. "Mmm."

"Sounds like a good idea to me, too. The question is, do you want to explain why we're late getting to breakfast?" He holds his hands up. "Hey, I have no troubles telling those dickheads I was shagging the prettiest girl in town. It's you I worry about." He walks to the nightstand, grabs the key card, and puts it in his wallet. He shoves it into his back pocket and I take that moment to admire his tight backside. I can't wait to see him in his soccer gear.

I throw my hands up. "What do I care? They'll be happy I'm not there."

He growls and comes toward me. "Lassie, if you're saying—"

I love when he gets all feral. Laughing, I put my hand on his chest. "But we should go. I don't want to make things easy on any of them."

He nods in agreement. I dress, put my hair back in a ponytail, and dab on a bit of lipstick. I'm not interested in wearing makeup while golfing in the hot sun, and my cheeks are tanned anyway. I finish and Tavish leads me out and to the elevator. Everyone is just getting seated as we enter the dining room, and I note the shock on numerous faces as we enter. I bite back a grin. My pretend boyfriend is a total badass and I like it. A few gasps come from the women, and I walk with a new kind of confidence. Is this what peacocking means? I bite back a chuckle.

As we approach, Tavish puts his arm around my waist and pulls me close and I glance at him, noting the warm way he's looking back. We're pretending here, a united front to show these guys I have support and can break through that glass ceiling, if only they'd give me the chance. The thing is though, nothing in the way Tavish is touching me, or holding me, or even looking at me feels like it's fake.

20

TAVISH

"I'm so glad you could join us, Tavish," Matthew says with a smile as he gestures for us to sit. I take in the twelve people at the table, and the two vacant chairs. I pull one out for Rachel and a little blush creeps into her cheeks as she sits. She glances around and I hate the uncomfortableness about her. She smiles and says hello to the other women.

"Happy to be here, and to be playing a round of golf." I drop into the chair next to Rachel and put my hand on her thigh.

"You golf?" Matthew asks.

"I play a little."

"What do you do?" a woman across the table asks me, drawing my focus. "I mean…" Her gaze rakes over my tattoos. "For a living."

"I work at Kilting Around, downtown Boston. Have you heard of it?"

"Oh yes, it's that new Scottish pub that opened last year. I have been so busy I haven't had the chance to check it out."

"Oh, you should, Dominique," Rachel pipes in. "The food is amazing."

"What do you do for a living?" I ask Dominique in return. It's a fair question, and I'm curious as to what keeps her so busy.

"I'm Matthew's wife." Okay, that doesn't really answer the question. Then again, maybe it does. She turns to the woman at her left. "Should we plan a lunch date?" She looks across the table. "Joyce, you too."

"Oh my, excuse my manners," Matthew booms from the head of the table. "I forgot you didn't know anyone here, Tavish." He does the introductions, and I greet everyone with a nod, and note the snarl on Jakob's face as he quickly informs the others that we already met. Clearly, I left a good impression.

Soon enough the server comes, bringing carafes of coffee and we all make our way to the buffet. Back at the table, the women fall into conversation about their kids and activities, and the men talk about work. The longer we sit here, the more I'm convinced Rachel should tell them to stick the job up their arses.

My ears perk when the guy beside me, Perry, I think, who, if I remember correctly, is a sales operation manager, mentions something about the branch in Seattle. I sip coffee and bite into my toast as he casually talks about waiting on word of his transfer.

I squeeze Rachel's leg and lean into her. "Did you know about this?"

She shakes her head. "I'm always left in the dark."

"Does that mean his position is open?"

She nods. "That probably means everyone is going to be golfing and schmoozing Matthew for the position."

"Are you going to try?"

She shrugs. "It's probably pointless."

I hate the defeat in her voice. "Is it a good position for you? Are you as qualified as any of the guys here?'

She snorts. "More."

"Okay, talk to Matthew about it on the course." If she doesn't get it, it might be the final straw for her. All I know is that she can't continue to work in a toxic environment. Rachel and I mostly sit in silence and conversation goes quiet as everyone finishes their breakfast. Once done, Matthew stands.

"I'll see you on the greens in..." He checks his watch. "Ten minutes."

Chatter erupts around the table as the women all huddle together and make a plan for the day, a plan that includes the spa, the pool, manicures and pedicures. A plan that does not involve Rachel. Nor should it. She's an employee of the company and this retreat is about networking, and that's what she should be doing. By rights, I'm the 'partner' and should be joining the women.

"I really dislike golfing," Rachel whispers to me.

I put my hand on the small of her back and we follow Matthew and the others to the clubhouse. "You were so good at it."

"That was mini golf."

"You've got this, Rachel."

She nods. "Thanks for the vote of confidence."

"Talk to Matthew about the job. See where you stand."

"I'm pretty sure I'd be a kick-ass operations manager."

"You'd be a kick-ass CEO and president, lassie." I bend and press my lips to her forehead. My phone pings, and I pull it from my pocket. "Can you sign out the clubs for me? I need to take this."

She nods and I walk away to read Brodie's text. I flip through the pictures of him and Fluffy, walking with the pet walking club, lounging in front of the TV, a beer in front of my rabbit. There's another pic of them having beer at the pub, with Fluffy getting all the attention. He sure as hell had a busy day with Brodie. I grin like an idiot and lift my head and note the odd way Rachel is watching me. I grumble under my breath and feel like a fool for worrying so much about a rabbit.

Tucking my phone away, I join her at the counter, and we sign out clubs. "Everything okay?" she asks.

"Yeah, just Brodie."

"Fluffy is good?"

"He is." I debate on showing her the pictures. Brodie was a fool for taking them. I, however, was the one grinning like the village idiot over them.

"All set?" Matthew asks and pats me on the shoulder.

"You bet." We head outside to the first green, and while it's a gorgeous course, it has nothing on a few in Scotland. Rachel might hate golf. She'd love the rolling hills and breathtaking views back home, though.

One of the guys comes up to me. He angles his head. "You're Tavish the Terror, aren't you?"

Shite. I really don't want to talk about my MMA days.

"Used to be," I tell him and pull a club from my bag.

"Dude, I knew it was you." He turns. "Jeremy, come here. I told you this was Tavish the Terror." I catch Rachel's gaze and she gives me an apologetic glance, like she's sorry she dragged me into this. While I've left my past behind, this could be a good time to get the attention on me, giving her an opportunity to talk to Matthew.

"Come on, give us your signature growl."

I never was much in to trash talk. It was simply part of the culture. "Nae, not the time or place." I take a few practice swings, and Jeremy calls a few more of the guys over. Rachel saunters off to chat with Matthew, and I stall. "Do you really want to hear it?"

"Sure do."

I hold my arms up high, my golf club in my hand like a sword. "Alba gu bràth," I yell, which means Scotland forever, and was a battle cry in Scotland's war of independence. Everyone claps and cheers me on and I catch Rachel's grin.

I fall into conversation with the guys about my time in the MMA as we take our shots and walk to the green. Rachel spends a lot of time with Matthew as I keep the guys entertained, and after a long while my phone rings.

I pull it from my pocket and I'm shocked to see that it's Sophie. I gave her my number for emergencies. I hope the washer isn't leaking again. I excuse myself and walk off toward a small pond and slide my finger across the screen.

"Hey Sophie, what's up?" I turn at a loud honking sound. Is someone coming at me with a cart. I don't see anyone, other than Rachel watching from the distance. The honk comes again, a bit louder this time.

"Is everything okay?" she asks.

"Yeah, just out golfing, what's up?"

"Oh, I'm so sorry, I didn't mean to catch you at a bad time. We were just having a few more plumbing issues. The laundry room sink is backing up. I was hand washing some of my... underthings and now the sink won't drain."

"I can take a look at it, but it will have to wait until tomorrow. Just try not to use it. It's probably a clog." Most likely it's all the bunny fur.

"I really appreciate it. I'm sorry to lean so heavily on you. I'm in between jobs and grandmother is on a pension."

"It's not a problem."

Honk.

Honk.

Bark.

Cackle.

Hiss.

I catch Rachel waving her arms wildly, and I look for a cart on the green. What the hell is making all that noise?

"Are you sure you're okay?" Sophie asks.

Something nips at the back of my leg. "Shite." I drop my phone, and turn to find a great big motherfucking bird attacking me, trying to hit me with its long neck and take chunks of flesh with its beak. A few more birds are standing behind it barking and hissing and flapping like mad.

"What the fuck, dude?" Holding my hands out, I start to back away. "It's okay, everything's okay." The bastard attacks again, running around me fast and taking a bite out of my calf. A few more fly at me, and I wave my arms wildly as they dive bomb.

I start to run, and they still come at me. Rachel and her coworkers start waving wildly and try to come to my rescue. The next thing I know, an employee with a cart comes racing over, scaring the birds back.

"Get in," the guy says. I hop into the seat as warm liquid oozes down the back of my leg. He takes off fast, putting distance between the birds and the cart. Once we're in the clear, he slows and Rachel and a few of the guys come running toward me.

"Tavish," Rachel says breathlessly. "Are you okay?"

"What the hell was that?"

"Canada geese," the driver says. "They must be nesting. Don't worry, we'll take care of it."

"Canada geese? Like geese from Canada?" Before he can answer, I shout out. "Aren't Canadians supposed to be over friendly?"

"I think they channel all their rage into the geese," Matthew answers as he approaches.

I stare at him, dumbfounded, until I catch the small smirk on Rachel's face. Oh, she thinks this is funny, does she?

"I think you need to get that leg cleaned and probably a tetanus shot," the cart driver suggests.

"Right after I prepare a goose dinner for us all tonight," I shoot back.

Rachel puts her hand over her mouth. "Tavish the Terror taken down by a goose," she mumbles, and I shake my head at her.

"Really?"

"Sorry…" she squeaks out. "Too soon?"

"I'm glad I could make your day."

She holds her hand out to me. "Come on, let's get you cleaned up and visit the resort's doctor."

The man behind the wheel of the cart speaks up. "Hop in, ma'am. I'll drive you both back. It's best he stays off his leg until it's checked out."

Rachel is about to get in and I stop her. "No, you keep playing."

"No—"

I pull her to me. "I'm a big boy, lassie." I drop a kiss onto her mouth and whisper, "Come find me when you're done, and I'll show you."

Her cheeks heat and she's winded when she points to where the goose attacked me. "What about your phone?"

"Leave it. I don't want you anywhere near those beasts."

"But—"

"It's fine, Rachel. I'll get a new one. I think it fell in the pond anyway."

She backs up and the driver takes me to the resort. This is not how I expected today to go down. He helps me from the cart and straight to the on-site clinic, where the doctor sees me right away. A few hours later, after a couple shots—tetanus and tequila—I lounge at the pool feeling no pain. Something or someone blocks the sun from my body, and I open one eye to find Rachel standing there.

"How are you feeling?" she asks. I note the tightness in her body, the worried look on her face. She doesn't need to worry about me, and if she's tense, I know how to take care of that.

"I'm good, lassie." I sit up a bit straighter. "Did everything go okay? You got to talk to Matthew about the promotion?"

"We talked. I told him I was interested." She hands over my phone and if I'm not mistaken her smile is forced when she says, "It didn't land in the pond after all."

She begins to back up, and I set my phone down and shade the sun from my eyes to see her.

I sense she's upset and trying to hide it. What really went on out there on the greens, and why do I get the sense she doesn't want to tell me?

21

RACHEL

I might have given myself a good hard lecture in the shower, reminding myself what was, and wasn't happening between us, but seeing that he'd excused himself from the greens to chat with Sophie sort of gutted me. As we drive home, he glances at me, and I smile in return. The last thing I need is for him to think I want more, and scare him off. Lucas needs him. Probably even more after spending the weekend with his father. We all know the promises Jason makes and never follows through with, leaving his child a little more broken.

"Did you have a good weekend?" he asks.

"I did. I had a good talk with Matthew, and he knows how much I want the new position. I guess we'll see." He shifts uncomfortably. "How's the leg?"

"Are you still laughing?"

"Nope," I say and bite my cheek.

"Why are Canada geese so angry?" He shakes his head. "I am never going to Canada."

"Banff is nice. Great mountains to ride your motorcycle."

"I hear New Mexico is good too, and I'd rather face off against a rattle snake."

I laugh at that. "You're scarred for life, are you?"

"Probably need therapy." As we drive along the coast, a beautiful lighthouse in the distance, he squeezes my leg. "What time will Lucas be back?"

I check my watch. "Not until dinner time."

"Want to go for a ride?"

I arch a brow and take in his grin. My body heats, recalling all the ways I'd ridden Tavish and how much I'd like to do it again. "What kind of ride did you have in mind?"

"We can take the bike out. Drive along the shore, grab some seafood at one of the restaurants."

"That sounds like a lot of fun."

"Wait." He grins and playfully wags his brows. "Did you think I had something else in mind?"

"Your grin was kind of cheeky."

"Geez, Rachel, do you think about anything other than sex?"

"Hard to do when I'm with you, Tavish," I tease, and while I'm being funny, or at least I think I am—and hey, he was the one who started it—I get the strangest sense I've hit a nerve.

"Have you ever been on a motorcycle?" he asks and scrubs his face.

"Nope, never. Lucas loved it. I assume I will too."

His fingers tighten on the steering wheel. "Do you think Jason is going to give you a hard time about me hanging with Lucas and taking him on the bike?"

My heart sits heavy in my chest. "He doesn't get a say, Tavish." It's true, he doesn't. It's not going to stop him from having a big one anyway. My stomach tightens, my morning bowl of fruit churning, and I flatten my palm over my belly to soothe it. Honestly, I hate confrontations of any sort, which is probably why I lasted as long as I did with Jason, and of course, never get ahead at work. Although, I was a little more forward with Matthew, stating my case as to why I'd be the perfect operations manager. I never would have done that if Tavish didn't have my back.

"Do you want me there when he brings Lucas home?"

"I do," I say honestly. "Except it's not a great idea." His body tightens. "Don't worry. I can handle anything he throws at me."

Tavish's eyes are murderous as he casts me a fast glance. "He'd better not throw anything at you."

"I don't mean it like that." I lean back in my seat as he takes a left and pulls into our quiet street. I stare at my neglected shrubs as he eases into the driveway.

"Put on jeans and a long sleeve shirt," he orders softly. "I'll head home and get changed and grab the bike and meet you back here. I might be a minute, though. I want to head to Brodie's and check on Fluffy."

I grin. There's just something about him calling the bunny Fluffy that gets to me. Maybe it's the fact that he's a warrior, big and strong, and fearless, and yet so gentle and caring when it comes to his new pet. It's freaking adorable, and if I wasn't falling for him before...

Nope, you are not falling for him, Rachel.

"Give him a kiss for me."

"You better be talking about Fluffy and not Brodie." I open the door and cast a glance over my shoulder. Was that jealousy in his voice? I really don't know anymore. He's a conundrum for sure. One minute all sweet, and handsy—not handy—in a good way, and encouraging me to start my own business, and in the next breath he's putting a measure of distance between us and reminding me he's with me because I hired him.

"Of course, I am."

I reach for my bag. He gets it first and carries it to my front stoop. I fish my key from my purse and open the door. "I'll see you soon." I turn to wave him off and in that familiar move I love, he puts his arm around my waist and pulls me against his hard body. His lips land on mine for a deep, mind-numbing kiss that's going to take a good ten minutes to recover from after he leaves.

He breaks the kiss. "I'll be as fast as I can." Instead of leaving, he stands over me for a second longer, his dark eyes moving over my face. "Are you scared?"

Scared? Yeah, I'm scared, terrified even—of the things this man is doing to me without even trying.

"You don't have to be. I'll go slow."

"Slow is good."

"I'd never take risks when I have someone on the back."

I blink. He's talking about our bike ride along the shore. "I… are you saying you take risks when you ride alone?"

"Maybe not as many as I used to."

Is he saying Lucas and I are the reason he's no longer a daredevil, or is that my ridiculous imagination hoping for things that aren't true? "Glad to hear it. I don't want anything to happen to you." He arches a brow, waiting for me so I say, "Lucas would be devastated."

His warm breath falls over my face as he exhales. "And you, Rachel, would you be devastated?"

"Of course. Who else is going to capture a family of racoons if they decide to nest in my attic, and who else is going to peek into my window—"

"If I find anyone peeking into your window, they'll have some explaining to do." He holds his hand up and curls his fingers, that murderous look back in his eyes. I sure wouldn't want to be on this guy's bad side. "To my fist."

I laugh and shove him. "Go get ready. I'm going to make a quick call to check in on Lucas."

He hovers for a second, his body close, a growl rising in his throat, like leaving might cause him physical pain. Again, that's probably all in my head. "I won't be long." He kisses my forehead and disappears out the door.

I take my bag upstairs and dump the dirty clothes into the hamper, glad the bonding weekend is done. It wasn't too much of a chore this year. Not with Tavish by my side, filling me with encouragement. I reach for my phone and shoot a text off to Jason. After a moment, when no reply comes, I consider phoning. I decide against it. He'll think I'm checking up on him, not Lucas, and nothing good can come from that.

In my closet, I pull out a long sleeve T-shirt and sweater and a pair of jeans, and head to the downstairs closet to dig out my ankle boots. They're stylish, not meant for a motorcycle, but they're the closest things I have and will do in a pinch. If I spend more time with Tavish on his bike, I'll have to think about getting some new gear.

Stop thinking long term, Rachel.

I walk around the house and tidy up a bit. It's strange not having Lucas here when I'm home. I check my phone again, and there's still no response from Jason. I put it down and head to the kitchen for a drink of water. My phone rings, and I run back to the living room and smile when I see who's calling.

"Hey, Mom."

"Rachel, I thought you'd fallen off the end of the earth."

"Haven't we talked about your flat earth conspiracies?" I tease, and she chuckles. "I've just been busy."

"I heard." There's a note of humor in her voice, and I guess she heard I've been busy with Tavish.

I drop down into my favorite chair, and try to recline. It creaks and groans and finally falls into place. "Tell me what you've heard."

"Heard some things about Mr. Sticky Buns."

"That's not his name," I blurt out and can't help but smile. "It's Tavish and you know that. Now what about him?"

"Eight wives and he murdered someone, Rachel." She makes a tsking sound. "How many times have I told you not to get involved with a man who had more than four wives. You know that's the line in the sand." I relax and laugh. Leave it to Mom to always help me see things clearly. "And as long as he murdered someone who deserved it."

"Oh, he probably did," I assure her.

"I'm sitting in the rocking chair Mr. Sticky Buns made, and it's lovely on my buns."

"Would you please stop calling him that."

"Fine, Tavish. By the way, I ran into Phillip and Sandra Anderson this afternoon, at the market." Her voice is a little more serious and I sit up straighter.

Ah, so the real reason for her call. "Was Lucas with them? Is everything okay?"

"He was. They were on their way to the Fairfield farm."

I smile even though my stomach is tight. Call it mother's intuition. "Lucas loves the farm. This will be a fun day for him."

"There was talk, whispers actually, about the new man in your life, and of course, all the rumor swirling around about him."

I huff. "What is wrong with people?"

"Oh so very much, darling. I just wanted to give you the heads up."

"He's a good guy, Mom. He actually helped me out with a work event this weekend and he's really good to Lucas."

"I'm sure he is, hon. I met him and what I know of him, I like. I don't really know him well, though."

Memories buzz in the back of my brain and I pull them forward. Long ago, when I got engaged to Jason, I remember her saying something very similar to me. I think way back when she saw something not quite right in Jason that I didn't. Oh, to have the wisdom that comes with age. Well, I'm older now too, and my wisdom tells me Tavish, even though he might not be looking for any sort of a relationship, is one of the good guys, and that's good enough for me.

"How well do you know him, Rachel?" Before I can answer, she says, "Oh, Brenda is here. We're off to bingo."

"Have fun."

I end the call and check the time. Tavish still isn't here, and it's a good time for me to head out and do a bit of gardening. The front flowerbed is overgrown with weeds, as Maize so kindly pointed out.

I spend a long time weeding, and when it grows too hot, I head inside to check my phone. Nothing from Jason, or Tavish. A bike engine rumbles, and I go outside to see him pulling out of Sophie's driveway. What the heck?

He eases into mine, and kills the ignition. I must have a strange look on my face, because he angles his head. "Everything okay with Lucas?"

Everything okay with Sophie?

Instead of shooting back like a ridiculous, juvenile teenager, I nod. "As far as I know. Jason hasn't texted back. I heard from Mom and she said they were going to the farm today. I'm sure they're busy feeding the animals."

He climbs off the bike and unhooks a helmet. He puts it on my head and my entire body tingles as his fingers brush my chin, pulling the straps together. "Sorry I'm late. I got Fluffy settled in back home, and I had to stop in to check on Sophie's plumbing. It took longer than I thought."

"She seems to be having a lot of troubles lately." Was that what they were talking about on the golf course before he was brutally attacked by angry Canada geese?

He latches the helmet and moves it on my head to check the fit. "Good?"

"Good."

"Her sink was clogged," he explains. "Bunny hair. There was a shite ton of it."

I note the water on his collar. "Is that why you're wet?"

He nods. "If you think I'm wet, you should have seen Sophie. She was drenched."

Do not go there, Rachel. Do not go there. He helped with her plumbing—her sink's plumbing.

"I don't remember Mrs. Potter having so much trouble." There's a part of me, a suspicious part, that thinks Sophie might be sabotaging the place just to get Tavish over. That would be crazy though, right? Or not. Tavish is a real catch.

"Her place is old, like yours and with three people now, instead of one, all showering and doing laundry, it can add extra pressure to the pumps and pipes."

Is he naïve? Maybe taken one too many hits to the head? I'm pretty sure it's clear that Sophie wants him. It was always a battle with Jason. I would bring up all the women wanting him and he'd gaslight me. Telling me I was the crazy one, only for me to find out later he was sleeping his way through every puck bunny at every away game.

He holds the bike for me to climb on, and once I'm stable, he throws his leg over. I instinctively put my hands around his waist, and he gives one a squeeze. He starts the engine and backs out of the driveway, and I relax against him as we travel along the coast, and admire the Cape Ann lighthouses.

We soon come to the fishing area, where many tourists are enjoying local cuisine, and he finds a parking spot for his bike. He puts his hand on my back as we move through the crowd, and he points to a quaint restaurant overlooking the water.

"How about there?"

"Perfect." The hostess seats us and the second we sit, my phone pings. I quickly pull it from my pocket. I read the message from Lucas, who clearly confiscated his father's phone, and give an exaggerated exhale as I glance at Tavish. "Lucas," is all I say.

"Is everything okay?"

"Not really?"

He pushes back in his chair. "What's going on? Do we need to go get him?"

I take his hands. "It's okay. It's just...he's asking if he can have a pet sheep." Confusion brims in Tavish's eyes. "He was at the farm today, and well...sheep."

Tavish laughs and settles in his chair. "I guess if you're going to have a pet."

Is he serious? "Uh, no. We are not getting a sheep, Tavish."

He lifts his finger to call the server over. "Look at me. I never thought I'd be caring for a bunny. Never say never, lassie."

"Tavish—"

He leans into me, his mouth close to mine. "Sheep are intelligent, playful, and affectionate. Probably better than a dog."

"Tavish—"

"A flock would keep the racoons away."

Is he really trying to sell me on this or is he just having fun? "That's what I have you for," I shoot back.

"Sure, but winter will be here soon. Sheep like to snuggle and will keep you warm in your bed all night. No sneaking out before Lucas wakes."

Is he saying he wants to be in my bed this winter?

I tap my chin and turn this around. "You might be on to something. A sheep might be a good idea. Intelligence, playfulness, and affection. Not to mention scaring off raccoons and keeping me warm. Honestly, why would I even need a man around?"

His eyes darken as they hold mine, heat flaring inside him. "Forget it. No sheep for you, and when I get you home, I'm going to show you exactly why you need a man around."

22

TAVISH

I can't believe how fast time flies when you're having fun. "Okay boys, go grab the balls," I say as we finish up football practice. I wipe the moisture from my brow and turn to find Rachel smiling at me. Her sweet, angelic smile always fucks me over, and while I signed on to be a stand-in for six months, that too is flying by.

I want more.

I can't fight it or deny it any longer. How the hell am I supposed to walk away from this small family? I don't want to, that's for sure, and when it comes right down to it, I'm not sure I can. Rachel hasn't once said anything about long term, and there were so many times I had to pull back, not believing I was the man she needed in her life, at least not on a permanent basis.

I spent my whole life worrying I wasn't good father or husband material—that I had too much of my father in me. Thanks to Dad for Hire, I'm starting to believe otherwise. Yeah, I beat the living shite out of a guy for hurting my friend

—I was a madman like my father—but I've grown up and matured, and have control of myself now. Right?

Lucas waves to me from the other side of the field as he collects balls. He's no longer getting picked on, and in fact, a few of the guys that had bullied him in the past have been over to the house, and I always make sure I'm in my kilt.

The kid is thriving, and when he's not at camp, I've been teaching him a few self defense moves, and of course, we have our secret project, and today is the day, Rachel is going to find out what we've been up to in my garage. I, of course, have been spending a lot of time at Mrs. Potter's place too, trying to come and go at odd hours, always under the cover of darkness so the neighbors don't catch me, or start more rumors—albeit this one would be true.

Rachel stands and starts my way and my heart beats a little faster. When was the last time I was this happy?

My phone pings and I pull it from my pocket. "What's up?" I ask Brodie as I shade the sun from my eyes and check for missing balls.

"I'm in the hospital," he blurts out.

Every worst-case scenario goes through my brain, and as the world closes in on me, I catch Rachel's eye. Her steps slow at the visible worry tightening my face, and she watches on with concern.

"What hospital?" I pull my keys from my pocket. "I'll be right there."

"No, it's okay, buddy. Nothing serious. I broke my foot."

"That's pretty fucking serious." I take a breath, able to fill my lungs again. Okay, it's serious but at least it's not life threatening.

Rachel reaches me and whispers, "What's going on?"

I put my hand over the phone, and say, "Brodie broke his foot. He's at the hospital."

"Go," she begins, immediately stepping up and into action. "I'll collect the cones and balls."

"No, you don't need to come." Brodie's voice comes through the phone. "I'm getting a cast and Gavan is here with me. I dropped a big can of tomato sauce on my damn foot at work." He curses. "I'm an eegit."

"Shite, Brodie."

"I'm going to be laid up for a few days."

"You can stay with me," I tell him. Rachel nods her head, an indication that she can help out too.

"Yeah, you'll help me out?" he asks.

"You know I will." I grip the phone tighter. "Anything. Name it." If he needs me to take his shifts at the pub, or help with his growing Dad for Hire business, I have no problem with that. I'll step in wherever he needs me.

He goes quiet for a second, and then I hear whispered words and a small chuckle. I grip the phone tighter, and whisper, "Shite."

"What?" Rachel asks stepping closer, trying to hear what Brodie is saying.

I brush my hair from my forehead, my body on high alert. "He's up to something and I can tell you right now I'm not going to like it. "Brodie, what the fuck?"

"The parade is Saturday."

I wait for more, but he goes silent. I hate when he gets cagey. "What about it?"

"I'm the town crier. I can't lead the parade with a broken foot." A few more muffled sounds and then, "You're going to have to do it for me."

"Yer aff yer damn heid," I automatically shoot back. Me? Town crier? Not fucking likely.

"All you have to do is walk down the main street in your formal Scottish attire and ring the bell. It's not that hard."

"He wants me to be town crier," I tell Rachel.

Her eyes light with excitement. "You should."

"No," I shoot back. "I'm not doing that. I'm never doing that. It's ridiculous."

"Tavish," Lucas says, coming out of nowhere. "I can do it with you if you're nervous." He puts his little hand in mine and gives it a reassuring squeeze, much the same way I do with him when he needs encouragement, and the fight drains out of me.

Well, shite.

I look at the little boy's big eyes, and the hope and support that lives there wraps around my heart and squeezes. How can I say no to that? Especially since his father hasn't been around in over a month. After he had him that weekend, he dropped him off at dinner time and I stayed away, like Rachel wanted. What she didn't know was that I was on the street, watching the exchange, staying close in case she needed me.

Jason of course had a lot to say about me, grilling her on our relationship, and my relationship with his son. If he doesn't like my influence, maybe he should come around more often, and stay a little longer. Oh, he'd promised Lucas more. In the end, it was lip service. Lucas was sad at his father's broken promises, and seeing him and Rachel hurt, hurt me. I did all I could to keep him busy and fill the void.

"Are you going to do it?" Brodie asks pulling my thoughts back.

"Did you really break your foot?" I ask my former best friend and glance around the field, as the kids all pack up and walk off with their parents. These families are all looking forward to the festival. Rachel and Lucas included. The town crier is a big part of the parade, from what Rachel had told me.

"You can't let all those kids down," Brodie says, hitting below the belt. The bastard knows me too well.

"Can you get one of the casts you can walk in?" I wave my free hand, not that he can see me. "It's like bubble wrap, or something."

"Eventually. As of right now the doctor says I can't put pressure on it for weeks." I grunt out a curse, and remember Lucas is standing there and I'm supposed to be setting a good example. "I didn't do it on purpose. I like being the town crier." A cackling voice comes over the intercom at the hospital, and when it finishes, he adds, "It's an honorable position, Tavish. You should be grateful I picked you."

"You picked me because there is no one else." I pull open my water bottle with my teeth and spray it into my dry throat.

"Wait, what about Gavan? Can he do it? He's lived here longer than me."

"He's serving up meals in one of the kiosks and can't."

"What about Finn?"

"Finn has a float in the parade, showcasing Finn-tastic-affairs."

"Why do they need someone to wear formal Scottish attire?"

"It's what the people want, Tavish." He blows out an exaggerated breath like I should know all this. "We have to give the people what they want."

I lower my voice. "What I want is to give you a proper beating right now."

He laughs. "That's an aye? You'll do it?"

Jesus. How is he always able to talk me into things I don't want to do? For some reason, he thinks he knows what's best for me. I guess at the end of the day, he knew Dad for Hire was what I needed and he wasn't wrong. I take a big, calming deep breath and let it out slowly,

"That's an aye," I grumble. Dammit, I had my own surprise planned for the festival. I guess I'll have to put them on hold. Before he can say anything else, or talk me into partaking in the mashed potato wrestling, I end the call and shove my phone into my pocket.

"Are you going to do it?" Lucas asks hopefully.

"Aye."

His big smile lets me know I made the right decision and my throat squeezes tight. I like when the kid is happy. "I get to do it with you?"

I ruffle his already mussed hair. "Aye."

"Ben," he calls out and takes off. "I'm going to be the town crier with Tavish. I get to ring the bell."

Rachel grins at me. "You know I don't like this one little bit." I glance around. "Maybe I'll move to a different city before the festival."

She nudges me, and her warm body sends heat straight to my groin. "You know this place has grown on you."

"Like a bad wart."

She laughs, and picks up the plastic container with orange peels in it. "I'll wave to you from the sidewalk and cheer you on."

"Oh, well then, that changes everything," I grouch. "Come on, Lucas let's go," I call out, and spot him talking to Ben and Sophie.

Sophie waves, and says, "See you later." My blood drains to my toes as Rachel stiffens beside me. Shite. Why would Sophie say that? Rachel's gaze goes from me to Sophie back to me.

"I didn't know you were doing more work at Sophie's." She frowns, like she's remembering something.

"Must have slipped my mind." I asked Sophie to keep my visits under wraps. She's going to blow this for me in a big way.

Rachel gives a dismissive wave of her hand and her laugh is a bit strained. "You're not accountable to me, Tavish. Your whereabouts are not my business. Just like mine aren't yours."

Is that a reminder that we're just hooking up? My body tightens, like I'd just received a good kick to the gut. "Her house is the same age as yours. Lots of upkeep needed and Mrs. Potter let things crumble around her."

"Sounds like the place will be completely remodeled by the time you're finished with it."

"Mrs. Potter is a lovely lady. I don't mind helping out."

"That's nice of you."

She puts on a smile. I know her well enough to know it's strained. Is she suspicious, thinking something is going on between Sophie and me? Nah, I've been extra careful, although Sophie doesn't seem to be as secretive as me, despite me asking her to keep things quiet. "I'm almost finished. Just a few more things," I assure her.

"Maybe she should hire her own Dad for Hire?" she finally says.

"I don't think they can afford it." I change the subject. "Speaking of hiring, anything on the operations manager position?"

"Nothing yet." We start toward the truck, and I toss the bag of balls into the back. Lucas comes bounding over, talking a mile a minute, so excited to be in the parade. Of course, I'm going to help Brodie out in his time of need. I'm over being the center of attention, however. I never even liked it when I was fighting.

Once everyone is buckled in, I head to Rachel's and drop her off. She reaches for the handle, and I stay in my seat. Her brow is furrowed as she turns back to me. "Are you coming in?" It's Saturday and we always hang out after soccer. It's insane how much I like that.

"No, actually my mate and I have some things to do. It's okay if Lucas comes with me?"

Lucas, who is not very good at keeping secrets, covers his mouth and starts to giggle. I grin at him in the rear-view mirror.

"Are you going for a bike ride? Lucas, you'll have to change if you're getting on the motorcycle."

"Not a bike ride," he shouts out.

She puts her hands on her hips. "What are you two up to?"

"Nothing, Mom."

"We'll be back shortly. Need me to pick anything up for dinner?" It's strange how much I love running errands for her.

"Nope, we're good."

She waves us off, and I drive straight to my place. "Do you think she's on to us, mate?"

"Nope," he yells as he bounces from the car, and I'm pretty sure she knows exactly what we're up to.

"Let's get a clean rag." We walk to the cabinet, and I pull out two clean rags. Last night I put the final finishing coat on the rocking chair, and Lucas and I need to wipe it down. "Okay, you do it like this." I show him how to smooth the cloth over the delicate chair, and his little hands work frantically. I love sharing my skills with my mate.

When we're finished, we stand back and I put my hands on my hips. Lucas glances at me and does the same. "What do you think?"

"Can I sit in it?"

"Absolutely. We need to try it out." He climbs into the small chair, which is big for him and runs his hands along the rails.

"I want to make chairs when I get big."

"What are you talking about? You're making chairs now." He beams at me. "Let's get this wrapped in a blanket and loaded."

He helps me get the blanket over the chair, and he grunts as we place it in the back of the truck. I bite back a grin, considering I'm doing the lifting. Once it's secure, we drive back home, or rather, his home. Crazy that I'm thinking of it as mine. Probably because Fluffy and I spend so much time there. At least with Fluffy to hang out with, Lucas is no longer begging for a sheep.

"You run inside and get your mom to put this on." I hand him a clean handkerchief and he excitedly runs into the house. I unload the chair and take it inside.

"What is going on?" Rachel asks as she walks down the hall, holding one hand out, as Lucas pulls her with the other.

"Stay right here, Mom."

I set the chair down beside her old broken one and Lucas and I take off the blanket. "Can I look now?"

I step up behind her, and release the blindfold and put my hand on the small of her back, simply needing to touch her as she looks at the rocking chair, her hands going to her face. "No way."

"We made it, Mom. Tavish and I made it." Lucas starts jumping around. "I helped cut the wood, and plane it and sand it, and we stained it. Isn't it beautiful?"

She turns to me, tears in her eyes. "It's absolutely gorgeous. What did I ever do to deserve this?"

"Hey, no tears."

"It's just such a nice thing to do."

I shrug. "Your other one was broken, and I thought you might like this."

"I do, I love it." She sniffs and Lucas jumps into the chair and starts rocking back and forth, so fast I'm worried he's going to fling himself out of it.

"Why don't you let your mom sit in it, mate. Let her see what a great job you did."

Lucas jumps up and Rachel sinks into the chair. She rocks and smiles a nostalgic look of contentment falling over her pretty face. "Lucas, when you were a baby, I had a chair like this. Not as nice as this of course. I used to rock you in it for hours when you couldn't sleep." She blinks up at me. "It broke ages ago, and I've always wanted to replace it." Why do I get the sense that there's a story behind the broken chair, and that Jason might have something to do with it?

She glances at her son and crooks her finger. "Come here." Lucas hops into her lap and she rocks him back and forth. The smile on her face is full of love and warmth, and I'm so happy that Lucas and I could put it there. Rachel hums, her mind clearly going back to Lucas' baby days and Lucas shifts, his arms and legs dangling, like a four-legged octopus out of water.

"I'm too big for this, Mom." He squirms out of her hold and jumps onto the sofa. "You need to have another baby."

She gulps. "Lucas, remember you need a mommy and a daddy to have a baby." They've obviously had this discussion before. "Daddy and I are divorced now."

He shrugs like he knows all the answers in the world. "Why can't Tavish be the daddy?"

Rachel looks like she's about to tip over in the chair as her gaze flies to mine, and I can't help but think...why not indeed?

It's a crazy thought for sure. When I moved to Massachusetts to be close to Brodie and live a quieter life, I had no idea I'd become the caretaker of a bunny, and fall for a little family of two. I haven't been this happy in...ever. Rachel is happy too. I see it in her eyes every time I look at her. I'm not Lucas' father. He has one, sometimes anyway, and I've been a stand-in for a couple of months now. I'd like to change that title to something else—if it's okay with Rachel.

Only problem is, I'm not sure if she wants the same things as I do.

I take one look at Tavish as he comes through my door, dressed in his formal Scottish clothing and my ovaries start dancing the macarena. Long ago I'd stopped thinking about having another baby. I was divorced and Lucas was getting older, and I resigned myself to the fact that I might become a cat or bunny lady long before my time.

Now, thanks to Lucas' suggestion that I have another baby with Tavish, and the sight of Tavish in his formal gear for the parade, my body is literally having a meltdown, wanting it all with the MMA Scottish prince, who owns a castle in a faraway land as he stands in my doorway. I take in the haughty way he puts his hands on his hips and the grumpy frown on his face.

"Happy Saturday to you too." He grumbles at my greeting. "You look amazing, by the way."

"I just want this over with."

I step up to him, press against his body. "Are you wearing anything under that kilt?"

"If I was wearing anything under it, it'd be a skirt. Not that there's anything wrong with a guy wearing a skirt." Rachel backs up at the sound of footsteps running along the upstairs hall.

"Tavish," Lucas yells, taking the stairs two at a time, and coming to a halt in the front entranceway. "Do you think I look okay?"

Tavish's gaze moves over Lucas' T-shirt and blue skirt, and he gives a disapproving shake of his head. "Sorry mate, you're going to have to change."

My stomach tightens. "Tavish?" Lucas hasn't worn a skirt in a long time, and I was sure, as a man who wears a kilt, that Tavish had no problem with it.

He drops his backpack, and pulls out a package. He holds it out to Lucas. "What is it?" Lucas asks, his eyes going wide.

"Open it and see."

He sits on the stairs and tears into the brown paper package. He gasps as he shakes out a kilt, one that matches Tavish's.

"Tavish," I whisper, my heart wobbling.

"What is all this?" Lucas asks and as he takes in all the different parts of the outfit, Tavish begins to tell him what they are and how to wear them.

"That's your kilt, mate. Right there is your shirt and tie." Lucas lifts a pair of shoes. "Those are your ghillie brogues, and you got your kilt hose and kilt flashes right there. Those are your socks and the flashes hold them up. That's your kilt pin and sporran."

Lucas pulls out another piece of the outfit. "It looks like a purse."

"Aye, a purse for men and it sits four fingers below the top of the kilt. I'll teach you how to do that." He takes out his waistcoat and jacket. "Did you know you never button a highland dress jacket?"

"Do I get a knife like you have in your sock?"

"Nae, mate. I didn't think your mom would like that. It's called a sgian dubh, and if you're left-handed, you put it in the right sock and if right-handed it goes in the left. We'll get you one when you're older." I smile at Tavish, and appreciate that he didn't get my son a knife while loving that he's talking about the future. "Now let's get you dressed."

Twenty minutes later, after Tavish helps him with his formal wear, Lucas stands before me, very proud of the way he looks. He spins around. "I love it, Tavish." He throws his arms around Tavish's waist and my heart beats a little faster.

I mouth the words, "Thank you."

"Okay mate, we need to get going."

Lucas dashes out the door, and Tavish hangs back for a second to give me a kiss. We've been keeping things pretty quiet, not showing affection in front of Lucas. I have no idea how long this is going to last, and I know Lucas adores Tavish and I don't want him to get his hopes up. But dammit, I'm tired of that. I want it to change and hopefully after today's big festival, we can find some quiet time to talk.

He wraps his arms around my body, drags me close, and I murmur, "Thank you for all this with Lucas, Tavish. I'm not sure I've ever seen him so excited."

"Come on, Tavish," Lucas calls out, and I turn.

"He has the patience of his mother," Tavish says with a laugh.

I wiggle my eyebrows. "You're right, and when it comes to tonight, and getting you out of those clothes, I can promise I'll have zero patience."

He growls. "Keep it up, lassie, and my boner will be leading the parade."

I laugh and follow him out the door. I stand on the stoop as he makes his way to his truck and I already miss his touches and kisses.

"Hi Tavish," Sophie calls out from her lawn, and as Tavish waves, my stomach tightens. I realize he's been hanging out over there helping her, yet there's a part of me—thanks to Jason's affairs—that fills me with worry and jealousy.

Am I entitled to feelings of jealousy? We're not a couple, we've never talked about being a couple, or being exclusive, and if he wants to be with Sophie, he can be, right? Oh God, I just don't know anything anymore, other than the fact that both my son and I love Tavish.

I work to push away those feelings, and wave to Lucas. "Go, have fun and I'll meet you at the bakery when you're done."

Tavish stops in the driveway and turns to me, his forehead bunched, his body tight. "Later, Rachel. We need to talk?"

We need to talk...

Those words...they're very familiar to me. I once spoke those exact words to Jason, when I knew we were over. I grip the rail and do my best to appear carefree. "Yeah sure," I say breezily, even though my gut is warning me that those four words signal that something very bad is about to happen, even though things have been going so great.

"Okay," is all he says as he climbs into the driver's seat and backs out of my driveway. Sophie and Ben start down the sidewalk, and I hurry inside, needing a moment to pull myself together. I step into my living room and drop down into my new rocking chair, taking a few deep breaths.

I think it's time I laid things on the line with Tavish, and told him how I really feel. If I do, and he doesn't feel the same way, though, does that mean I'm jeopardizing his relationship with Lucas? Dammit, the last thing I wanted to do was come between them. That's what Dad for Hire was all about in the first place. But what if I do tell him how I feel, and he feels the same way?

I run my hand along the smooth wood. If he didn't care, he wouldn't have made me such a gorgeous piece of art. Although, he could just be doing a stand-up job of being a stand-in dad and this project was for Lucas.

I put my hand over my tight stomach. I'm not sure what's going to happen. All I know is Tavish wants to talk and I have to come clean with him. I push to my feet, grab my purse and keys and lock up. Since the main street isn't far, and the roads are shut down for the parade, I decide to go on foot. Maybe a good brisk walk in the sunshine will help clear my head.

As I get closer to the main street, the volume of the crowd gets louder. It cheers me up a bit, and the truth is, I'm excited to see Tavish and Lucas lead the parade. In the big park behind Mom's bakery, numerous kiosks and tents are set up. Mom always leaves her bakery open during the day of the festivities, and she usually sells out.

Since the street is crowded and so is her bakery, I walk around the building and go in through the back entrance. I've been so busy lately, I've barely seen her, and of course, while she supports me, during our last conversation, she did ask me something that stuck with me.

"How well do you know him?"

"Mom," I say coming from around the back.

"Rachel." She turns and hugs me, and I grab an apron, ready to help.

"You're almost sold out," I say and step up to the counter, happy to see business is going so well for her. It makes me wonder about my job, and why Matthew hasn't picked the new operations manager. Is it really possible that I could start my own business? I'm close to thirty. Is that too late? I'm about to ask my mother when I realize who I'd be asking. Heck, after Dad left, she picked up the pieces of her life and single-handedly—zero support—opened a bakery, putting her skills to work. I spent many days after school doing homework at one of the tables.

I wouldn't be doing it single-handedly though. Tavish was quick to point out that he'd support me. My stomach twists. Unless he's about to break things off with me during our talk. I put that out of my mind for the time being, and we hurry to serve all the customers. I check my watch.

"The parade should be starting soon." I untie my apron. "Let's get out there."

The bell overhead chimes and in walks Belinda. "Sorry Belinda, but all we have left is one pinwheel," Mom says. "If you want it, it's on the house."

"Actually," she says, her wary gaze going from Mom to me. "I was hoping I could talk to Rachel."

"Oh, absolutely," Mom says tossing me a concerned look before backing up. "I need to wash up anyway."

"Is everything okay?" I ask, instantly worried about my son. "Did you see Lucas? He's with Tavish. They're leading the parade." I'm rambling, I know. I can't help it. My intuition is warning that something is very wrong.

She puts her hand on mine on the counter. "This isn't about Lucas, it's about you and that young man you've been seeing."

"I haven't been—" She angles her head and I stop. She lives across the street from me. She obviously realizes how much time Tavish spends at my house—even overnight. Also, I'm tired of hiding it. I don't have the energy for it anymore.

"You know I like to keep to my own business and don't gossip."

"I know."

"I've known you since you were a small girl, Rachel." Fine lines crinkle around her blue eyes as she frowns. "I care about you. You've been through a lot, and I don't want to see you hurt again."

Did the lights in the bakery just dim, or am I feeling a bit faint? I lean against the counter. "What's...going on?" I ask, not sure I want to hear the answer, or perhaps there's a part of me that already knows what it is.

Her hands are a bit shaky as she takes her phone from her pocket. She sets it on the counter. "I had a security camera installed last year, it was before you moved home. There were some kids causing mischief in the neighborhood." She pauses, and takes her hand away from her phone, like she can't bear to show me what's on it.

"Belinda, please."

She gives herself a moment, and after a curt nod, she presses play, and shows me video footage of Tavish coming and going from Mrs. Potter's—Sophie's—place late at night.

"He's doing some work for them." Even though I'm quick to come to his defense—I did the same with Jason—there's a part of me that warns something is off.

She puts on another video, and after he leaves Sophie's, he uses his key to enter my place. I check the time on the camera, and that would be long after I was asleep. My God was he sneaking out of my bed, into hers, and then back into mine.

I move away from the counter, and she picks up her phone. "I'm so sorry, dear. I didn't know what to do or if I should tell you. I figured if it was me, I'd want to know."

I take a breath but there's no oxygen left in the bakery. The sound of bells jingling out on the street pull my attention and I walk past Belinda, a familiar kind of numbness about me. Out on the street, I spot Tavish and Lucas. Lucas rings the bell proudly and smiles and waves at me. I plaster on my best smile, and wave back. Tavish's steps slow briefly as my gaze flickers to his, and everything about him tightens.

He knows I know.

Jason gave me the same look when I found out about all his affairs. Tears form in my eyes, and I swipe them away. As the blur clears, I scan the crowd, looking for my best way out. I can't seem to breathe.

That's when I spot Jason. Speak of the devil.

He comes storming my way, rage all over his face. Oh God, what is going on with him? I haven't heard from him in ages and now he looks like he wants to murder me. "Rachel," he screams over the crowd.

"What...I didn't know you were back home," I say, trying to sound normal, and not like the rug was ripped right out from underneath me.

"Is that why my son is in a skirt? You didn't think I'd find out? How many times have I told you he's a boy and shouldn't be wearing skirts?"

"It's a kilt," I correct. "It's fine, Jason."

"Oh, for fuck's sake, Rachel. It's not fine. I should call child protective services and have him removed from you. This is ridiculous."

Panic erupts inside me, anger filling my every pore. How dare he say things like that to me? He's been absent most of Lucas' life. I'm the one who's done the heavy lifting and know what's right for my son. "How dare you," I shoot back, my voice bordering on hysterics. The crowd parts, and I cover my face, not wanting to cause a scene, although it looks like it's too late for that.

"Dad," Lucas says, running up to us. "Dad, did you see me? I was ringing the bell."

All Jason does is scoff at Lucas and the hurt look on my son's face breaks my heart a little bit more. "Get yourself into some proper clothes, Lucas. You shouldn't be in a fucking skirt. You're embarrassing yourself and me."

Lucas goes still at his father's harsh words, and the deep horrified sadness in his eyes guts me. My fingers fist. I have never, ever wanted to hit someone so badly. Lucas starts crying and I pull him to me.

"Stop your crying, Lucas, and get out of that skirt."

"It's a kilt and it's traditional Scottish battle wear," Tavish's hard voice says from behind me and I spin, gasping as I take in his murderous eyes.

Jason laughs and glances the length of Tavish. "You look ridiculous too."

"That's better. Pick on someone your own size. I can handle it." Lucas tucks into me tighter and Tavish puts a supportive hand on his shoulder. "What kind of man makes his son cry like this?" I turn Lucas, not wanting him to see any violence, and he buries his face in my stomach. "Why don't you walk away?" Tavish suggests.

"He's my son." Jason jabs his thumb into his own chest. "You're the one who needs to walk away." He shakes his head and looks at me. "Why the fuck would you bring a guy like this asshole into Lucas' life? No wonder the kid is fucked up, wearing skirts." He walks toward me, everything about him threatening as he looms over my body. "You're doing a shit job of raising him, Rachel. You don't deserve custody."

Tavish, who looks like he's struggling to stay calm, takes a threatening step toward Jason and a tortured sound crawls out of my throat as my heart nearly jumps from my chest. "She's doing an amazing job," Tavish says through clenched teeth. "And if Lucas wants to wear a skirt, or a kilt, he can wear a skirt or a kilt."

Jason squares his shoulders and glares at me. "You're making him soft. No wonder he gets picked on."

Tavish's calm begins to fray around the edges when Jason calls Lucas soft. Jason reaches for Lucas, roughly grabs him by the shoulder and tries to drag him from me. As soon as Lucas cries out in pain, something in Tavish breaks, the last of his calm replaced by red hot rage. It fills his eyes, his face, and seeps from every pore in his body. Air races from my lungs as panic erupts inside me.

"Tavish," I yell, but I don't think he can hear me. He smacks Jason's hand away from Lucas' shoulder.

"You're hurting him."

Jason tries to shove Tavish. "Back the fuck off, asshole. You have no say here." He reaches for Lucas again, and the next thing I know, Tavish is between us.

Fear grips my throat, and someone pushes against my back, trying to get a better view. I stare at Tavish, but I don't recognize the man before me. He shoves Jason back and Jason stumbles to the ground. The next thing I know, Tavish is on him, pinning him to the ground, his fist in the air. Pure rage forms a cloud around him. Ohmigod. He's going to kill Jason.

I scream Tavish's name at the top of my lungs, as my body shakes and tears run down my face. I have never been so frightened in my entire life. "Stop."

Seconds before his hand barrels into Jason's face, he stops, his entire body shaking with rage and fury. "Tavish," I plead. "Please..."

He goes still for a good ten seconds, his body still tense, and Jason shoves him. "You'll be hearing from my lawyer, fucker."

Tavish stands, his shoulders slumped as he turns to me, hurt, sadness and raw fear brewing in the depts of his eyes.

"Tavish," I choke out, never having seen anyone so broken before. He stares at me, and after a long moment, his gaze drops to the back of Lucas' head as I keep him nestled against my body.

"Rachel." He reaches for me and I flinch. Warrior Tavish disappears and the man I know—or thought I knew before Belinda showed me the video footage—stands before me. One thing becomes very clear as he hovers close. My mother was right…I don't know this man.

He stares at me for another second, his gaze searching my frightened face, and then he gives a curt nod. "Right," he says quietly, like he's reminding himself of something. The next thing I know, his back is to me as he walks into the crowd and out of our lives.

24

TAVISH

I pace around my garage, kicking empty cardboard boxes out of my way. My hands fist, and I spread my fingers and take deep breaths, trying to find a measure of calm. I lost my shite yesterday big time and I can't expect Rachel to forgive me, not when I can't forgive myself. I swore a long time ago never to react or fight with emotions, yet I did just that.

But the second Jason put his hands on Lucas and told him he was soft, my entire childhood came back in a flash and all I wanted to do was pummel him in a way I couldn't pummel my own father. I scoff. I guess I was right after all. I *am* like my father, and if I can lose my temper like that, I'm not fit to have a family of my own. I guess it's a good thing I realized that before I told Rachel how I felt.

Christ, not only did I fuck up on the sidewalk outside her mother's bakery, I fucked up spectacularly. There were dozens of phones recording the fight and I can't imagine anyone in this small town wanting me around anymore. I heard the rumors about me, that I was trouble, and in the end, I guess I lived up to them.

I stomp around and curse under my breath as I grab the box I just kicked and start packing it with my meager belongings. Everything I own can get donated. I have no intentions of dragging any of my things, not that I have much, back to Scotland with me. As much as I'd like to take Fluffy, he's better off with someone else. I'll try Mrs. Potter, and if that doesn't work out, he'll have to go to a shelter. I never should have kept him in the first place.

Have I not learned anything over the years?

"Hey."

I turn at the sound of Brodie's voice, and I don't want to look at him, don't want to see the disappointment on his face. Rachel is his friend. He cares about her. He's not going to like that I frightened her by going caveman on her ex. I lift my head and clench down on my jaw as I take in his frown. My first instinct is to ask about Rachel and Lucas. I want to know how they're doing.

You gave up that right when you jumped her ex, mate.

"Hey," I say back and run my shaky hands through my hair. Fuck, I'm tired. Last night in bed, I played the day over and over in my mind, considering all the other ways I could have handled the situation—without fists.

Brodie glances at the boxes. "What's up?"

"I'm leaving."

He opens a packed box and peers inside. "Where are you going?"

"Back to Scotland. I don't belong here." I lean against my work bench, expecting him to try to talk me out of it. "You know it and I know it."

Using crutches, he walks over to my bike. "Are you taking this with you?"

"No."

"Can I buy it?"

What the fuck?

"You can have it." Putting down his crutches he throws his leg over the bike, and puts his hands on the bars, pretending to rev them and it reminds me so much of Lucas it hurts my head and my heart. "You don't even ride, Brodie."

"I can learn." He glances at me. "I thought you loved this bike."

"Not attached." A snort of disbelief sounds in his throat. "Is there anything else you want?" I ask, my annoyance level rising.

He climbs off the bike and using his crutches again, slowly strolls through my garage and lets his gaze rake over the tools I bought when I moved here. "I always liked this wood planer."

I shake my head. "Really?" Honestly, I'm surprised he even knows what a planer is. "Since when have you been interested in woodworking or tools."

"Just now."

I walk over to the planer and pull the plug before he accidently turns it on and loses a finger. "Do you even know how to use a planer?"

He runs his fingers along the machine. "No, but I can learn. Can I have it? I remember when you got it, you told me how much you loved it." He arches a brow. "You sure you don't want to take it with you?"

"Not attached, take it." I gesture with a nod toward the door leading into the house. "How about Fluffy? Do you want him too? I'm not taking him with me. You can go get him if you want him."

"Are you kidding me? You love that little guy."

"That wasn't the question, and I don't love him. I was temporarily taking care of him until someone came for him."

He tosses me a look that suggests I'm full of shite. He's not wrong. I glare back as I fold my arms across my chest. "What do you want, Brodie?"

He lowers himself into one of my rocking chairs and runs his hand along the wood. "Can I have this?"

"You can take whatever the hell you want. Just say whatever it is you're here to say so I can get back to packing."

He leans forward and puts his elbows on his knees. "Tell me why you're running away, leaving all the things you love behind."

I hate the question, but at least we're getting somewhere.

"I'm not, I don't—"

When did I forget that I wasn't supposed to love anything? Oh right, when I met Rachel and Lucas.

"Funny, I've never seen you run from anything." He stretches his legs out, like I'm not in the middle of packing and have all the time in the world to entertain him. "You never tapped out. You always fought."

"Leaving where you're not wanted is not running away. You weren't there yesterday. You didn't see what happened."

"Oh, I saw. Hell, everyone saw." He rocks back and forth and casually adds, "Everything is documented today, Tavish. We can watch it now if you want." He pulls his phone out of his pocket,

"I don't need to see it, I was there." He runs his finger along his phone, scrolling for the video, no doubt. "Was the look on Rachel's face recorded, too? Did you see that?" I pinch my eyes shut. It does nothing to erase the horrified look on Rachel's face as she stared at me. It's imprinted on my brain and will be forever. Unable to help myself, I ask, "Have you... talked to her?"

"Just left her place, actually."

My heart jumps. "Is she okay?"

"Not really." He frowns and glances down.

My blood drains to my toes and the room sways before me. A tortured sound catches in my throat as I bite back a sob. I fucking hate myself for hurting her. "Is Lucas...okay?"

"He will be. He's pretty resilient. I bet he'd like to see you."

I snort. "Yeah, I'm sure Rachel doesn't want me anywhere near him or her." The garage grows warm with the sun beating in and I walk into the house. Brodie follows and I grab two beers from the fridge, handing him one. I crack mine open and drink half the contents in one gulp.

"What are you going to do back in Scotland?"

I wipe my mouth with the back of my hand and my gaze goes to the picture Rachel framed of the boys and me on the field. My chest tightens and I turn away. "I don't know yet. Maybe I'll raise sheep."

Brodie walks over to Fluffy's cage and takes him out. "Hey little buddy." Fluffy wiggles his nose. He holds him out to me. "Are you really going to leave this guy behind?"

Even though it feels like someone took a cheese grater to my heart, I work to harden myself. "Yes." I drop down into the kitchen chair.

Brodie puts Fluffy on the floor and the stupid bunny hops over to me, sits on my foot and stares up at me with those big brown eyes. Christ.

I rest one elbow on the table, my head hurting. "I'm not running away, Brodie. I don't belong here."

"This is exactly where you belong."

"I wanted to kill him. I swear if Rachel hadn't screamed, I would have beat him to death. Just like I almost..." I let my words fall off as my throat tightens. "I lost it."

"Yeah, maybe you did for a second. But let me tell you, if I had been there, I would have done the same thing. The man deserves a good beating and for the record, you didn't lay a hand on him."

"I wanted to."

"But you didn't. You pulled it together, when many others probably couldn't." I pick Fluffy up and start petting him, my throat too tight to talk, so instead I just sit and listen. "He was hurting Rachel and Lucas. If you watch the video, you'll see what I saw, and what a lot of other people saw too." He gives me a moment and when I don't respond, he says, "Do you want to know what we saw?"

"No, but I'm sure you're going to tell me anyway."

"I saw a man who was once afraid to love, fight to protect those he loved."

Love...

He's right. I do love Rachel and Lucas, and even Fluffy.

"Back when we were kids, you were protecting me, because we're brothers and you love me. I'm the only one you ever let get close, and you weren't going to let anyone hurt me. Your father was right, Tavish. You were soft, like your mother. You still are." I steal a glance at him to find intense eyes staring back. "Any man who calls his bunny Fluffy has to be soft, and it's not a bad thing." Fluffy climbs up my stomach and puts his head on my shoulder. Brodie smiles as Fluffy snuggles into me. "You lashed out because you care, not because you don't."

"The point is, I lashed out, like my father." My throat squeezes tight. "What if I...what if I hurt them, Brodie?"

"Ah, see, you're nothing like him. He was a weak man, weak of character. You're a man of strength, and the best guy I know. You would never hurt the people you love, Tavish. You protect them. It's ingrained in you." My chest grows tight, making it hard to breathe. "Do you really think I'd pair you up with Rachel and her son if I thought you were anything like your old man? I knew you two were perfect for each other and you were the man Lucas needed in his life."

I scratch my neck where Fluffy's whiskers tickle me. "You put us together, on purpose...you thought..."

"Everything we ever loved was taken from us, so we learned not to get attached. I get it, mate. This time though, you got attached, like I hoped you would—and you're scared shitless because of it." He takes a big swig of beer. "Only thing is, Rachel and Lucas aren't going anywhere. No one has taken them from you. You're the one walking because you're afraid. We always knew it was better not to get attached or love anything or anyone. Now though, maybe you're walking because you did get attached, did find love, and it might be easier to turn away from it before it's taken from you."

"I was going to talk to her, Brodie. After the festival. I was going to tell her how I felt, and it did scare me." Is he right? Did the fight with Jason give me an out, an excuse to run before I got hurt? "Now I'm not sure she'll ever speak to me again."

"If you love her…"

"I do."

"Then maybe now is the time to fight, harder than you ever had to fight before."

I nod. He's right. I've taken down some pretty big bastards in the cage, yet if I want to win Rachel and Lucas back, the most important fight of my life is still before me.

I search his face, seeking help. "What do I do?"

"You'll have to figure that out yourself, mate." I see no answers on his face as he stands and finishes his beer. "Oh, and Belinda showed her video footage of you coming and going from Mrs. Potter's house at strange hours. She thinks you were sleeping with Sophie, so there's that too."

What the fuck?

25

RACHEL

It's been a few days since the fiasco at the festival, and I can't seem to pull myself together. Not only did I lose Tavish, my son did too, and that's not all I lost. Nope, I lost my job too. Maybe loss isn't quite the right word. On Monday morning, after Lucas' camp called, telling me he was sick, I went to see Matthew to tell him I had to leave. My words were met with a disapproving growl and an announcement that the operations job was going to Kent. That's when I quit.

What the hell was I thinking?

I can't just quit my job. In fact, I'm likely going to crawl into Matthew's office before the end of the week and beg for it back. I hate, absolutely hate that it's a boys' club and I keep getting overlooked. While I'd love to start my own company... A noise crawls out of my throat. That was a ridiculous dream and not something I can take on now.

I swipe at the tears in my eyes, and try to focus on the road ahead. I'm not surprised the camp counsellor called on

Monday to tell me Lucas wasn't feeling well. He was still shaken up this morning, but I insisted he try to go to camp as I thought it would help take his mind off things. Obviously, it hasn't. It's just a little after lunch and I'm on my way to get him again. I realize that though he's mad at his father for yelling at him for wearing a skirt—or rather kilt—what he's really upset about is Tavish.

He can't understand why he just walked away, why he's not been around. We always spend Sundays together, and Tavish was nowhere to be found. Instead, it was Brodie who came to check on us. He'd seen the video of course, and repeatedly told me Tavish was one of the good ones. I thought so too, until I saw the footage of him sneaking out of Sophie's late at night.

Honestly, do I really know him?

I'd never seen the violent side of him before. I know he's protective, and his instinct to intervene and remove Jason's hand from Lucas' shoulder came from down deep—a result of his hard childhood. I'm grateful he didn't hurt Jason. For his own sake. I know he worries about turning out like his father. He's nothing like him. I see the way he is with Lucas. My heart hurts just thinking about what they're both losing in each other.

I pull into the parking lot at the camp and wipe the tears from my eyes as I walk inside to collect my son. He's holding his stomach when I find him in the office, and he jumps up and gives me a hug, even though there's disappointment in his eyes.

"Hey," I say.

"I was hoping Tavish would be picking me up."

Pain sears my heart and I work to steady myself. What am I supposed to tell him? "Not today, kiddo." I grab his backpack, shoulder it, and smile at the receptionist as I sign him out. I work to sound happy, like my life isn't a hot mess as we walk to the car. "If you're up to it, want to go get a sticky bun at the bakery?"

God, just thinking about sticky buns brings Tavish to mind.

He nods. "Okay. Can we get one and bring it to Tavish?"

"We'll see, okay." I can't bring myself to squash his hopes. Lucas goes quiet for a long time and I cast him a glance. "Is your stomach bad?"

He nods. "I don't want to see Dad anymore."

His words hurt the hollowed-out part of my heart. "Your dad is back on the road. It will probably be Christmas before he's in town again."

"He was mean."

Yes, he was, and I'll be going to the courts to ensure there's supervised visits—if and when Lucas decides whether to see him again. I'd rather Lucas have no male influences in his life over having his father berate him for what he wears. The kids on the playground aren't just bullies, his own father is one, and Lucas doesn't need that.

I pull up in front of the bakery, and Lucas unbuckles and jumps out. He's already inside before I get myself out of the driver's seat. The delicious smells of fresh pastry and dark roast coffee fill my senses. I smile at Mom as she holds her arms out to Lucas. She takes one look at me and worry crinkles around her eyes.

She gets Lucas a sticky bun. "Why don't you head to the playground?" I do love that the playground is right behind the bakery and we can keep an eye on him through the big glass windows. That's how I saw him walking with Tavish that day and pulled my ridiculous karate moves.

"Okay," he says and happily walks out the back door. I drop into a chair that faces the window and stare after him until he's on a swing. Mom brings me a big steaming cup of coffee and I take a much-needed sip.

It takes all my strength just to say, "Thank you." She puts her hand on mine, and gives it a squeeze. "I quit my job yesterday," I blurt out.

"About time." My head rears back. Okay, I wasn't expecting that. "That place makes you miserable. You'll find something else, Rachel. Something that makes you happy."

I blink my eyes and try to fight back the tears. "I'm not sure I'll ever be happy again."

"Tavish, he made you happy, didn't he?" Her eyes are wide and full of worry as she watches me carefully.

God, hearing his name is killing me. "I didn't know him, Mom. You were right."

She doesn't look happy about being right. "Tell me what you did know." I take another sip of coffee and consider her question.

"I know he loves spending time with Lucas and he was really good with him." A slight smile touches my lips as I remember the surprise rocking chair. "He had a hard upbringing, and never thought he could be a good dad."

She crosses her legs and her chair makes a squeaking sound. "Do you think he could be a good dad?"

I smile and nod as tears fill my eyes. "I do, actually."

"What else do you know about him?"

"He's a former MMA champion, but doesn't ever want to hurt anyone." I shake my head, finding that so odd and...admirable.

"He almost hurt Jason."

I swallow, hard, and instantly come to his defence. "He was protecting Lucas and I think if he wanted to hurt him, he would have. He wanted to stop him from hurting us."

"What else do you know?"

"He's a good friend. He'd do anything for Brodie. Even sign up to be a stand-in dad." A laugh comes out of nowhere. "And lead the parade in a kilt."

"Being a stand-in dad. Do you think he did that for Brodie... or for you and Lucas?"

I glance into my coffee cup. It was after he came across Lucas getting bullied that he changed his mind. "Maybe for both."

"Tell me what else you know."

"He's looking for a quiet life."

"Like you."

I nod and tears fall. "He loves his pet bunny, even though he won't admit it."

"Why do you think that is?"

"I think...I think he's scared to love anything. I think he was tossed around a lot as a child and he's afraid...afraid of getting hurt." My heart pounds a little faster.

"Do you think that's why he walked away?"

"I don't know what to think." I sniff and as my body chills, I wrap my hands around my warm coffee. "Maybe he walked away to go be with Sophie."

I saw the video with my own eyes, and there's still a part of me that can't quite believe it. Tavish doesn't seem like the kind of man to sneak around. He's nothing like Jason.

Fine lines deepen around the corner of Mom's eyes as she frowns. "Do you believe that?"

I exhale loudly. "No, Mom, I don't."

She pats my hand. "Maybe you do know more about him than you think."

"I miss him. I love him," I croak out, and tears fall hard.

"Maybe it's him you should be telling that to."

"He walked away from us, Mom. It wasn't the other way around." I take another sip of coffee.

"Yes, and maybe you need to show him he doesn't have to be scared, that you guys aren't going anywhere."

"What is that sound?" I lift my head to check on Lucas, and stand when I find him walking toward the town's piano. I can't see who's playing it, but the music has to be coming from the park. No one in town plays that well, which means Lucas is walking toward a stranger.

I bolt out the back door and spot Lucas. I run toward him, and he waves to me, a big smile on his face as he keeps walking.

"Lucas, get over here." Music fills the park and my gaze shifts, my heart jumping into my throat when I spot Tavish at the piano playing *Ain't No Sunshine*. What the ever-loving hell. Lucas keeps walking and Tavish shifts on the bench, making room for my son, and seeing the two of them together fills the void in my chest with all the love welling up inside of me.

Tavish stops playing, and his head lifts, his gaze on mine. "Lucas," my mother calls out from behind me. "Come on inside. I made some hot chocolate."

Lucas jumps up and gives me a big grin. "Tavish is here, Mom," he says as he runs past. "I'm going to get him a hot chocolate too. And a sticky bun."

"You do that," I say, my legs heavy beneath me. I stand perfectly still as Tavish pushes to his feet. I admire his Scottish dress attire as he comes toward me. He looks as tired and messed up as I do. "Tavish," I whisper breathlessly as he closes the distance and hovers over me, his entire presence and scent completely overwhelming me.

"Hi," he says back and glances around the empty park. "I was looking for you."

"You found me."

"I went to your work earlier."

I swallow. "I quit."

"I heard. I'm sorry you didn't get the promotion." He scrubs his face and my insides ache as I study his big fingers, missing his touch so much. "You deserved it."

"Why...why did you go to my work?" I spot the pet walking club in the distance, all slowing to watch us. Great, an audience.

"I wanted to talk to you." He looks out into the street. "I saw your car and saw Lucas on the swing. I thought I'd play you a song I learned."

I stare at him in confusion, and then suddenly understanding hits like a punch to the face. "Mrs. Potter." My heart gallops in my chest and I'm even more breathless—probably from relief—when I state, "You were getting lessons."

"I was helping her a lot and she wanted to pay me." He points to the piano. "You told me you missed music in your house. I thought two birds, one stone, you know." He grins. "That's how Americans say that, right?"

I grin, my heart wobbling in my chest. I can't believe he was taking music lessons for me. Could the man be any sweeter? "Yes," I respond, my voice a low soft whisper.

"I was going to play for you at the festival—show you what I was secretly up to, which wasn't me sneaking into Sophie's bed." Shame overcomes me at the hurt in his voice. "I thought you knew me better than that."

The sheer pain in his eyes guts me. "I do." He takes my hand, and using the rough pad of his thumb, he lightly rubs my wrist. "Old insecurities..." His gaze searches my face. "I think maybe we were both battling them the other day."

He exhales. "Yeah."

"I never should have thought that about you, Tavish."

He pulls me closer. "I'm not my father," he says with assurance. "I would never, ever hurt you or Lucas."

"I know that." I'm so happy to hear he knows that too, because I wasn't sure he did. "You protect those you care about."

"I'm not in the Dad for Hire program anymore. I don't want to be Lucas' dad for hire, or stand-in dad, or whatever it is you want to call it, anymore."

It takes every ounce of strength in me not to drop to my knees and sob. "Okay, I understand."

"Actually, I don't think you do. I can never be his biological father, Rachel. I can only be his stepdad and I'd like that very much."

Ohmigod, is he saying what I think he's saying? "Tavish."

He drops to one knee and pulls out a big diamond ring. I gasp and briefly close my eyes. Is this really happening? I resist the urge to pinch myself. If it's a dream, I don't want to wake.

"I would have come to you sooner," he says, his eyes locked on mine. "It killed me not to, but I needed to find the perfect ring first. I love you, Rachel. Will you make me the happiest man in the world and be my ninth wife."

I burst out laughing and drop to the ground with him. "I would love to be your ninth wife."

He smiles, slides the ring onto my finger and brushes tears from my face. My heart swells as I take in his handsome face. "How about my first?"

"Even better," I tell him and admire the ring that fits my finger to perfection.

His lips find mine for a soul-searing kiss and my chest expands to make room for my pounding heart.

He breaks the kiss and cups my face. "I've never felt like I belonged anywhere until I met you and Lucas. You guys are home to me, Rachel. It's the most amazing feeling in the world and the scariest. I don't want to be afraid anymore—"

I put my fingers to his lips. "You don't have to be. We're not going anywhere, and you have made me the happiest woman in the world. I love you, Tavish, and Lucas does, too. You are going to be an amazing stepdad. The best in the world."

He stands, pulling me up with him and drags my body to his. "We're going to work together to create your own company, and fill our house with love, music, bunnies, sheep and children."

"Wait, what?"

His grin is adorable and sheepish. "Oh, you caught me sneaking the sheep part in there, did you?"

"No, I caught you sneaking the children part in there."

"Well, come on, Rachel." He playfully rolls his eyes at me. "You have the rocking chair."

"You want me to have a child because I have a rocking chair?"

"I want you to have a baby or two because I want a family with you. Lucas was on to something when he saw you in that chair and suggested you have a baby. I haven't been able to stop thinking about that." He kisses me. "Do you want those things with me, Rachel?"

"Yes," I say dreamily as my Scottish MMA prince who owns a castle in a faraway land kisses me with love and passion and throws me off kilter.

He laughs. "You know you just agreed to the sheep?" He angles his head, his eyes moving over my face. "Actually, you kind of look like you'd agree to just about anything right now."

"Uh huh," I murmur as all my dreams come true. "Just no racoons."

"Not even one?"

"Okay, maybe one. As long as we can get a Canada goose," I tease with a grin.

He laughs and scoops me up. "Let's go tell Lucas, and your mom and then Brodie." He gestures to the pet walking club. "I'm sure they'll spread the news to the rest of the town." I put my arms around him and he winks at me. "I think earlier there was some mention of sticky buns, too."

"Sticky buns...yes..." I whisper and he slides his hand down my body and gives my backside a pinch. It doesn't wake me because I'm already awake, and while this isn't a dream, it's a dream—a fairy tale—come true.

S cotland, one year later:

From the back patio at our Scotland castle, I set down a tray with bread, cheese, grapes and meats beside a fresh pitcher of lemonade I just made. I glance around at my small family—which is about to get bigger—as they run through the herd of sheep that wandered onto our lush property. I hired a landscaping company to plant flowers and shrubbery and upkeep the ground before we came. I wanted the place as perfect as I could for my family.

Family...

I smile as my heart overflows with love. I have my own family. Sometimes I still can't quite believe it. With her hand wrapped around her tummy, Rachel turns my way and waves and my heart beats against my ribcage. My love for her grows stronger every day, and all I can say is I must have done something great in another lifetime to have Rachel and Lucas in my life.

I wave back and Lucas, who insists he'll wear only kilts while in Scotland, calls out, "Can I have a sheep, Dad?"

My heart tumbles. After I adopted him, I told him he could call me whatever he wanted, and he wanted to call me dad. I secretly wanted that too. His own father isn't in the picture much and like I said once before, sometimes an absent father isn't a bad thing. When he saw Lucas last Christmas, the visits were supervised. Rachel made sure of that.

"Can we, Dad, can we?"

I make eye contact with Rachel as she rolls her eyes and gives me a warning glare. No, we did not get sheep back in Massachusetts. We did however get a racoon, or rather a half a dozen of them. After a big storm that tore off some shingles, they once again found their way into the attic, and I carefully removed them and fixed the damage.

After we got married, we decided to sell my place and I built a big workshop in Rachel's back yard for my woodworking. Not that I've had a lot of time for it lately. For the last year, I've been busy helping Rachel get her business off the ground. She's been working hard, too hard, which is why I insisted we take a vacation to Scotland. She'd been wanting to see the castle for a long time, but building a business from the ground up, even though it's still very small, required all our focus. I'm so proud of her successes, and how she's helping other women break through that glass ceiling.

We spent the last week touring Scotland, visiting all the touristy spots Rachel wanted, and I even took her to some hidden gems and old haunts. The pain of the past is now in the past—where it belongs. Rachel's love has helped heal old wounds, just like my love has helped her, and now, being here with her and Lucas, has helped me create new happier memories. I have to say I'm really glad I didn't sell this castle when I moved to the States. I guess fate knew all along that I was going to want to come back to it someday.

Rachel makes her way over to me as Lucas runs around with the sheep. She looks warm and tired, and I take her into my arms. "You need to get off your feet." I pull a chair out for her, and she drops into it and I sit across from her and take her feet into my lap. My gaze rakes over the flush on her cheeks, but I think it has more to do with her pregnancy than the warm heat. "Did we overdo it today?" I ask.

"Nope," she insists. "I loved everything about today and Lucas is still going strong." She rubs her stomach, cradling our little baby girl, and glances up at me. "We're going to have to get a sheep, aren't we?"

I laugh and rub her feet. "How about we just promise him a vacation here every year? That might satisfy him."

She sighs and takes in the majestic view. "I do love it here." I pick up the pitcher of lemonade and pour her a big glass. She presses it to her forehead before taking a big drink. She sets her glass down and glances at the stack of decorating magazines. The castle is big and old and has been lacking a female touch and I want her to make this place her own. The only thing I insist on having is a piano so we can both fill the place with music and love. Even Lucas has been learning to play, and once we have our little girl, and I plan to be a stay-at-home dad, I'll be able to spend even more time teaching Lucas many new things.

It's funny. I went from never thinking I could be a good father to having the title of stand-in-dad, then stepdad, to a stay-at-home dad and I think that's going to be my absolute favorite role yet. Rachel's stomach grumbles and I laugh. Now that the morning sickness has passed, she's been ravenous.

I stand, break a piece of bread, and add some grapes and hard cheese to a plate and set it in front of her. She smiles as she glances at her son. "He's going to be such a great big brother."

I bend and kiss her. "He'll forget all about the sheep once he has a little sister to play with."

Lucas comes running over, and snatches up a grape. He takes a big bite and it squirts everywhere. He laughs and throws his arms around my waist, giving me a big hug that wraps around my heart and squeezes. God, I love this kid. "Thank you for taking me here, Dad."

I hug him back and catch the way Rachel is smiling at me, love, respect and appreciation dancing in her eyes. While I own a big, gorgeous castle, I have never considered myself a prince, but Rachel, she's definitely a princess, and I plan to spend the rest of my life treating her like one.

"So where were we on getting a sheep?" Lucas asks and grins up at me. I smile back, and despite Rachel's groan, I'm pretty sure my next title might be sheep farmer.

***

Thank you so much for reading Rachel and Tavish's story. I hope you enjoyed it as much as I loved writing it. Please check out "Also by Cathryn Fox, to find more romantic comedies, and sexy contemporaries!

ALSO BY CATHRYN FOX

Hot Scots in Kilts:

Kilting Around

Kilt Trip

Off Kilter

Crazy Canadians:

Crazy Apologetic Canadians.

Scotia Storms

Away Game (Rebels)

Warm Up (Rebels)

Crash Course (Rebels)

Home Advantage (Rebels)

Shut Out (Rebels)

End Zone

Fair Play

Enemy Down

Keeping Score

Trading Up

All In

Blue Bay Crew

Demolished

Leveled

Hammered

Single Dad
Single Dad Next Door
Single Dad on Tap
Single Dad Burning Up

Players on Ice
The Playmaker
The Stick Handler
The Body Checker
The Hard Hitter
The Risk Taker
The Wing Man
The Puck Charmer
The Troublemaker
The Rule Breaker
The Rookie
The Sweet Talker
The Heart Breaker

In the Line of Duty
His Obsession Next Door
His Strings to Pull
His Trouble in Talulah
His Taste of Temptation
His Moment to Steal
His Best Friend's Girl
His Reason to Stay

Confessions

Confessions of a Bad Boy Professor

Confessions of a Bad Boy Officer

Confessions of a Bad Boy Fighter

Confessions of a Bad Boy Doctor

Confessions of a Bad Boy Gamer

Confessions of a Bad Boy Millionaire

Confessions of a Bad Boy Santa

Confessions of a Bad Boy CEO

Hands On

Hands On

Body Contact

Full Exposure

Dossier

Private Reserve

House Rules

Under Pressure

Big Catch

Brazilian Fantasy

Improper Proposal

Boys of Beachville

Good at Being Bad

Igniting the Bad Boy

Bad Girl Therapy

Stone Cliff Series:

Crashing Down

Wasted Summer

Love Lessons

Wrapped Up

Eternal Pleasure Series

Instinctive

Impulsive

Indulgent

Sun Stroked Series

Seaside Seduction

Deep Desire

Private Pleasure

Captured and Claimed Series:

Yours to Take

Yours to Teach

Yours to Keep

Firefighter Heat Series

Fever

Siren

Flash Fire

Playing For Keeps Series

Slow Ride

Wild Ride

Sweet Ride

Breaking the Rules:

Hold Me Down Hard

Pin Me Up Proper

Tie Me Down Tight

New York Times and *USA today* Bestselling author, Cathryn is a wife, mom, sister, daughter, and friend. She loves dogs, sunny weather, anything chocolate (she never says no to a brownie) pizza and red wine. She has two teenagers who keep her busy with their never ending activities, and a husband who is convinced he can turn her into a mixed martial arts fan. Cathryn can never find balance in her life, is always trying to find time to go to the gym, can never keep up with emails, Facebook or Twitter and tries to write page-turning books that her readers will love.

Connect with Cathryn:

Tik Tok: @cathrynfoxwriter
Newsletter https://app.mailerlite.com/webforms/landing/c1f8n1
Twitter: https://twitter.com/writercatfox
Facebook: https://www.facebook.com/AuthorCathrynFox?ref=hl

Blog: http://cathrynfox.com/blog/
Goodreads: https://www.goodreads.com/author/show/91799.
Cathryn_Fox
Pinterest http://www.pinterest.com/catkalen/